Time-Crossed Christmas

Guardians of the Stones Time Travel Romance

Jane DeGray

Leavesly Park Publishing

All rights reserved by Leavesly Park Publishing, Friendswood, Texas.

ISBN-13: 9781735239859

Cover design by:Jane May/Servian Images
Library of Congress Control Number: 2021919038
Printed in the United States of America

To Robert, Maryn, Ava, and Jaida who inspire me daily.

To my husband Jim for his unending support throughout the writing of each book.

Contents

Chapter 1

England, 1813

Lady Caroline Wyckham blinked dreamily as she imagined the warm, loving eyes of her husband opening a gift from her on Christmas morning. Always tender, he—

"Caro?"

Blissfully immersed in her fantasy, the sound of her name on her cousin's tongue popped her dream bubble and Caro plummeted to earth with a thump.

The reality hurt. She had no gift to give or husband to receive it.

"Will Hugh like this one, Caro?" Louisa, Lady Bowson pulled her eyes from the heavy gold Brown and Wilkinson pocket watch in her hands long enough to seek a response from her cousin. "Caro? Have I lost you again, dear?"

Caro blinked twice more, squinted, and did her best to focus her errant attention on the pocket watch swinging from Louisa's hand. What should she say? Really, she had no experience gift-giving for a real husband.

Two hours earlier, a sudden downpour had sent the women dashing into the tasteful and welcoming confines of Love and Kelty Jewellers to escape the wet. Since then, the storm had turned into a persistent drizzle while they perused every imaginable gift for men from rings to snuff boxes and everything in between.

The embellished gold-cased watch reminded her of the one she had given her beloved Lord William Lowther, the second son of the Marquess of Westdale, before he left for India. It had the same hidden compartment that when opened had space for a miniature portrait as well as an inscription. In William's, she had placed the tiny painting of herself opposite the message, "Yours for all time. Love, Caro."

She smiled at Louisa, but a thrum of emotion stole her answer. In her mind's eye all she could see was William's handsome face their last night together in her parent's garden. His usually calm gray eyes had sparked fire as he begged her to wait for him.

That was two years ago.

Shaking off thoughts of William that dogged her like a faithful hound, the scene in front of her materialized once more. All she needed to do was help Louisa select a present for Hugh— a task not as easy as one might think. As far as Louisa was concerned, no item was good enough nor rich enough for her dearest husband.

The cost of the splendid watch would support an average London family for years. Caro could think of several similar pocket watches she had seen the baron wear over the time she had known him. But that hardly mattered to Louisa.

When Caro had given William the new pocket watch, he had given her the one his grandfather had passed down to him. Touched as she was by the gift, she did not think he should have given her a precious family heirloom. William assured her she would be in the family as soon as he returned, so she was only holding it for him.

Now the watch was a part of William she kept forever close to her heart. Resting her hand over where it was pinned to her chemise, she debated how best to answer Louisa.

Would the baron like the watch Louisa held? Probably. William did love his. Did Hugh need another pocket watch? No. However, it was nearly Christmas and the season of gift giving, so Louisa would purchase something for her husband. Why not this?

If truth be told, Caro found herself simply not interested in the answer. She wished she were in the Christmas spirit, but she was not. William's whereabouts had been unknown for well over a year, so without a direction to send a gift, shopping for him was not an option. She had no other male to buy for but her father who happened to be the Duke of Rowland.

In the first five minutes inside the store, she had found the perfect gift for him. The cravat pin, featuring a large round ruby surrounded by a plain gold band, was wrapped and in her reticule. Not very imaginative on her part, but she knew the pin would suit her father's staid style.

This morning she and Louisa had visited seven stores in search of gifts for her cousin's children. At each stop Caro's heart had tugged in her chest as she considered purchasing valiant toy soldiers or darling baby dolls in frilly outfits. She longed for children and a family of her own. Oddly, no one ever stopped to think about that as they dragged her along to take advantage of her availability and expertise in shopping on Bond Street.

Perhaps they thought seeking her opinions on gifts would include her in their family circle. Did they think it would prevent her from missing William? No, it made her feel depressed and restless. She was not proud of that.

Caro sighed, dug deep, and found her words. "I'm sure it would be just the thing, Louisa!" Had she summoned enough excitement in her voice to sound convincing? Seriously, she could not take another hour of this. She had mentally trod through her relationship with her almost-betrothed at least three times in the last hour.

Exhausted, she could not risk another flight of fancy. To ground herself in the present, she ran her finger through a bowl of crushed cinnamon sticks and cloves sitting atop the counter. The pungent scent she stirred up lent the air a seasonal touch. Still, it did not over-power the smell of damp wool that arrived with each jingle of the door as new customers entered on this drizzly day.

A fastidious man, Mr. Kelty had straightened his intricately tied cravat and adjusted the sprig of holly berries on his lapel before greeting Louisa and Caro. With a cheery smile and a bounce in his step, he had insisted upon serving them personally. So sure was he of a good sale, he had happily twirled his jeweler's loupe like a quizzing glass.

Now even his ardor had dimmed. Exasperated, he mopped perspiration off his forehead with a monogrammed handkerchief. His toothy smile had shrunk to a thin line with his lower lip held in place by the bite of his front teeth.

"I'd be happy to wrap this up special for his lordship, my lady." The poor man flushed, his worried eyes darting at the line of other fine lords and ladies milling about the small shop, each vying for his attention. It was his busiest season after all.

One peek at Louisa, however, and Caro could see indecision still ruled her face. Perhaps a change of tactics was in order. A diversion, perhaps? Caro decided to try for everyone's sake.

"Oh, Louisa, is that not the most elegant diamond necklace you have ever seen? And look, it has a matching bracelet and cunning little eardrops." Caro pointed to a case beside them and did her best to flash enthusiasm over her find. Backed by black velvet, brilliant diamonds shimmered and gleamed through the glass as if calling to them.

It worked.

Louisa stepped to Caro's shoulder and studied the sparkling diamond set. Caro thought it was exquisite and would be thrilled with a gift like that from her husband—if she had one. She stifled the sigh that wanted to surface, choosing a different survival tactic in its stead.

"Perhaps I can drop a word or two in Hugh's ear, and he would purchase it for you for Christmas," she teased, drawing a raised eyebrow from Louisa. "You know he'd be delighted to buy you something you like."

Louisa smiled the silly, besotted smile she always smiled when she thought of her darling Hugh. It made her appear years younger, a glow from within lighting up her blonde, blue-eyed beauty. The two were an unfashionable pair of lovebirds after six years of marriage and three children.

Caro held her smile in place and promised herself she would not let her envy show. She loved her cousin dearly, and Hugh had never been anything but kind to her as the spinster relation. Still, it was hard to be around them and not feel jealous of the family they shared.

Caro's offer hung in the air waiting for a response to rescue it. Instead, her stomach chose that moment to announce to all it had been too long since breakfast. *How embarrassing!*

Gentleman that he was, Mr. Kelty pretended not to hear the unladylike grumble, but Louisa burst out laughing. That made Caro blush even deeper when the majority of the store's patrons turned to stare at her.

Successfully diverted, Louisa sprang to life, her mind made up. "Mr. Kelty, please wrap this handsome watch for my husband and deliver it to our townhouse this afternoon." She shot a sly glance at Caro before adding, "I believe Lady Caroline and I are late to luncheon." Her smile widened as she turned her attention back to Mr. Kelty. "Should my husband happen to stop by looking for a Christmas gift for me, you may direct him to this lovely diamond parure." She winked at Caro, grabbed her by the arm, and pulled her out of the shop quite before either Caro or Mr. Kelty knew what had happened.

A good diversion was a useful tool indeed.

∞ ∞ ∞

After luncheon and a short nap, Caro decided to stop by the kitchens to be sure Cook had her favorite lemon tarts for teatime. Papa had summoned her to meet him in the library for tea. Whatever he wanted to talk with her about would go down much easier with her favorite tarts on the cart. Papa loved them, too, but he could sour any sweet with his dour predictions of misfortunes to come. Proper fortification was necessary to survive what lay ahead. Besides, Cook loved to make them for her, and Caro loved being spoiled. It worked out as mutually gratifying for the pair.

Turning down the hall to the kitchens she heard what sounded like a baby. The untempered sound of one unhappy child echoed off the walls, underpinned by adult voices shushing in sing-song rhythm. Whoever could be visiting down below with a baby in tow? Her father never allowed infants to be kept on the premises since they distracted his servants from completing the work for him that he employed them to do.

Caro tiptoed into the kitchen by a side door, surprising the staff by seeming to appear from nowhere. Milly, a kitchen undercook, shrieked and nearly dropped the poor babe, so startled was she by Caro's, "Hello there, little one!"

The child's response to all that was to arch its tiny back and turn beat-red in the face with an ear-splitting wail. Now everyone from Cook on down to the scullery maid held a sheepish expression and wished to be anywhere but facing the lady of the house.

Caro struggled to keep her mouth in a firm line like her mother always had when dealing with servants, but it was not to be. The corners of her mouth insisted upon tipping up, giving her a demonic grin. Now she had the servants really concerned. All except the child, whose lungs were healthy and strong and insistent upon whatever it was it desired.

What a din it was making! Caro wanted to know everything about this little demon, but she must calm it if she were ever to be heard. Holding out her arms she bobbed her head at Milly, signaling the girl to hand over the human contraband. Milly obliged, but she was visibly stricken with guilt as she did so. Her red curls drooped out of one side of her mob cap as big blue eyes blinked up at her employer through stubby lashes.

"There, there, sweet thing," Caro crooned. "What has got you so upset? Hmmm?" She bounced and patted the baby, feeling its solid weight snuggle against her body and its face nestle into the space between her chin and shoulder. Was it odd that the tiny being fit against her body perfectly? The snuffling and snotty little face emitted a huge, snorty sigh and subsided into a noisy sleep.

The servants looked stunned and chagrined. Cook was the first to speak, her round, heat-reddened cheeks beaming a smile. "Well, would you look at that, Milly. Our Lady Caroline has the magic touch." She smiled at Caro who was absurdly pleased by the compliment. "That little sweetheart has been fussing for over an hour and none of us could get her to stop."

Milly's face displayed her conflicted feelings. Unsure if her employer was angry about a baby in the house or happy that she had quieted the child, Milly's expression settled on concern. Caro decided to help her out by taking matters into her own hands.

"Milly, my dear, would you be so kind as to introduce me to this precious child?" She patted with a steady rhythm the little fanny that tipped up and over her breast as she swayed side to side on her feet. Something about this was supremely satisfying.

"The babe belonged to my cousin Rose, m'lady. Her name is Lucy."

"Belonged?" Caro's eyebrow lifted.

"Rose and her husband were kilt in an accident a week ago, Lady Caroline. 'Twas during that bad rainstorm. Her man had the reins and Rose was sittin' in the bed of their old cart on the way to market when a wheel come off. It sent 'em tumblin' down a ravine." Milly sniffed and wiped her eyes with the skirt of her apron. "Rose lived for two days but Jem died right then from the fall. Little Lucy was with a neighbor at the time, due to her bein' a bit colicky that day."

"Oh, you poor little thing," Caro murmured. "Is she still a nursing babe?"

"Yes, m'lady. 'Tis why we've had such a time coaxin' her to eat. She still wants her mum."

"Who will be her mother now, Milly?" The question sounded more accusatory coming from her lips than she intended, since the maid visibly cringed.

"I dunno, m'lady. I hav'na found a home fer her yet. I sent word to me oldest sister in Shropshire who I think will take her, but it will be days before I hear back. Then someone must accompany her there." Milly's eyes darted between Caro and baby Lucy at an alarming speed.

Such a sad state-of-affairs for such a little tyke. Caro looked about the area and signs were apparent everywhere that Lucy's squall had upset the usually smooth operation of the kitchen. Flour was smeared across Cook's forehead and into the grey-steaked brown curls sneaking out from under her cap. Worse, not a tart was in sight. That did not bode well.

Milly's apron had come untied from her small frame, and the smell of sour milk seemed to waft in the air. Every set of eyes in the kitchen, including those of the pot boy and one of the footmen, carried a haunted look. They tried not to appear to keep an eye on the proceedings, but they, too, wondered if they were in trouble. The problem was they all were painfully aware no one had asked permission for Lucy to stay even for a short time.

Well, from the look of things, she needed to initiate a rescue. Teatime was fast approaching. If she did not want to anger her father, she had better get everyone back on track. The practical approach was always best, according to her late mother.

"Cook, please make sure you have a healthy plate of lemon tarts for tea and add my favorite Darjeeling tea to the cart. If the duke is not in a good mood, I am sure to need it." Already Cook had resumed her work at her table, the flour flying into a bowl and two eggs cracked into the mix before Caro had finished her instructions.

"Yes, m'lady."

That left Milly frozen and awaiting her fate like a prisoner her sentence. Not yet ready to surrender the sweet bundle in her arms, Caro decided to put off the discussion with Milly until later. Why not let her squirm a bit longer for not having shared her dilemma with her father or at least with her? Did she think them ogres? Of course, they would have been willing to work out an arrangement for the child.

"Milly, you may return to your work. I am certain Cook needs your help." One hand waved in a dismissive manner across the wreckage that was the kitchen. "I will handle this one until she awakes."

Caro sneaked a peek at the baby now snoring softly in her arms. "Then you may attend her in the nursery. Ask Mrs. Oates to be sure it is clean with fresh bunting and bedding installed for the babe. It has not been in use since my nieces were here during Lady Bowson's lying in. Lucy may shelter there until other arrangements have been made. You must sleep in the nanny's quarters, Milly, while Lucy is here."

Caro raised her eyebrow imperiously, not wanting to appear too soft in front of the servants. "Does that sound acceptable to you?"

Milly all but fell on her knees thanking her for not putting her out and without a reference at that. Caro suppressed a grin, wheeled about, and stole away with the darling child now cradled securely in the crook of her arm.

"Thank you, m'lady, thank you! You shan't regret it. Thank you!" A whoop of relief went up from the kitchen as she sped around the corner and up the stairs into the main house.

Wanting time to herself to admire the fine bones and soft skin of the sleeping Lucy, Caro padded down the hall hoping to find an empty sitting room. Sadly, before she got there, Jennings, her father's old retainer, met her at the door.

Which room he had come from was a mystery, but then it always was. How he walked without a sound on marble floors was a secret he did not share. She never heard him coming. Ever. She would simply look up and the old man with the kindly eyes in an otherwise expressionless face would be staring at her. She should know by now what to expect, but he had successfully made her jump out of her skin once again.

He had been with her family since long before she was born. Over the years she had formed a suspicion that part of Jennings' job was to track her actions both day and night. Did he miss anything that went on in her life? Doubtful.

This time her start made Lucy start as well. To Caro's relief, the little dear smacked her rosebud lips twice and then settled back into her exhausted repose.

Determined to keep Lucy sleeping at least until teatime, Caro calmed herself and addressed the butler in a whisper, "What is it you wish to say, Jennings?" There was no point in chastising him for sneaking up on her. He would do it again anyway.

"Your father wishes to see you in the library immediately, my lady."

"What? No. I mean, why now? We are scheduled to have tea in less than an hour." Her fluster made her bounce Lucy a little more roughly with one arm as she pulled out William's watch from her pocket to check the time. Lucy objected with a snort but did not awaken. Caro took a deep breath and tried again. "Why now, Jennings? What is going on?"

"I am sure I do not know, my lady." His lips were set in that firm line she knew all too well from her youth. She would get no more from him even if he were dying to tell her all. He answered to no one but her father.

"Fine! But what am I to do with baby Lucy? Would you care to take her while I speak with the duke?"

Ha! She had finally elicited a reaction from Jennings beside his usual. The man's face showed sheer horror. The thought of taking the little bundle reeking of sour milk and spit-up into his pristine, white-gloved hands and pressing her to his crisp black uniform was too much. He would do it, but it would cost her. No, she had better keep the child with her.

"Oh, all right. I shall keep her with me, but you will owe me a favor, Jennings, for letting you off this time." There, she had neatly turned the tables on the man, and he was not complaining.

"As you wish, Lady Caroline." He turned and escaped at a pace far faster than his norm, terrified she might change her mind and award him the baby. She noted she still heard not a footstep as he retreated.

Whatever did her father want that could not wait until teatime? Had she overspent her allowance? She did not think so. No untoward behavior or *faux pas* came to mind. She bent her head and whispered to Lucy, "We shall just brave the day and see what Papa wants, won't we?" Somehow it was comforting not to be alone, but to enjoy the silent backing of the little one in her arms. She knocked on the door and waited for her father's gruff answer.

"Enter."

What would he think when he saw what she carried? She contemplated that for only a moment before he launched into a snorting, indignant response.

"What is this? Your idea of a surprise?" he blasted. Hoping her father's blaring voice did not awaken the child, Caro hurried to cover Lucy's ears. "What did you get yourself into now?" He sat back in his chair and crossed his arms—never a good sign.

"Now, Papa—"

"Don't *now, Papa* me, child. You know you are supposed to marry before you have a baby." That jab found a tender spot, and she felt her skin flush. Well-aware that her father objected to her spinster status, she knew he loved her and had not meant to be cruel, but still, it hurt. Seeing her pained expression, his face became a thundercloud of compressed emotion. When he opened his mouth to plead his case, a rasping cough stole his words.

Caught between pique and worry, Caro examined her father while waiting for his fit to pass. As he tried to speak, it only worsened. The duke bent over his knees, red-faced, and struggled to breathe. She hastened to the back of his chair and placed a hand between his shoulder blades hoping to quiet his cough. In seconds, he was able to take a breath as the cough eased. Should she be concerned about these episodes? He did not seem to have them often, but when he did, they had a rough, chesty quality that worried her. His ice blue eyes, now watering from his exertion, sparked at her as if mere tears would never put out their fire.

"You inherited your mother's calming touch." His gruff

voice wheezed, still too loud at only half the volume. Fortu-nately, his color quickly returned to normal, relieving the worst of her anxiety.

"Well, shall we begin again, Papa dearest?" Caro responded in a loud whisper. "I should warn you, if you wake this child nei-ther of us will be able to hear the other."

The duke faltered for a moment, but acknowledged the wisdom of her words, motioned her to be seated, and mopped his eyes with his pocket cloth. When ready to begin, he raised an imperious eyebrow at his only child. My, but that raised eyebrow had a familiar feel to it. Had she not used that tactic only a few minutes ago in the kitchen? She had better be frontal here and cut off any chance of being denied Lucy for the time being.

"My dear Papa, this little lamb is the niece of Cook's helper Milly. It seems Milly's sister and husband met their demise last week in an accident during that dreadful rainstorm." Her father lifted a second brow but said nothing, so she dashed on before he had time to reconsider. "With nowhere else for her to go, Milly was forced to take the child until other more suitable ar-rangements could be made for her care. Cook insisted she clear it with us, but Milly had not yet had the opportunity to do so. The poor thing is still a nursing babe and cannot understand why her mother is not here for her."

Unable to resist patting Lucy, she clucked a soft croon to her. The duke's brows had inched higher when she looked up. "This little girl had them all undone in the kitchen with her wail-ing when I dropped by to be sure your favorite lemon tarts were on the tea cart. I decided to do what Mother would have done had she been here, and ordered the nursery prepared for the child until her family members can claim her."

Caro adopted her best imitation of her mother delivering orders to her staff. "We cannot have the household at sixes and sevens because of a mere baby. However, we cannot turn her out with no place to go and lose a loyal servant like Milly in the pro-cess." She finished with an imperious look at her father that had the corners of his mouth twitching.

"You are so like your mother, Caro, sitting here ordering me about. Even those flashing green eyes and your fiery auburn curls match hers." He shook his head as if needing to shake off the memory of her mother, too. "If you have already secured those arrangements for the child, I shall not contradict them. Besides, you look lovely with a babe in your arms." He grinned.

Caro blushed knowing this was as close to an apology from her father as she would get for his earlier bluster. She nodded her acceptance and continued to gently bounce Lucy in a steady rhythm. Still, something was not right. Why had a baby in her arms set him off? "Why is it you wished to see me, Papa?"

"Yes, about that. Lady Chatham invited us to attend her musicale this evening." Caro turned to give her father her full attention. Something was up. To her mind, her father had no use for the over-bearing lady or her husband. She noted he was sitting rather rigidly in his chair, his graying hair brushed carefully from his face. There was something a bit wild in that wealth of hair surrounding his head that gave him a leonine look. Many a woman would like to have called this handsome man her husband, but he steadfastly avoided marriage, even though it had been four years since her mother's passing.

"We are due to attend the Woodington's dinner party this evening. Why have you changed your mind?" He loved the Woodington family. Yes, something was afoot. Definitely.

"Do you remember the baron, Lord Tremont?"

"Cornelius Tremont, your friend? The one you call Corney?" His name conjured up a burly man with thick red hair, bushy eyebrows, and even bushier sideburns. In fact, the man seemed to be made mostly of curly red hair. The only other trait she could recall was that he spoke loudly as if everyone should be interested in what he had to say. Other than that, she had never given him a thought. He was one of her father's acquaintances. Not one of hers.

"Well, yes. He has come to London to look for a suitable wife and has asked about you."

Her stomach dropped to her knees. Her father's true intent

was all too clear.

"Oh, no. Not him, Papa. You cannot mean you would marry me to him? He is older than you, is he not?

"Well, madam, I am not yet on my death bed, am I? Nor is Corney. The baron is a wealthy man with beautiful estates and is well-liked among his peers. You could do worse."

"I am sure he is liked among his peers which are those of your era, Papa. You know I have not accepted any offers from those near my own age, so why would I accept the baron?"

Her father's hopeful expression dimmed as his brows met in a V above his nose. "You must give up this notion of waiting for a suitor who has not acknowledged you in years. Whatever happened to him, I do not know. But I do know it is time you got on with your life. You cannot continue to waste your time minding me and my estates. If I should die before you are settled in a marriage of your own, you will stand to lose everything to my heir. You will have no home except that as a spinster relative. Is that what you wish?" His scowl deepened. "I have never met Cousin Patrick because he does not visit from Ireland. Even so, he and his sons will inherit all that I have. That will leave you with only a small portion from your mother's family and a pittance of an inheritance from me. As you are aware, all my funds are wrapped up in lands and property that are entailed."

"But Papa, you said yourself you were not in your grave yet. Why must I rush into a loveless marriage?" Caro's heart was beating faster, and she could feel it throb in a vein in her neck. Had he truly forgotten he was the reason she was unmarried? That thought made her even more angry. Surely, her father had not drawn up a marriage settlement with the baron without asking her, had he?

"Bloody hell, Caro, I am not a young man. I have no guarantee from above that I will be here in ten days, let alone ten years. I would like to see you married, with children of your own in your arms and grandchildren on my knee." His voice had risen with each word. "You need not live the life of a spinster. You are a lovely young woman. You have only to decide on a husband to get on with a family life of your own. For my sake and yours, stop this incessant waiting for a man who clearly does not want you!"

The moment the words slid out of his mouth, he grimaced and looked away. His face told her he knew his arrows had found their mark. Stunned by the venom in them, she stood stiffly in front of him with tears welling in her eyes.

William Lowther had wanted her. She knew this for certain. He had asked her to marry him, and she had said yes, promising to wait for him. Plus, he had given her his grandfather's pocket watch to keep until he returned. To Caro it was as good as a betrothal ring. But that was before he had left for India and after her father had refused his near penniless offer.

William had drawn the duke's ire when he continued to press his suit, and everything had fallen apart after that. He had had no choice but to seek his fortune abroad and hope the duke would change his mind and accept him as Caro's husband if he prospered.

So far, he had not returned. She had been distraught when William left for India, promising to write him every day once he had sent his direction to her. Correspondence between the two existed for a short time. His letters had been warm and loving and filled with the excitement of discovering a new land. And then they ceased to arrive.

Caro never understood what had happened. Her last letter from William described him as busy guiding East India Company soldiers through troubled areas and caring for sick or wounded in the absence of a medical doctor. He had not described heavy fighting, but other medical hazards of life in India, like fevers or snake bite. Was William still alive? Had he been killed by one of the many maladies present there, not the least of which was a people who objected to the British-backed company? Was she waiting for no one?

Gossip abounded about the missing William, but no one returning from India seemed to know anything for certain. After an absence of two years was it time to give up on William?

She sneaked a glance at Lucy. Did she want a chance to

have a child of her own? Could she accept someone she did not love as a husband? She needed more time to think. What could she say to dissuade Papa from husband hunting for her until she knew her own mind?

Lucy stretched out her little body to twice its previous length as luxuriously as a housecat on a divan. Her eyes flicked open, and she squinted up at Caro as if the light hurt them. By the time she finally succeeded in opening them fully, many blinks later, she also remembered just how hungry she was and let out a couple of warning cries. This discussion, or interrogation, with her father would have to wait.

"So, you are demanding we attend Lady Chatham's musicale this evening. Have you sent out our rather late regrets to the Woodingtons regarding dinner? No hostess approves of reneging this close to her dinner party."

"I sent a note around several hours ago. It should be fine." Her father's growl indicated he was none too pleased with her line of questioning. Lucy was warning with increasingly loud squawks that any further delay would cost Caro the last of her peace of mind, so she did not pursue the point.

"Be ready by nine and we shall depart shortly thereafter," her father noted with finality and directed his attention to the papers on his desk.

Well, she had been summarily dismissed! She wheeled on her heel and strode out of the room, deciding those lemon tarts would never see teatime in her father's presence today. She would eat them all herself if she had to.

Chapter 2

1863 Civil War Tennessee

William Lowther knocked through the ice capping the top of the rain barrel to free the dipper. It reminded him that Christmas was only days away, and snow was sure to fall before long. He measured out enough frigid water into the bowl of his mess plate to wet his hands to wash them.

Damn, but it was cold!

Pulling out a sliver of lye soap from the pocket of his jacket, he set to scrubbing himself. The harsh concoction of fat, ashes, and vinegar carried a strong smell, but got the job done. Somewhere he must commission a new supply of soap. Operating with filthy hands was unacceptable.

He examined the blood stains on his clothing and sighed. All the soap in Tennessee would be insufficient to tackle the residue of past medical work. He could not waste what little still existed on the fabric of his shirt and pants, or even his jacket. Besides, the abrasive ingredients seemed to cut into the material and leave it so frayed holes popped up everywhere.

He had forgotten what it was like to feel clean the last two years. As a medic for the Union army, he was lucky to obtain any tools to work with, let alone soap. Cleaning wounds was only part of what he had learned from his friend and mentor Rick Duvall. Before being assigned to different divisions, Rick had taught him most of what he knew about survival and medical care of the wounded.

War made strange bedfellows, but his relationship with Rick had been in a category of its own. What would Caro think if he told her exactly how he had spent the last two years? Was there a chance she would believe him? He went over the details of that first meeting in his head.

As a guide for the East India Company regiment nearly two years ago, William had been surprised by a witch—a figure he thought only existed in children's bedtime stories. He knew better now. The word *witch* rolled easily off his tongue today because there was no other name for the woman who had put him here.

He had been living near Benares in Bihar-Bengal while working to open new muslin and silk trade routes for the East India Company. When a new Company regiment arrived, they offered him a job guiding them through the territory near the border with Nepal. He was familiar with the area, and since their private army was filled mostly with British recruits, they encouraged him to go as a scout. He welcomed the better income, but the encounter with the witch was totally unexpected. She would change his life—perhaps forever.

He had been scrubbing up as he had today after tending the wounds of a British soldier downed in a skirmish with some locals. A dried-up voice cackled in his ear making him spin around on alert, wondering if he should go for the throat of the interloper.

What he saw was so unanticipated he had merely gaped at the woman, speechless. When he recovered himself, sensing she meant him no harm, he gazed down at her in wonder. A tiny thing though she was, her aura proclaimed a power he recognized but did not understand. Draped in a voluminous black gown that covered her from chin to ground, only the toes of her black boots poked through her skirts to show she had feet.

"Aren't ye the clever one, sir, caring for wounded when no one else is about to do so. This one here is a mighty precious person."

He nodded and waited for her to continue. Why was she addressing him?

"I believe ye saved this man's life, no?"

When it was apparent she wanted a response from him beyond a simple nod, he gave in and answered, "Mayhap. 'Tis the charitable thing to do when a man is down, is it not?" He raised an eyebrow in challenge, unsure if he should treat her with deference or ignore her.

The old lady looked into his eyes with the most disturbing orbs he had ever seen. Clearly an old woman—a hag by anyone's standards—she looked into his soul with a pair of lively blue eyes that sparkled with youth and vitality. That is the moment he decided she must be a witch. What other explanation made sense?

A shiver of apprehension shot through him. Searching the area, he realized all the others had long ago left to find food and their beds. He was entirely alone with the crone. If she did mean to hurt him, he had not a single weapon with him. He doubted it would do him any good anyway if she were truly a witch.

"Well, young sir, I have an offer for ye I fear ye cannot refuse."

That garnered his attention. "Go on."

"Ye have been worryin' yerself 'bout makin' a fortune so's you kin marry the young lady ye left back home, am I right?"

Both his eyebrows stretched up to his forelock. "How do you know of the young lady?" Had Caro sent this old woman to him? Should he recognize her? He did not recall ever seeing anyone like her before. Surely, he would remember someone this unusual if he had.

"I know 'bout most things ye do, young man, as I've had me eye on ye for some time now. I knew yer granddaddy."

That left him feeling even more at a loss. Where would his grandfather have met a woman like this? It was time to cut to the heart of the problem and confront her. "What is it you want of me, madam?"

"Ah, so impatient, ye are! No one hast told ye of yer duty as a Guardian of the Stones, have they?" Her head cocked to the side as she watched him digest that piece of information.

"I have no idea of what you are speaking, . . ." He waved his hand not knowing how to address her.

She replied with a grin that displayed a startling lack of teeth but left her looking years younger, nonetheless. "I am Olde Gylda of Hampshire to most folks. Ye may call me Gylda since we shall be workin' together."

Oh, this was not to be borne. "I am not in need of employment . . . Gylda. As you might have noticed, I am in service to the British East India Company, at present."

The old woman chortled like a young girl. "Nah, ye won't have to deal with them again, young sir. They cannot track ye down where I am sendin' ye."

He should have known then to turn around and run from her, but she had intrigued him. The more she told him of the work she wanted him to do, the more fascinated he was. Had his grandfather really worked with this old woman? Why would the man never have shared that information with his grandson if he were to follow in his grandfather's footsteps?

Old Gylda told him the East India Company would be battling Nepal along the border with India in 1814, and his skills as a surgeon would be needed. How could this be true when it was a whole three years in the future? That conflict would be a warm-up for an even bigger need at a battle she called Waterloo. What? He had no skills as a surgeon. He simply helped people to the best of his ability and left nature to do the rest.

Ah, yes, but Gylda only chortled over his modesty. She would send him to America to train under someone with the odd name of Rick—a man far advanced in the care of injured soldiers. America did hold some appeal, but he had no idea what he would do there to further his goal. His job here was to make a fortune so when he returned to England, he could marry Caro. That was plenty daunting to keep him from adventuring wherever the spirit led him. He did not see how Gylda's plan would further his. To win Caro's hand, he had to return victoriously to London as a wealthy man to show the duke he could keep his daughter in style. That was his focus.

His mistake was thinking he had a choice in any of this.

The sound of voices headed their way spurred the old woman to action. She told him she would explain the rest later. Had he known what she had in mind for him, he would likely have fought her. As he stood with his head tipped to identify those coming closer, he was startled to see Olde Gylda clutched a flat rock to her chest. Where had that come from?

To top it off, the old lady chanted something under her breath that sounded like *ar-goll-mewn-ahm-sir*. Before he had time to think more about it, a wind whirled from behind nearby rocks all but knocking him off his feet as it swirled around him.

Worried the old lady would be blown away, he grabbed her in a bear hug and held her tightly. The wind sucked all the air from his lungs leaving him gulping for breath. When his body lifted off the ground, his world went dark.

At that moment, he had not a clue what the future would hold for him over the next two years of his life. If he had known, would he have changed things? Could he have?

Chapter 3

"You look lovely this evening, Lady Caroline. And you, Lady Violet." Christopher Duncanby, Viscount Danson, bowed to each, displaying a finely formed leg, and finished with a kiss that grazed each gloved hand. What a charmer. He was careful to hold each woman's gaze while performing his gentleman's greeting with absolute grace.

Dressed in a gown of shimmering pale blue with dark-blue ribbon trim, Caro curtsied and maintained her poise. To her dismay, Violet, a vision in her signature shade of purple, once again unleashed a giggle that betrayed her obsession with the man.

The viscount was handsome with perfect hair, coiffed in the latest style, and a cravat so intricately tied it must have taken his valet an age to master. His blond good looks and light blue eyes complemented a strong chin, featuring a slight dent that must have been where the gods had kissed him goodbye at birth. In short, the man was beautiful, particularly in his black evening dress.

So far Lady Chatham's musicale was not a disaster, but the evening was still young. The place was a crush with each room of her large townhouse overflowing with guests. Caro's best friend, Lady Violet Lowther, had met her almost immediately once inside the door, so the evening started well.

Violet, William's sister, was a sweet, giggly girl who created fun wherever she went. One could not stay in a bad mood in her presence for long. She adored Caro and was completely supportive of her waiting for William since she wanted Caro to be her sister.

Tiny and doll-like with dark hair and rosy lips, Violet also adored the viscount, hence her inability to keep from giggling when near him. To complicate matters, Lord Christopher displayed a marked preference for Caro.

Negotiating the evening with the viscount and Violet would be a challenge. Might she find a way to encourage the two to sit together without her around? It would take some skill, but she was sure she could accomplish the goal without either being the wiser.

Having said their hellos to mutual friends, the three decided to work their way toward the seating well ahead of the start of the musicale. Standing room only awaited late arrivals and was to be avoided according to rules for young ladies. Not a fan of these amateur musicals, Caro would gladly forfeit her seat to anyone who wanted it. Waiting out the event in an adjoining room visiting with friends was much more pleasurable.

Too often, the children of the *haute ton* were not pitch-perfect and charged through classical pieces with,out the joy or ability the works demanded. She had never mastered listening to a slightly off-key soprano or a sour note on a pianoforte as though nothing were amiss.

That pain was still a source of amusement for Violet who giggled as she reminded Caro of their unbecoming decorum as youths attending musicales. The two young ladies, along with William, had been banned from sitting together by Caro's mother who found their overly pained expressions inexcusable. Their duty as guests was to suffer through with dignity no matter how horrid the sound. Sadly, suffer was still the appropriate word, more often than not.

Leading the way toward chairs near the front, Caro spotted the opportunity she had hoped to find. From the left side, she slipped all the way through the row of empty chairs to the center aisle, with Violet right behind her. That placed the viscount next to Violet. He was not happy and pantomimed his displeasure over Violet's head.

Caro blinked in innocence at his narrowed eyes and pretended not to understand the cause of his chagrin. Now if she could get Violet to stop her giggles long enough to talk to the man in full sentences, the evening might not be a waste.

As much as she loved Violet, she would rather have spent time with her other close friend, Charlotte, Lady Woodington, at her dinner party. The conversation there would have been interesting as well as entertaining. No cringe-worthy events at all. She would have to think of some way to make it up to Charlotte for throwing off her numbers at the last moment. Really, what was her father thinking?

As if her thoughts had conjured the answer to that question, the man she did not want to see tonight above all others, took shape in the aisle beside her. His stealthy arrival would have made Jennings proud. She would much have preferred her butler surprise her once again.

"Good evening, Lady Caroline."

Meeting his eyes, she froze, unable to reply. Cornelius Tremont, Baron Tremont, in all his sartorial splendor, grinned down at her with his untamed red hair surrounding his head like a halo. Was it the unruly sideburns clashing with the orange brocaded waistcoat glittering unrepentantly beneath the evening blacks that made her mute?

His collar points were so high she wondered they did not cut the rolls of fat under his chin. Smelling of brandy and cigars, his intimate perusal of her person claimed ownership of her he did not have. At least, she prayed her father had not promised her to this alarmingly atrocious man.

To think she had been open to possibilities like wedding the baron only a few hours ago! She had, indeed, lost her mind. Even dear Lucy and her desire for a child of her own were not sufficient to spend five minutes in this man's company.

Any thought she had entertained about settling for someone at hand instead of waiting for William disappeared in a heartbeat—even if he never returned. One glance at the baron standing above her, ogling her breasts, had squelched that possibility forever. She would never marry a revolting old man like Lord Tremont. Never! She shivered at the mere thought of it.

"Are you chilled, Lady Caroline?" Chivalrously, the baron attempted to shrug out of his jacket, but it fit him too tightly, and he only proceeded to wiggle like a fuzzy worm on a hook.

"No, no, not at all." Caro searched for an excuse for her action when all she wanted to do was tell him to leave her alone. "I am simply excited to be here to enjoy what is sure to be a delightful evening of entertainment." She felt her smile stiffen on her face and heard the lack of enthusiasm in her voice that belied her words. Not surprisingly, the baron did not take the hint.

"Might your friends shift down a seat? I should be happy to keep you warm," he smiled, revealing teeth yellowed from tobacco and white spittle coating the corners of his lips.

A couple she did not know strolled in from the other end of the row and seated themselves next to the viscount who was busy glowering at the baron. She sighed in relief.

"Thank you for your concern, Lord Tremont, but I am quite comfortable." Her eyes darted behind the baron, and she exclaimed, "Oh look, is that my father with Lord Chatham? You should say hello. He shall be happy to see you." She did not wait for his response but turned back to Violet and launched into a monologue on the performances listed in the program.

The baron, now openly sulking, had no choice but to stomp up the aisle in search of the duke who appeared not to be where his daughter pointed.

Violet could not contain her giggle. "Caro, you can stop babbling now. He is gone."

"If you are cold, Lady Caroline, you might be warmer if you switch—"

"—No, I am fine, I assure you." After all that, she would not dream of switching places with Violet to sit next to the viscount. Would this musicale never start? Might she be left alone to sit and pretend to listen to the music, carefree of personal problems, for at least an hour? This social maneuvering was exhausting. At least it answered one question with certainty: she would not marry the baron.

Chapter 4

Tennessee, December 1863

Reveille shook William from a troubled sleep. As usual, after lying awake most of the night, he had just drifted off when that bloody bugle sounded the call. In truth, he had not slept well since leaving India. The jarring horn shattered his nerves every morning, but it did get his blood pumping. Nothing else had the power to force him up and moving and ready for a jolt of coffee—if a brewed cup could be found.

The Union division he served had been traveling northeast in hopes of reaching winter quarters near the Tennessee border before the first snowfall. At present, however, they were camped a few miles outside of Bean's Station, Tennessee, waiting for the infantry to catch up with the cavalry that had moved much faster. With a lull in the fighting, William thought it was a good time for him to leave America and return to his own time.

His friend and mentor, Rick Duvall, had gone home a few months ago, but it seemed more like years had passed in William's head. He missed Rick and his calm leadership. The two had become solid friends, being thrown together to mend the many casualties of the Union army with few resources and fewer tools.

The man was a genius at saving lives. Rick had taught him

dozens of ways to patch up a soldier so the man might live with all his limbs still attached. Other military surgeons chose to chop off a damaged arm or leg, claiming gangrene would set in otherwise. To them, it ensured the man would live. William preferred to see his patients leave his field tent whole.

He would be anxious to teach others in India what he had learned from Rick. He hated to admit it, but Olde Gylda was to thank for that. At least, he should thank her for the opportunity to learn, but would he thank her for separating him indefinitely from communicating with Caro? Would his love be waiting for him, or would she have given up and married someone else by now?

He truly had no way to reach her since she lived in 1813. How did anyone grasp that notion? As he did every day, he imagined how he would sound struggling to tell her his story without appearing stark-raving mad. There was no way to soften it. The tale was bizarre.

The only one who understood it was Rick, another Guardian of the Stones. He would understand how William's introduction to a new time period fifty years in the future might still play nightly in his head. Like a vicar reciting his psalms, William's mind recounted his first meeting with Rick nearly two years ago.

Knocked out by the whirling storm, he had awakened afterward with the old woman prodding him gently in the chest with a spindly finger. He sat up and pushed her away with a groan. His whole body hurt. Perched on a rock beside him, Gylda seemed to be quite chipper, unaffected by having been picked up and blown away by the wind. Giving him a gap-toothed grin, she pulled him up and dusted him off with an enormous pocket cloth like it was the usual thing one did after whirlwinds.

As he peered closer, he realized she no longer held the stone, but in searching for it elsewhere, other things struck him as wrong. He was no longer standing in a British camp with tents nearby, but in a wilderness surrounded by trees. Looking for something familiar, he could see the trees and grasses around him were not those of India. He panicked, sniffing the air. It did not smell or feel right, either.

Olde Gylda had watched him closely as he made these observations, her lively blue eyes twinkling the whole time.

"Ha! I knew ye'd be a sharp one. I was a bit worried when we passed through London and ye ne'er woke up. I had a devil of a time transferring us to the next stone with you a lump on the ground. 'Tis a blessing I am a witch, or Abasi and his men would have captured us for sure."

William's jaw dropped open a tad further with each sentence of her screed. What was the old crone saying? He had been back in London and did not know it? So close to Caro? This was quickly becoming a disaster. Did he know anyone named Abasi? Why would he want to capture them? Where were they now? If this were a dream, everything around him was disturbingly real.

"Ye know 'tis different, don't ye?" She cackled and punched him again in the stomach.

"Yes, I do," he gritted out, not amused at all. "Would you mind telling me where we are and what just happened?"

She squealed in delight. "I told ye that ye were a Guardian of the Stones, right?" She waited for him to nod. "Ye also know that ye are to help soldiers of war recover, yes?" Now his impatience started to slow boil. Was she determined to drag out every little point? His face must have shown his tolerance level was depleted because her next words tumbled out in a rush. "My good sir, ye are now in America in the year of eighteen-hundred and sixty-two."

He stayed frozen in shock so long, that same gnarled finger poked him twice to see if he still breathed. How did one respond to something like that? His eyes examined the land around him which only confirmed he was not in India. That did not explain how he could have whirled across half the world to America and landed fifty years into the future. None of this made any sense. It did not end there.

With his mind still reeling, a man approached from over the ridge dressed in a uniform he did not recognize. Who was this? Friend or foe? In alarm, he looked for guidance from Gylda, who happily shrilled a friendly greeting to the newcomer. He relaxed slightly and waited to see what this man would say.

"Call me Rick," the man offered, thrusting out a hand for him to shake. Not certain what he should do, he accepted the hand presented to him and was surprised by the solid grip of the man before him.

"Well, laddie, this here is Doc Duvall. He's the man ye'll learn all ye can from before goin' back home." Gylda patted Duvall on the back like a favorite child.

Rick was bearded, and wore a dark blue uniform trimmed in what looked like brass buttons. The jacket had seen hard times with the sleeves frayed and wear apparent in every fiber. He looked like no doctor William had ever seen. This was the man who was supposed to teach him advanced medicine? It did not look promising.

"I see you've met Gylda. From your expression you aren't quite clear why you're here, are you?"

William snorted. "You might say that, yes." He paused and caught his breath, recognizing the man's accent was a near match with that of an American friend from London. The nationality part seemed to be true. Before he could reconsider, he decided to simply ask, "Am I really standing in America and is this the year 1862?"

The man chuckled and shook his head at Old Gylda. "You enjoy this time travel business way too much, don't you? You might make it a little less shocking for the new recruits, you know!"

Gylda thought that was hysterical and went into fits of laughter while Rick grinned, and William frowned. Had the doctor just confirmed time travel? Was he fifty years ahead of his own time as the old crone said? He felt all the blood leave his head as the truth of his situation sunk in.

"Wait! If this is so, how am I to return home? I am betrothed in England. I never intended to stay forever in India. I-I never agreed to any of this!"

That was the last thing he remembered before his world

went dark . . . again.

William shook his head over how naïve he had been when he arrived in America. It seemed like a century ago rather than two years with so much happening to him in between. His arrival in the new world had been a shock to his system, but Rick Duvall had an even bigger shock still waiting for him.

∞ ∞ ∞

"Caro, you will wait for me, won't you?"

"Of course, William. You know I will never love anyone but you."

"I must leave for India now or nothing will change for us, and you will be lost to me." She nodded her head in misery. He held her face in both hands and looked deeply into her eyes. "Know that I will return to you, no matter what."

Caro awoke in a sweat, the words *no matter what* echoing in her mind. How often had she dreamed of that exchange? All her insecurities pushed open the door her heart tried to keep shut and rushed in. What if William had found a new love in India and had a family of his own? Had his words only mattered to her? After all, theirs had never been an official betrothal.

Her mind wandered over last evening's musicale. The baron's rusty brows had hovered over glaring eyes that rarely left her person throughout the evening. Meanwhile, the viscount had managed to seat himself beside Caro for the second half of the program. Much to her displeasure, the attention he paid to her had become obvious even to Violet, whose giggle and glow diminished as the night wore on.

Her father caught Caro's eye during an exceptionally long aria and had the nerve to waggle an eyebrow at her and then at the viscount and grin. Actually grin, as if no one else could see him! She sighed and fanned herself with the top bed sheet to cool her body. At least it was not the baron he was so enthused about. Still, she did not want the viscount either and certainly not when Violet pined for his regard.

Everything was so much harder to deal with as an adult. She longed for the days when William and Violet had joined her in all kinds of mischief. Her friends had supported her and made her days fun, regardless of the trouble the three spawned.

Her history with musicales was not a good one, but Christmas musicales were the worst. Caro had a pitch-perfect ear and a voice to match. Her mother had been delighted to feature her in one musicale after another all year, but she hated performing. The most unforgettable night was the Christmas spectacle when she was sixteen. Her mother had her singing "The Holly and the Ivy" with Lord Gerald, a seventeen-year-old reprobate who pinched her bottom whenever no one was looking. She complained bitterly to her mother who refused to rescind Lord Gerald's invitation to sing. It simply was not done.

Hearing of her dilemma, William and Violet hatched a plan that would satisfy Caro's wildest dreams of retribution. As she and Lord Gerald took the floor, somehow the boot boy's pet mouse darted into the room with her mother's King Charles spaniel snapping at its heels.

The ensuing melee had been a thing of wonder. Women of all ages screamed, stood on chairs, or fainted at the sight of the mouse that ran for its life at top speed over the toes of jeweled slippers. The snarling Rufus, although not a large dog, rampaged through rows of people, oblivious to gowns, feet, and the hands trying to catch him.

At one point the poor mouse thought it had found the perfect hiding place with an inside run up Lady Bethany's leg. The snooty, high-strung girl nearly tore off her gown in front of the entire audience in her efforts to dislodge the beastie.

Her shrieking mother was too fearful of the vermin to be of much help, but her father dashed to her side for the rescue. When he got there, however, he could only think to pick her up and shake her in an unseemly fashion as if she were a rag doll. To add to the family indignity, the mouse dislodged itself after much struggle and flipped out of Lady Bethany's skirts right into the face of her mother who promptly fainted.

It was a spectacular moment. The evening's unscheduled entertainment abruptly ended when the footmen chased the terrified mouse from the room, and the yapping spaniel was captured and removed by her mortified mother.

This unparalleled lapse of decorum had the ton suspended in frenzied speculation for what seemed an eternity for her mother, but in fact, was only a few days. The Lowther siblings claimed to have heard Lord Gerald was behind the debacle, since he and Caro had quarreled before their performance, but the young man swore he had nothing to do with the scene. Her mother was so upset, she had not hosted another musicale or allowed Caro to perform in one for a full year—a year of freedom her daughter had enjoyed immensely.

Looking back, Caro thought perhaps she had fallen in love with William that night. While Lord Gerald chased the overwrought little dog around the room, William had given her a conspiratorial wink as he stuck a foot in Gerald's path. The boy who could not keep his hands to himself had gone sprawling across three rows of chairs, landing in Aunt Augusta's lap. She cuffed his ears as if he were the errant dog until he howled for release.

It was a perfect evening. William had defended her honor and rescued her from a hated duet. Thereafter, her sixteen-year-old heart beat only for William.

What a pity those simpler days were gone.

Chapter 5

Riding at the back of the Union cavalry with a medical wagon and two other medics, William noted some changes that disturbed his peace of mind. On the plus side, the Union troops were fresh off a victory having defeated the Confederates at Chattanooga in the Battle of Missionary Ridge at the end of November. They also had held Knoxville against a Confederate assault a few days later, thus ending the Knoxville Campaign. Those successes had sent the Confederates into retreat with the Union troops following them out of the area.

The downside troubling William was the location of the Union infantry. Led by General Parke, they were supposed to travel right behind the cavalry for support. Over several days, however, the foot soldiers had drifted out of sight until he knew not how far behind the cavalry they were. It left him and his fellow medics feeling very vulnerable from the rear.

To add to his concerns, General Burnside who had led the Union troops through their previous successes had been moved elsewhere. In his place Brigadier General Shackleford was the new commander now in charge at Bean's Station. The change-over seemed to leave the Federals open to the machinations of the cunning General Longstreet, one of General Lee's favorite officers. He was only a short distance ahead at Rogersville and could claim a much larger force than Shackleford held at Bean's

Station, especially if Union forces were spread out. And they seemed to be. It did not bode well from William's perspective.

He hated worrying about these tactical issues, but his time working with the Company military in India had taught him to be aware of what was going on around him. Still, he constantly had to remind himself this was not his fight. He was only in America to learn from Duvall, not help the Union win.

All he really wanted to do was go home to London, or even back to India—anyplace in his own time, so he could communicate with Caro again. Every day apart increased the chances they would never be together again. Duvall was gone, so he was learning nothing new. Why then was Olde Gylda keeping him here?

By nightfall, the scene William feared had begun to unfold. General Shackleford sent a message after dark to Parke's command asking for infantry support to protect the rear. Union pickets reported the Confederates moving back toward Bean's Station from Rogersville. Without an infantry directly behind them, Shackleford's cavalry was in danger of being surrounded and overwhelmed by Longstreet's superior numbers before relief could arrive.

That news had William contemplating how he might leave the area. Who could stop him if he walked away and disappeared without a trace? Privately, he begged Gylda to send him a Guardian Stone. No response. Every day he hoped one might appear, yet nothing resembling the stone that sent him into the midst of this terrible war had presented itself.

Not even Duvall's accounts of his own travels back in time had changed William's viewpoint. He wanted to go home from the moment he had arrived. It was not until he learned the details of Rick's time walking and his life in Texas that William was stunned by the enormity of his situation. After Rick's account, he listened raptly to whatever the man told him.

As he recalled, it had been in November of 1862 when Doc had let slip the secret he had not meant to share. The two had been working on the wounded somewhere near a place called Cane Hill in Arkansas. Their afternoon had seen hundreds of wounded and there had been little time for talk. The tent was hot, and the smell of unwashed bodies, blood, and disease was enough to turn even the strong stomachs of the doctors.

The unsanitary, crowded camps featured a raft of ills. Syphilis and dysentery were the chief offenders, but typhoid, pneumonia, mumps, measles, and TB were right behind them in killing soldiers.

An experienced doctor, new to their unit, pulled out a bottle labeled "Calomel/Mercury Chloride" and prepared a big spoonful of the tincture for a syphilis patient. The soldier looked to be about seventeen.

Doc happened to see it and realized what the man called Silas was about to do. Horrified, he had only enough time to swat the spoon from the surgeon's hand, sending the liquid in a splat across the front of the patient's filthy jacket.

Incredulous, the surgeon's fists clenched, and for a moment William expected him to punch Doc in the face. Instead, Doc calmly said, "I apologize for not seeing what you were doing soon enough to stop you verbally. A dose that large will kill this young man. Mercury Chloride is toxic."

The surgeon scowled and shook his graying head as if that were the most ridiculous notion he had ever heard. Reaching into his beat-up black bag on the table behind the patient, he pulled out another bottle, this one full of pills labeled "Blue Mass."

He displayed the tincture in one hand and the pills in the other before tossing the bottle of pills to Doc Duvall to examine. "I've been treatin' patients with syphilis with these two medicines for years." His lips curled into a snarling challenge.

"Right, Silas, and how many of them became healthy and lived?" Doc only gave the pills a cursory glance while he waited for a reply, an eyebrow of his own arched to counter the challenge.

The surgeon glowered even harder at Doc through narrowed eyes. "It's syphilis, Duvall. Most patients don't live long with it no matter what we do."

The young man with open sores all over his body moaned, leaving William to wonder if it was pain from the disease or what the doctors had just said.

"True, but I see no need to poison our patients, do you?"

It was tense for a time between the two doctors until finally Doc broke the silence.

"Make him as comfortable as you can, Si, but lay off the mercury pills and tinctures. They won't make him feel any better, but they will make him sicker as time goes on until they kill him."

"What makes you think you're so damned smart, Doc? Why should I believe you when mercury like this has been used as a medicine fer hunnerds o' years?"

The man glared intently at Doc having used as insulting a tone as he could muster. He sneaked a glance at William to see if he might be of support, but unsure of what to say to any of this, William kept his mouth shut.

"I've had advanced studies on this you haven't had. Trust me, it's all new and there are labs working on a cure for syphilis that won't use any mercury in the medicine they make." He stopped and shook his head as if to clear it. "Right now, the mercury will only make it worse. Why don't you ask your patient what he wants to do?"

Silas growled in the direction of the young man who by now just wanted off the table before someone killed him on the spot.

"If it be all right, sir, I think I'll jus' be goin' on now. I don't need nuthin' what's gonna kill me. Least not today." He slid off the table like a worm off a hook and scooted for the tent door. A ragged trail of stained bandages flapped behind him as if he were an excavated Egyptian mummy.

Silas snatched the bottle of Blue Mass out of Doc's hands and threw it back in his bag in a fit of temper. He jammed the bag shut and stomped off to find a new location where he would not have Doc Duvall interfering with his next patient. Doc let him go. Too many men were waiting for care to let one troublesome encounter slow them down for long.

William sidled up to Doc a short time later when they had a small break in the action. "Where did you study about a syphilis cure, if you don't mind my asking?"

"I trained in Houston, Texas," Duvall drawled.

"Oh, isn't your family from there?" Doc nodded, his mind occupied by the search through his bag for a missing tool.

"When was that?"

"In 2005 and 2006."

William watched his friend suddenly go still. Color crept up his neck and onto his face.

"I m-mean about ten or fifteen years ago," he corrected. Doc's head came up with his face doing its best not to look guilty.

It was too late. William was on to him. "You haven't been completely honest with me, have you, Doc?" It was not a question. Duvall shrugged and gave him a boyish grin.

"Nah, I haven't. The truth is I come from about 150 years in the future, son. I know mercury kills people, and a drug called penicillin will cure syphilis and a host of other things as well."

William's eyes were huge. That was not at all what he thought his friend would say.

"Olde Gylda has had me here to try to stop all the death not caused by fighting the war, but by rampant illness and unsanitary conditions. It's why you are here. She hopes by having me teach you and a few others some new skills, many lives and limbs of soldiers can be saved.

Digesting this mind-blowing information had William struggling to put his thoughts together. "Is that how you know so much about sanitation? And what to do to keep patients from getting sick when operated on?"

"Yeah, I can't do everything I've been trained to do here, but I can do enough to keep lots of these guys alive to go home to their families. That's the important thing."

"Is that why she hasn't let you go home?" William's face scrunched with a new, unsavory thought. "Am I keeping you here?"

Rick laughed and rolled his eyes in William's direction. "Who knows what's in Gylda's head, but you may be right. I know I'm ready to leave this hellish war and see my wife and kids again.

"Me, too!" William flushed. "At least I'd like to have a family someday to go home to see. If I do not return to Caro soon, I am worried she will have married someone else. I have no way to tell her where I am, if I am well, or when I shall return."

"Same here, Willy, my boy!" Rick shook his head in frustration. "My wife doesn't know if I'm alive or dead, but she does know I'm a time traveler. Still, I hate that I've put her through all the worry. My kids probably think I deserted them." The pain in the man's eyes told William just how much that separation hurt.

Neither had a chance to speculate further because the next round of wounded came straggling in. William practiced the method Rick called triage and sorted the patients into three groups: those mortally wounded, those slightly wounded, and likely surgical cases. He wondered if that was from Rick's world far into the future or this one. Either way it was a skill he would take back with him.

With a new perspective, he turned to help the next patient.

∞∞∞

A full year had passed since then. He had parted with Doc Duvall near Pineville, Missouri around midsummer, 1863. Rick had been sent to join up with Major Plumb and the 11th Kansas Cavalry regiment. William had been shipped east by railroad from St. Louis to Louisville, Kentucky. From there William was assigned to General Burnside and then General Shackelford.

The news of Rick's departure from Lawrence, Kansas, had hit William like a hammer. Just knowing Rick was in the same time period with him had fought off his sense of isolation. He was happy Doc and his family could go home to their own time and thankful Rick had alerted him to the event by letter. Despite Doc's assurances he would be sent home soon, too, William was not so sure it would happen.

That left William to wait alone tonight for the trouble sure to strike in Bean's Station. Doc's legacy, however, lived on with William. Silas had asked to be transferred to a different unit about two weeks after their mercury exchange, so he had not been a long-term problem. William had made it his mission to pass on the message to other medics that mercury was not the cure-all they thought it was. Silas's replacement and others were not easily persuaded either, but he and Doc had managed to make progress on several other fronts over that year whether together or apart.

He climbed onto his field cot inside the medics' tent and tried to relax his tensed muscles. So much had changed, yet so much stayed the same. Nothing was ever easy in wartime. Sleep, least of all. It was always hard to sleep knowing a battle was imminent. He rarely felt in danger himself since their medic tents were routinely set up behind the lines far enough away to be out of the fray. Occasionally, a retreat would send them all scurrying for their wagons to get ahead of the trouble.

That was the source of his anxiety tonight. The camp rumor was that Longstreet planned to cut the Feds off from retreat and hold them in a vice while the Confederates annihilated them. How did one accept that fate? Should he try to call up Gylda and a Guardian Stone again, or simply wait it out? Supposedly, the old crone would not let a time walker die.

Right now, all he knew was he was tired and dispirited. His nightly salvation was to open the pocket watch Caro had given him and talk to her miniature in his head as though she were in front of him. They had wonderful conversations. Caro was her lovely, intelligent, witty self. His friend. He imagined where she was, what she was wearing, and how her eyes would sparkle when she saw him. He would walk her through her day, shopping on Bond Street, or visiting friends. She would expect lemon tarts for teatime with her favorite Darjeeling tea. He would pretend he did not notice when she ate twice as many tarts as he did. To tease her, he would help himself to the last tart just to see her expression. He loved her indignant response that would turn to sunshine when he cheerfully shared the treat with her.

Would she be off this evening, looking divine and smelling of roses, to a dance or a rout, or perhaps the theatre? He should have enjoyed those events with her when he'd had the chance. Instead, he had "suffered" through them, complaining of matchmaking mamas and warm lemonade at Almack's to fit in with all the other young bucks about town. What he would not give to have that time back to spend with Caro all over again.

Whose arm would she be on tonight and what were her thoughts regarding this gentleman or that one? Those were the questions plaguing him every night when he tried to rest his weary soul before the labors of the next rigorous day. Kissing her picture and reading the inscription one last time, he sent up to heaven the same quick message he sent every night.

Wait for me, Caro. Please wait.

Would she hear it? The loud click of the watch cover as it closed said she just might.

Chapter 6

Caro was pleased with herself. It had taken a bit of finagling to get Papa to go along with her plans, but in the end, he was excited about the trip, too. Her friend Charlotte had invited them to a Woodington family Christmas in South Yorkshire.

The estate, called Woodworth, was grand with a wonderful place to skate, sleigh rides to be had, and all the rituals of a traditional family Christmas down to the Yule log. Woodington Christmas holidays were legendary among the ton, and it was a treasured invitation to join them.

The downside revealed itself upon presenting the house-party arrangements to her father for approval. Apparently, her father was more than serious about seeing her married soon and intended to force the situation, even over the holiday. He had insisted that Cornelius Tremont be invited as well as Christopher Duncanby, or they would not attend.

Caro had rolled her eyes at her father when he told her those would be the conditions for their visit. That small action made him so furious with her that he sputtered and coughed for a full quarter of an hour. He turned so red and frowned so fiercely she thought his eyebrows might permanently be joined in the center. Only when she had rubbed his back had he calmed down. After that it had taken her half a day and most of her lemon tarts to put him in a better mood.

Knowing two unsuitable suitors would be at the house party to complicate her enjoyment was troublesome. Searching for a way to keep the holiday from ruination, Caro applied a little persuasion of her own. She pleaded with Charlotte to add Violet Lowther and her parents to the Woodington guest list. That Violet's parents would also be attending was purposely not divulged to her father. With Violet and Charlotte beside her, she could fend off any amorous beaus.

A solid two-day drive from London—three if bad weather factored—it promised to be a cold journey to Woodworth. Caro had cajoled her father into allowing her to invite Violet to ride to the house party with her. He had suspected Violet would be in attendance due to her close friendship with Charlotte and Caro. The thought of having to listen to two chattering young women for two days straight in a confined space was enough for him to readily agree to separate traveling carriages.

Since Violet's parents would be coming from Bath, it was convenient for both to have Violet traveling securely with the duke's entourage. Plus, Caro could honestly say that Violet would have been forced to travel by herself without Caro's assistance. The duke would never have argued for the girl to make the trip alone no matter who her parents were.

When Caro suggested that Lucy might ride with them some of the way, too, that sealed the deal for separate conveyances. The duke did require his peace and quiet. Thus, ready to get out of the city and enjoy the countryside, Caro and Violet, plus their maids, occupied one carriage, with the duke and his valet in a second. Not quite as splendid an equipage as the duke's, the young ladies' coach was still warm and plush for a heavy traveling carriage.

Caro was satisfied with most of the details for her Christmas holiday. She found it disquieting, however, that William and Violet's parents, the Marquess of Westdale and his marchioness, were not friends with her father any longer. As one might expect, they had been distressed with the way the duke had handled William's offer for Caro, especially after the two families had known each other for so many years.

Why the duke had turned down William had never been explained beyond a brief statement of "The boy is not ready to wed her." Frankly, William might have been a second son, but the insult stung since the Lowther family was a proud one in good standing with the ton.

Caro had never gotten much more out of her father either. The strain once William left for India had been enough to dampen relations with the Lowther family even more. Then, when William's company listed him as missing with his whereabouts unknown, it had been enough to sever any friendly ties between the two families.

Caro feared her father's reaction when he learned William's parents had been invited as well. She prayed he would not make a blustery scene of it when that time came. Surely, he would agree that pushing her at two other suitors in front of William's family would be insensitive, if not poor form. Her beloved may have been gone for two years, but his parents and sister were not at all ready to assume him dead.

Two more traveling coaches trailed the duke's entourage with all the luggage and other servants, including Milly and Lucy. Only a few days ago, Milly had heard from her sister who had agreed to take Lucy into her home in Shropshire. They arranged to meet them at the coaching inn near Stilton late the first day to deliver Lucy to her aunt.

Caro was not looking forward to that since she had bonded with the child more than she cared to admit. She had found it most satisfying to be the only person able to get Lucy to calm down if the baby girl got too upset. All Caro had to do was pick her up and hold her close. Lucy would suck in a big, shaky breath, plop her head on Caro's shoulder, and drop off to sleep seconds later. It worked every time. How could she not love that?

Any time, day or night, Caro relished having them bring the child to her as needed. She dreaded the separation from the sweet baby, but she knew Lucy needed a permanent home with a family who would love and care for her. She would find that life with Milly's sister. At least she hoped so.

The morning that had begun clear and crisp got darker and grayer as the day wore on. Caro thought it might be a metaphor for parting with Lucy. Even the child seemed to be aware of the atmospheric pressures around her. Each time they stopped to change horses along the Great North Road, Lucy's happy baby babbles turned a little crankier. Milly had packed enough food and drink for several days in each of the vehicles for all to enjoy, but none of that satisfied Lucy.

By the third stop, Caro was secretly pleased that Lucy had passed the fussy stage and was now ready for the switch into Caro's carriage. As Milly predicted, Lucy tuckered out and slept within minutes once they were back out on the road. The little darling snuggled in like she was home at last. It was heart-breaking and endearing all at once.

During the last few miles before stopping for the night, the weather turned nasty. At first, scattered flakes of snow fell gently and melted upon hitting the earth, but then it turned into sleet that soon was pinging sideways off the doors of the coach, creating hazardous travel. The lamps had been lighted at the last coaching stop but did little to erase the dim view of the world around them.

Lucy must have intuited their collective angst because she awoke screaming at the top of her lungs. This time, nothing Caro tried made her stop for more than a few minutes. Every time the babe quieted to sleep, the carriage would groan or slide, and she would awaken screaming.

The snug vehicle had foot warmers and many blankets, so they were not unduly cold inside. However, the freezing temperatures outside had either the horses sliding on the ice or the carriage wheels dragging in a skid every few minutes. It was terrifying. The back of the carriage would swing left or right and then tip side to side as it recovered its course, sometimes sending its occupants on a similar tipsy trajectory inside.

Violet and Caro kept their eyes on each other in the dwindling light, hoping these would not be their last moments. Their maids huddled together opposite them with eyes closed and prayers on their lips.

At last, the carriage slowed to a stop and the brightness from outside torches told them they had arrived at their stop for the night at The Bell in Stilton. Caro took a deep breath and discovered she had been holding it for what seemed like miles. As her muscles unclenched across her body, Lucy echoed her stretch and settled into a whimper before she, too, gurgled a huge sigh. All were thankful to have arrived in one piece.

Sounds of the steps being pulled down prepared them for the carriage door to open next, but it did not immediately happen. They heard scraping and pounding before the ice that sealed the carriage door popped off to free the door to open.

Caro was touched to see her father greet them with a somber bear hug for Caro and a fatherly pat on the back for Violet—a huge display of affection from the dispassionate duke. He had been worried, too.

What a relief to step inside the toasty inn with its fireplace roaring and the smell of roasting meat and yeasty bread mixing with the fruity scent of ale. Even the thick layer of tobacco smoke hanging in the air could not darken her enthusiasm for the place. Caro insisted Lucy accompany her and Violet to their room for a wash and a change of clothes before they returned to the main rooms for dinner. A short time later, spirits were high with Lucy happily blowing bubbles when they found the duke in the private dining room assigned to them.

That happy interlude ended swiftly, however, when Caro realized there were others in the room. She promptly lost her appetite as her stomach slid up to clench her throat. On a bench on the far side of the room sat Milly with an older woman and four children.

The woman had to be Milly's sister since she had the same bright hair and blue eyes as Milly. With fine lines hatched across her face, her skin had the texture of a newspaper that had been crumpled up and then flattened out with an iron. Her clothing was clean and tidy, but it, too, had a worn quality as if it had had its seams turned more than once. Sadly, the woman's face looked dead, as if all emotion had been beaten from her face.

The children lined up beside her, from smallest to largest —a boy and three girls. They, too, sat with their hands in their laps over clothes that had obviously been passed down from child to child since their well-mended sleeves, skirts or pant legs were mostly too short or too long. The littlest child, a boy, had a round hole in the bottom of one of his shoes. The only bright spot she could see, as she watched them watch her and Lucy, was the air of expectation on the part of the children. Their excitement broke the tension in the room.

Milly hopped up from beside her sister and rushed to her mistress. "My lady, I was worried Sybil and her young'uns would be caught by this dreadful storm, but it turns out they was all here afore it got bad."

"I see." The words stuck in Caro's throat. She was not ready for the exchange to take place. Not yet. She squeezed Lucy closer to her breast and stared as Milly's sister stood from her place by the wall and curtsied. Her girls did the same, but what touched Caro's heart was the little boy who did a well-practiced bow and then grinned at her from ear to ear. He was a beautiful child with the same red hair and freckles, but his beaming brown eyes looked golden in the firelight of the room and set him apart from his siblings.

The children were bursting with repressed energy and ready to hop up and down if she did not introduce them to Lucy soon. Still, observing no signs of warmth in Sybil, Caro decided to break rank with protocol and let the children meet the baby first. Caro motioned for a footman to pull out a bench from the trestle table, so she could sit down and hold Lucy on her lap for the introductions.

"This, dear children, is your cousin Lucy. Come say hello."

They did not have to be asked twice. Caro found herself holding her free arm out to keep the girls back at a safe distance, so they did not smother the child. The smiles and exuberance on their faces told her they did not suffer the reprimands as a scold, but their mother had quickly had enough. Stepping through the many small hands that pushed to pat and pet baby Lucy, Sybil held out her arms to Caro to take the child from her.

Caro's breath caught as she was still forming several reasons why she should still hold Lucy when she looked up and spied the tears in Sybil's eyes. All the air whooshed out of her as she realized Sybil was mourning the loss of her sister at the same time she was meeting her niece. Lucy was all that remained of her sister's family. What a bittersweet moment!

Tears flooded Caro's eyes when Sybil's face morphed from a frown into a delighted grin. The woman's face had transformed from frozen and expressionless to warm and joyous.

"Oh, Milly, ye did not tell me she was the spittin' image of Rose! Look, her eyes are the same color and the shape of her lips, too."

Milly's tears flowed, but they were happy tears. "I knew ye'd be glad ta see that fer yerself, Sybil."

The two sisters huddled over the baby with the four children pushing each other and tucking themselves into any crevice to see baby Lucy. Everyone now smiled and cooed at the little one in their midst, so Caro stepped back and took a seat beside her father. In only a moment, Lucy no longer belonged to her. She pulled a neatly embroidered handkerchief from her sleeve and dabbed at her eyes. Her work was done. Lucy had a new home and a new family.

Violet sat down beside her and whispered into her ear. "You should be proud of yourself, Caro. Not every employer would have taken such an interest in the offspring of a relative of a servant. Baby Lucy was lucky to have you."

"No, Violet, I was lucky to have her." Caro's lips wobbled as she whispered back to Violet, so she did not continue the thoughts inhabiting her mind.

She did not tell Violet how much she wished Lucy had been William's child. That if William were truly gone from this life, and she could never be with him again, how having his child would have kept a part of him alive. All of that would have broken her heart once again, so she pursed her lips to keep the trembles at bay and watched Lucy settle in with her new family.

Talk during the meal that followed had her father squirming in discomfort, but since they had a private dining room, he did his best not to complain. After all, it was not every day a duke shared a meal with the servant class at the same table. Caro would have it no other way and adored getting to know the children. Bess, Bea, Tisha, and Bertie were well-behaved and charming in their plans for the new baby in their household.

The family would leave at first light the next morning unless the weather prohibited, so goodbyes had to be said before they parted for the night. The duke hurriedly bid his guests a good evening and left the room, not wishing to witness any of the emotional outbursts he believed would follow. He instructed Caro and Violet to come by his private sitting room off his sleeping quarters upon leaving Lucy with her family.

Once the duke had gone Caro nodded to her footmen to cart in a trunk full of bottles, blankets, baby clothes, and toys. Included was every item of baby paraphernalia Caro had purchased for Lucy in the short time she had resided in the duke's household.

Overwhelmed by this generosity, Sybil and Milly cried anew, and the children were agog. Never one to be stopped by a few tears, Caro emptied her pockets of every coin she had with her, including all her pin money, and made Sybil promise to let her know if Lucy ever needed anything.

"Good heavens, Caro, stop now. Next thing you know you shall be shedding your clothes to give away, and I'll have to find a blanket to wrap you in just to get you to your room!" Violet giggled and so did Sybil and Milly, allowing everyone to take a breath.

Sybil smiled at Caro with such warmth in her eyes that Caro's fears of a loveless home for Lucy vanished completely. "Milady, thank ye for all ye 'ave done for our sister's child. Rose would be pleased. Our family thanks ye fer seein' 'er here in such grand style. We will treasure Lucy as the best present Rose ever gave us."

Sybil curtsied, leaving Caro to nod, her eyes full of tears as she choked back her emotions just long enough to make a dignified exit. Then she ran to her room with Violet trailing behind. Her father must have been listening from his quarters for them to pass by, because he knocked on their door moments later.

"Won't you ladies join me for a nightcap in my sitting room?" His eyes roamed over Caro with some sadness surfacing from their usually unreadable depths. "You will sleep better after the events of the evening, I believe."

Caro whimpered and flung herself into her papa's arms to be comforted, and he obliged, patting her back rather awkwardly. It was Violet who said, "I believe that is a yes, your grace." The duke grunted in agreement and detached Caro from his person. "Wash your face and dry your eyes, daughter, and I will expect you both shortly." With that, he nodded to Violet and exited, his ducal armor back in place.

A few minutes later, Violet and Caro were seated in a comfy little sitting room before a blazing fire. No one had much to say while the duke poured some sherry for the ladies and a brandy for himself. With drinks in hand, the mood was still somber, so Violet decided to tell them the rousing tale of Dick Turpin, the infamous highwayman of the last century. She was an excellent storyteller and even had the duke laughing at her ripping account of Turpin's derring-do. It was a perfect choice because the very inn where they now slept had been the thief's hide-out for weeks before he had jumped out a window to escape the law.

Somehow the much-exaggerated legend was just what they all needed to relax. Soon Caro's eyelids fluttered, and her yawns were cavernous, so she and Violet retired for the night.

Caro's dreams were lucid and not at all restful. She and Violet found themselves in the dead of night traveling at a rapid clip down a deserted road. The lamps were lit on the carriage, but they shed little light on the lane ahead. Suddenly, an old, old lady with glowing blue eyes stepped onto the highway and planted herself firmly in their path. Her voluminous black gown blew in the nighttime breeze forming a silhouette framed by the moonlight. With Violet jerking back with all her might on the reins and Caro glued to her side, the coach miraculously rolled to a stop only inches from the woman. Searching around for help, their coachman and all the footmen were nowhere to be seen.

The old crone called in a rusty, cracked voice for Caro to leave the coach and walk to her, something Violet pleaded with her friend not to do. The duke and the other carriages were no longer behind them. She and Violet were indeed all alone in the middle of the night on a lonely road. Still, Caro could find nothing particularly worrisome about this person dressed all in black, so she complied.

The old woman grinned at her with only half a dozen teeth twinkling in her head like stars, but still Caro was not frightened. Reaching into the pockets of her capacious gown, the crone pulled out three items for Caro to see. The first was a pocket watch made of gold. She popped it open to show Caro but did not allow her a glimpse of the picture inside. The second was a map she unfurled labeled America, with the third nothing more than a strip of clean white cotton material. The witchy woman said nothing about each item but clearly wanted Caro to have them. Not seeing any reason to decline, Caro shrugged and put her hands out to take the offering. She would figure out what it meant later.

As the old woman stretched out her arms to hand the objects to Caro, a black-caped rider on a huge black horse galloped up from behind the coach. In a single motion, he swooped down and stole all three items from the witch's hands.

Violet screamed that it was Dick Turpin on Black Bess as the thief disappeared into the dark even faster than he had appeared. Caro heard the old woman swear loudly, but when she turned to look at her, the woman was gone. Just gone. Not a trace of her left behind. That is when Caro awoke.

"Do you suppose it was the sherry or the tales of Dick Turpin that caused my dreams to be so vivid?" Caro asked at breakfast after regaling her father and Violet with her dream. This one she remembered in detail and enjoyed telling them about it. Despite the dark of night and a witch-like character, it had been more frustrating than scary. She was happy when morning had dawned with a blue sky and warmer temperatures. The roads would be much improved today.

"I'm sure it was my expertly told tale of Dick Turpin that rattled your brains, dear girl," Violet joked, diving with relish into a plate heaped with coddled eggs and some plump sausages.

"Hmm," her father agreed. "No doubt that is why Turpin was in your dream." He paused for a moment in thought as he pushed a kipper about his plate with his fork. "But where did the witch come from? I have never seen anyone like her, have you?"

Caro and her father liked dreams. This was not the first time they had analyzed one of their own, enjoying the mind's nighttime wanderings with as much delight as a sweet from Gunther's. Her father believed all parts of a dream stemmed from recent interactions in the normal course of life, while Caro skewed more toward the fantastical side, believing messages were told in dreams for a reason.

"I have no idea, Papa. I have never met anyone like her, and I think I would remember if I had."

"I am more interested in the items she tried to give you," Violet said. "Do any of those hold any significance for you?"

"Well, I did go shopping with Louisa not long ago when she bought a gold pocket watch for Hugh. Would that count?"

"It certainly would," her father answered, nodding sagely. Then his demeanor hardened, and his eyes narrowed. "I do hope the map does not mean you are thinking of running off to America."

Caro understood the underlying message there without having it spelled out for her. Perhaps her father was softening on throwing her at potential husbands? Why make it easy on him. She chose to respond by lifting an eyebrow and letting the corners of her mouth turn up slightly. She was not above keeping him guessing on that score.

Her father *hmphed* and let it go. He turned to Violet and changed the subject. "What do you think the white cloth represents?"

"Good question, your grace. If it is a bandage, might someone be wounded?" When Caro sucked in a breath of concern, Violet added, "Or it might signify a surrender. Like waving a white flag, perhaps."

The duke smiled indulgently at the young women. "You two will have all day to consider it, so let us be gone now while the day is young."

"You are so right, your grace." Violet delivered her best dimpled grin which left the duke a little flushed but pleased. Few could withstand the force of Violet's dimples when fully unleashed.

Caro devoured her last triangle of toast, gulped a swallow of her now cooled tea, and gathered her belongings to head for the carriage. It would be another long day no matter when they started out, but without baby Lucy to entertain them, it would seem even longer.

As they picked up speed turning out of the inn yard and onto the Great North Road, Caro blew a kiss toward Shropshire and the highway Sybil's family would have taken. She made a silent wish for Lucy and her new cousins to have a safe journey home. The darling babe would be missed.

Would she ever hold a baby of her own in her arms?

Chapter 7

Waiting, waiting, waiting. Was there ever a harder thing a soldier had to do? Charging into battle was always a relief. It required no thought other than doing the job as assigned. Sitting and waiting for a battle to start meant far-ranging thoughts roamed unfettered through a man's brain. Would he be killed? Maimed? Sent home too mentally damaged for any decent future life? When battle was imminent, the desire was to get on with it and let the outcome be determined by the fight.

William and the other medics had not set up as usual for the coming battle for Bean's Station. They had been told there would be no safe place behind the lines if, in fact, Longstreet's army surrounded them. Not even the yellow flags with green H's marking them as hospital wagons would protect them.

If General Parke's Union forces arrived too late to shore up Shackleford's weak side, their only option was to hope a breach occurred somewhere in the Confederate's offensive around Bean's Station. Then a retreat out of the area could be orchestrated to avoid being caught and slaughtered. If the day favored the Confederates, there would be no time to break down any kind of tent or camp. They must be prepared to flee at a moment's word in any direction they were sent.

That meant the surgeons would tend to the wounded out of the back of their hospital wagons as patients appeared. Only the direst cases would be put into the wagons for travel. The other casualties would have to rely upon friends and other soldiers to move them to safety. At best, it would be a race to safer ground for Shackleford's forces.

After a long, uneventful morning, tension had ratcheted to a peak when several riders galloped in from the northwest. They were identified quickly as Union pickets whose report would launch the awaited action. The camp took notice and sprang to life, poised to hear the next move.

William flipped open his pocket watch and found the time was ten minutes after two. Orders from officers blasted through the camp, setting up for the fight that would come from all sides, if reports were accurate. William braced himself for the battle. Silently praying he would live to see Caro again, he snapped the cover closed and placed the timepiece in the pocket over his heart. That was his last moment of quiet for the next few hours.

Fighting was indeed from every side, but William did not care, trying his best to concentrate on saving as many lives as possible in the onslaught. Both Union and Confederate soldiers appeared at his wagon. He never bothered to ask a question other than a medical one. It did tell him the likelihood of winning this battle was slim to none. Soldiers by the hundreds gathered around the medics with casualties mounting faster than they could account for them. The fighting intensified to the point William feared he might not survive the day.

Then, out of the din of battle, bugles signaled retreat, and the already chaotic scene around the medical wagons became riotous. Sergeant McCullum circled them, riding at a gallop, to order the wagons be moved immediately.

William had no choice but to stop in the middle of stitching up a gaping slash in a soldier's upper arm before it was completely closed. He hurriedly wrapped the arm as tightly as he could and promised to tend it as soon as they regrouped in a safe area. The soldier was as anxious to be gone as William, so he did not fight the order as he melted into the melee.

As William pitched the last of his medical equipment into

the back of his wagon, his driver was done with waiting. The wiry Scot, known only as Mac, giddy-upped the team and started off without William. He had to run to jump up and slide inside or be left behind. All around him wounded men cried out, realizing their chance for medical attention was leaving. Some tried to hang onto the sides of the wagon but were easily bumped off or pushed off by Mac to keep from tipping over.

The retreat was terrifying in its scope. Troops rushed in confused, disorderly haste in all directions. Shots skidded overhead with one cutting through the top of the wagon, leaving a sizable hole in the canvas.

William examined the one patient left inside, hoping to make him as comfortable as possible. Judging from the man's sickly countenance, the bumping and jangling of the wagon over rough terrain was not helping his pain. He was about to administer a dose of morphine when the man passed out. With luck the poor sod would stay out cold through the worst of the retreat before regaining his senses.

The wagon tipped precariously to one side before slamming hard the other way. William's medical bag went airborne, landing just out of reach. Before he had a chance to grab the thing, the wagon careened on two wheels in a sharp pitch that sent them headed in the opposite direction. When it banged back to earth, it sat eerily still with one corner clearly lower than the other three.

William guessed a wheel had broken or come off. Now what? As he crawled over his patient to the front to confer with Mac, the canvas cover was ripped back. Three Confederate soldiers pointed guns at him from three different sides.

"Hey, Doc, where ya think yer goin'?" the biggest man hollered at him. William chose not to answer until a second man prodded him with the tip of his bayonet.

"Just following orders, sir," William glared back. Mac was no longer on the wagon seat. Was he wounded? Dead?

"Well, no point worryin' bout that no more. Yer comin' with us. The gen'ral will be mighty glad to list ye on our side." He laughed and motioned for his buddy to pull William out.

"What about my patient?" William was loath to leave the man for dead.

"He'll git to take his chances like ever'body else, English!"

Before he could form a retort, the men had pulled William out of the wagon and set him on his feet. He pointed at some of his medical equipment in bags and scattered on the floor of the wagon. "If you want me to do anything for your wounded, you'll need to bring those bags too. I cannot do without them." The third soldier dutifully loaded himself down with the items William wanted.

"We best be gittin' him outta here, afore they realize we stole one of their docs. Put him up behind ye, Jeb. Sam, load them bags behind yer saddle."

"Yassir, Captain." Jeb and Sam had followed orders and charged off with the captain leading the way before William even spotted Union soldiers. The hospital flag the captain had removed and now waved seemed to clear a safe passage for them as they wended their way along the edge of the fighting.

In which direction were they traveling? North? South? William was no longer sure. The sun had been lost behind clouds socking them in, and darkness would soon be upon them. How would he ever be found by his Union troops? Olde Gylda better be coming to get him out of this mess in a hurry, or he might just be lost forever.

∞ ∞ ∞

The Confederate camp was jubilant as they celebrated their victory. Shackelford's troops had been pushed into retreat. The win was not the one General Longstreet wanted, however, because two divisions failed to make the battle in time to surround the enemy and cut off their escape.

William's captors had happily dragged him to the general's tent in hopes of appeasing the man's temper. Surgeons were a precious resource after all. But it was not to be. Furious with his subordinates for disobeying his command and allowing the enemy to retreat, the man was in the full fury of a rant as they neared his tent.

William was unable to make complete sense of the diatribe, but it sounded like the general wanted to chase the Union troops until they caught up and slaughtered them. Good lord, what a waste of mankind if they did as he raged! Traveling through the thick of the fighting, William's practiced eye at assessing casualties had placed the number between one and two thousand already. And for what? Bean's Station? Nothing was there but an old trading post left from years gone by. No land or strategic ground had been captured that would further the cause. This had been an opportunity to catch the Union troops unaware and do human damage. The Confederates had suffered a huge loss as well. Where was the honor in that?

As William listened along with his captors outside the tent, Longstreet ripped into a man he addressed as Grumble. William had heard of a Confederate general called Grumble Jones. Could this be the same man? If so, no wonder there was a hot argument going on inside. Jones was known even to Union soldiers as a strict disciplinarian who was as quarrelsome and irritable with his superiors as a cornered badger. Apparently, neither side was budging in this argument.

Right in the middle of a stream of vitriol, the man called Grumble made a sound that resembled that of a dying animal. William winced. He glanced at Jeb and Sam who were holding him on either side and their worried eyes told him they wondered what was happening, too.

General Longstreet himself, his face contorted around his heavy dark beard, poked his head out of the tent and bellowed, "Doctor! I need a doctor in here now."

It took the big captain behind him about two beats to shove William forward.

"Got one right here, sir. Captured him in the battle today. Got his medical bags and ever'thing."

Longstreet only grunted and stepped aside, allowing William to be shoved into the tent.

"Tend to him, Doc. He just hollered and collapsed." He paused for a moment and bent to stare at the bloodless face of the man. "Is he dead?"

William knelt by the officer on the ground and checked for a pulse. He found none. The man likely had suffered what Rick Duvall called a sudden cardiac arrest. His friend had told him this happened when a heart misfired and beat out of rhythm. That caused the heart to stutter and then stop. If rescuers revived a patient fast enough, he might survive; otherwise, he simply died.

William swiftly unbuttoned and removed the jacket which held the markings of a general and positioned himself to begin the procedure he had learned—a technique Duvall called C-P-R. He'd forgotten what exactly the initials stood for beyond the C for cardiac.

The details he remembered involved pushing on the chest of the person as hard as possible and then giving him breath with yours. The method was supposed to revive someone whose heart had stopped. He had never executed the procedure by himself before, but now was the time to try. Rick had been successful using the technique, and William had assisted once. Still, his body shook with the stress of a man's life in his hands—literally.

He positioned his palms in the center of the man's chest. With his fingers interlocked, he began pushing down hard for a moment before letting up, only to repeat the movement again and again. With each push he pressed down at least a couple of inches, counting at a steady pace. When he reached thirty, he stopped and tilted Grumble's head back so his mouth fell open. Then he proceeded to take a breath himself and blow it into the man's mouth. After two such breaths, he repeated the motions.

William glanced up as he switched back to pushes only to see the shocked faces of the men watching him. Longstreet voiced their concern. "What in God's name are you doing, man?"

"His heart has stopped. This method can start it beating

again if it is not too late." William answered speaking in rhythm, trying hard not to lose his count.

A man behind him guffawed, but Longstreet only *hmphed* a response and motioned for William to continue. He was aware of the general's eyes on him intently watching his actions. After the fifth round of pushes, he felt the restlessness of the men huddled around inside the tent. Finally, one of them blurted, "Stop it, mister. He's dead."

Without warning the downed man's body jumped, and his hands formed fists. A collective gasp went up from behind him. The general's eyes opened showing confusion at finding himself on the ground looking up into the face of a stranger.

"Welcome back." William grinned, wiping the sweat from his brow before it dripped on his patient's face. Grumble tried to sit up, but William put a hand on his shoulder and gently pushed him back. "You have suffered a shock to your system, Sir. You need to rest for a time where you are." He folded the man's jacket and placed it under his head as a pillow. "Just breathe in and out slowly and try to fill your lungs before letting the air go."

"Doc, you saved General Jones's life! I could have sworn he was gone." Longstreet's voice quavered slightly, showing his amazement at what he had witnessed. The others in the tent were trying to make sense of what they had seen, too, mumbling their shock to one another and watching William with new respect.

"It does not always work, Sir, but it is always worth trying."

"Where did you learn to do that?" Longstreet's ice blue eyes were sharp, searching William's face for answers.

"I was taught by another doctor I worked with a while back."

"How do you know what to do?"

"Well, if a man is not breathing, you try to get his heart pumping and his lungs working. By pumping the chest and breathing into his mouth, I tried to supply the heartbeat and breath until his body could decide to take over and do the work again."

"Yer English, ain't ye?" This question came from one of the men behind him. "Did ye larn that at some fancy school in Lunnon?"

William decided to let that be the case since he could not very well tell him it came via a time-traveler from 150-years into the future. No point in saying where Rick had come from or that he learned it as a doctor serving in the Union army.

"Yes, something like that." He smiled and hoped the subject dropped. "Might someone fetch some cool water? I imagine the general could do with a drink of water and a face wash."

Water in a tin cup, a small bowl filled with clean water, and some drying cloths were thrust under his nose several minutes later. William held the general's head up and let him drink the cold well water. The man did not object to having his face washed, either. Having done all he could for his patient, William helped Jones sit up for a few minutes before General Longstreet insisted he be lifted from the ground and settled on the cot at the back of the tent.

"He needs to rest for a few days to recover his strength, but he should be fine if he doesn't try to overdo it for a while."

"What happened to make him do that, if I might ask?" General Longstreet's eyebrows puckered in thought. "He dropped like a rock in the midst of our argument."

William nodded. "Sometimes the heart gets excited and skips a beat or two. When that happens, the organ can get out of rhythm so much that it stops. I think that is what happened here."

"Hmm, I suspect you are right. Grumble and I seem to hold our," he halted and searched for the right word, "discussions at canon-blast level. We shall have to be careful to keep them more in the rapid-fire range in the future." His attempt at levity sobered. "The General is a good man. We cannot afford to lose him."

Not knowing what else to say or do, William occupied himself by wiping his hands on a fresh towel that someone had handed him. What would they do with him next? Waiting to find out felt awkward.

"We need ye, Doc. We lost a sawbones today, and we have too many casualties to count." Longstreet did not wait for a response but signaled for the man called Sam to report. "You! See that our new doc gets a change of uniform. Since you and your partner captured him, you two will find him a wagon and drive him. Take care, soldier, this one is special." He slapped William on the back and dismissed him by turning his back on them to examine papers on his travel desk.

"Yes, Sir," Jeb cried with a snappy salute. "Let's go, Doc."

The smaller of the two, Jeb pulled back the tent flap and gave William a gentle push out into the night where the hulking Sam waited. Stars shone above in a clear sky, untroubled, as if hundreds of men below had not been killed in a battle that had raged for hours. How would their families learn of the deaths of their loved ones? Would it take months for a letter to reach them? Did they feel the loss tonight as they looked up at the stars?

William's eyes watered. Was it the cold? Or was it the fear he might disappear into the ranks of the Confederates where he might not be found or identified if he failed to survive the war? He had not chosen to come to America at all. Would Gylda rescue him? Or was he truly alone?

Chapter 8

The weather the second day cooperated most of the time, dropping only fat, puffy flakes of snow on Caro's carriage for short periods of time. It was, however, enough to create a winter wonderland to drive through. With the usually rugged road frozen solid, dust was not a factor. The trees boasted a frosting of snow on their branches decorated with an occasional icicle dangling beneath like swag. The best part was mid-morning when the sky shone a bright blue and the icy land twinkled like diamonds on the water.

It was enchanting.

For a while.

No matter how well-sprung the duke's carriages, two long days of travel over dangerous roads with everything from mud holes to icy patches left everyone exhausted. Relief flooded Caro and company when the outlines of Woodworth appeared against the orangey-red fingers of the setting sun. By the time their entourage had passed through the gates and up the snow-cleared drive, Caro was tempted to dive out of the coach whether a footman was there to catch her or not.

Perhaps she should have been a bit more careful. She had spotted Charlotte emerging from the huge, double front doors at the top of the stairs behind the six columns of the portico. Unfortunately, she had not seen who else might have passed through them first. What was that old expression about *look be-*

fore you leap?

In her rush, Caro did not check if the steps were down before she stepped off into . . . nothing. As a result, she all but flung herself into the arms of Cornelius Tremont who caught her with exaggerated exuberance by swooping her off her feet and holding her tightly.

She smelled his distinct odor of tobacco, horse, and unwashed male before she recognized the man's furry face. As for the baron, his eyes glowed like a demon's in the light of the torches, sinfully delighted at his good fortune in having Caro fall from the coach into his arms.

"Well, hello, my lady! I am most happy to greet you, too." He gave Caro's thigh a healthy squeeze as he spoke, sending her hissing and squirming to get down like a wild cat picked up against its will. Caro knew she should keep her claws sheathed, but she was horrified to be in the grip of this aging Lothario.

"Lord Tremont, put me down at once."

Loath to do so, he nuzzled into her neck. "Why, my lovely, did you throw yourself into my arms if you did not wish for me to catch you?"

Beyond words, Caro's anger emerged in a low growl and narrowed eyes as she flailed her feet. How dare this man grab her and manhandle her like she belonged to him? That thought stuck in her throat like a bite of dry fish. Did he think he owned her?

Thankfully, her father approached from his carriage and the baron had no choice but to put her down. To her further vexation, the duke's presence made the man nearly drop her on her backside in his hurry to rid himself of the spitting tabby he held. She scampered to her father who rescued her with an arm around her waist. There she held her ground, glaring at the baron from the safety of her father's side.

"I see you are recently arrived as well, Corney," the duke greeted dryly, raking his eyes across the baron and noting the man still wore his hat and many-caped traveling cloak. A raised eyebrow from the duke was enough to freeze even the most ardent suitor in his tracks, and his longtime friend was no exception.

"I-she-w-we," he stuttered rather lamely, before giving up the explanation entirely. "Your s-servant, your grace." Caro smirked at the baron's obvious fluster. At least her father had not deserted her in a time of need. Perhaps he had not already traded her off like an unentailed estate in a card game after all.

Charlotte, Lady Woodington, had been watching the action with genuine interest but decided it was time for her to intervene. "My darlings, it is freezing out here and you must be so very weary from your travels. Leave these gentlemen this instant and come warm yourselves inside. They may join us at their leisure by the fire in the great hall when they are ready." She gave her husband a pointed look to attend to the men, while she ushered her charges inside.

Violet was laughing openly by the time the threesome reached shelter and closed the door behind them. "My goodness, Caro, what were you thinking?"

"I was thinking I wanted out of that dreadful coach, if you must know." Her equanimity restored at having reached their destination and with her two best friends flanking her, Caro's smile flashed anew. "I thought he was a footman!"

That admission sent Violet into titters again and this time Caro and Charlotte were giggling with her. So much so, that Pruitt, the unflappable Woodworth butler, was forced to all but wrestle their pelisses and bonnets from them as they flapped about the entryway like henwits. Violet found his consternation highly amusing which launched her into more spasms of laughter until the hall fairly echoed with high spirits.

"I have sorely missed you two and just this kind of silly fun," Charlotte chortled, her chocolate brown eyes dancing with mischief. "Robert is truly a dear, but he cannot compete with a good giggle among bosom bows, can he?"

Through fits and starts as she worked to regain her composure, Caro confessed, "Oh, my, Charlotte, while I am sure that is true, did you not see how the baron pinched me? He was convinced I had dropped into his arms on purpose. On purpose! How will I ever make it through the holiday with that man on my heels?"

Violet fought to keep from falling into another bout of laughter at Caro's exasperation. "All joking aside, dear Caro, my job will be to shadow your every move, so you do not have to be squeezed by the roué again."

"And I, too, will do the same." Charlotte fingered a glossy chestnut curl back into place as she checked her appearance in the massive mirror of the entrance hall.

"Thank you. You are my dearest friends whom I trust to do exactly as you say. You do not know how much that means to me."

"Do remember, though, that Lord Tremont was invited as part of the agreement you struck with your father, and as his hostess, I cannot be rude to him."

"How can I forget?"

"I can, however, herd him wherever I choose and as a gentleman, he is required to follow where I lead." The unholy spark in Charlotte's eye gave Caro abundant faith that the baron could be managed by the three of them without untoward trouble.

She surely hoped so.

As they warmed their fingers by the fire, the housekeeper, Mrs. Pembroke, arrived to ask if they were ready to find their rooms. A short, well-rounded matron with a genial air, she exuded an aura of competence about her. With pride, she explained that every room at Woodworth had fires round the clock, so they would never feel the cold while here.

Caro was reminded again of the immense size of the place. The exquisite furniture and thick carpets stretched about the great room as if royalty were expected. How they ever kept the enormous house warm was a mystery, but it was always comfortable inside. But then Charlotte was a genius at household management, having been weaned managing an estate almost as large as Woodworth before her marriage. Perhaps it was only right that Charlotte be mistress of a place like this.

Unlike her friend, Caro had little interest in the trappings of décor. She preferred people to things. Marrying a second son without prospects of grandeur had never been her concern. Her father had not seen it that way.

Shaken from her reverie by Mrs. Pembroke's voice, Caro realized she had been woolgathering again. Following the woman up the grand staircase, she passed a dozen portraits of Woodington lords from years gone by to reach the guest wing above. She and Violet would have just enough time for a bath and a rest before dressing for dinner.

∞ ∞ ∞

Woodworth had been something of a ramshackle place when Charlotte and Robert married. She brought the much-needed funds into the marriage to take the huge, shabby estate and restore it to its former magnificence. Charlotte had done a marvelous job supervising, and Caro could see improvements even in the six months since last she visited the estate.

The guest wings of the grand place filled rapidly with family—mostly Charlotte's cousins, who were of an age with Caro and Charlotte. Caro especially looked forward to meeting Charlotte's cousin Alexander, Viscount St. John and his viscountess and bride, Elena, who were already in residence.

As with the majority of the *haute ton,* Caro and Charlotte's families were related through marriage. Charlotte's beloved cousin Hugh, Baron Bowson would arrive with his family a day later. He was married to Caro's cousin Louisa. Had Hugh bought the diamond parure she and Louisa had found while shopping for Hugh's pocket watch? She had a bet with Violet that Hugh would show up with the diamonds in tow.

More families with children would arrive throughout the week to fill the nursery to the rafters, but no family holiday was ever complete without Aunt Augusta, who made sure everyone's business was hers.

Robert's side of the family was much smaller. William and Honora Fitzwilliam, the 4th Earl Fitzwilliam, and Christopher Duncanby, Viscount Danson, comprised the only family attending from his side.

Caro and Violet, as Charlotte's best friends, held a high place among the guests, and of course the invitation extended to their parents as well. The lone guest seeming to belong to no one in the eyes of most of Charlotte's family was Cornelius Tremont. By the end of the first evening, it was not a mystery why the baron had been invited. The attention he focused on Caro at every opportunity told the tale for him. That was worrisome for those who knew Violet's parents were on the guest list. The whereabouts of William Lowther was a subject most had been avoiding for at least a year.

Dinner was a relaxed, family affair even though it was served with many removes in a formal setting. Chatter went across the table and from end to end in a most shocking lapse of manners as family members enjoyed their time together. Caro was relieved to be seated between Alexander St. John and Hugh Bowson. Charlotte had placed the odious Cornelius Tremont down the table and away from her. Caro would have to remember to thank her for that.

Lord St. John, or Alex, as he asked to be called, was an entertaining guest. A world traveler, he told fascinating stories that were most diverting. Caro did observe, however, that it was his wife, the lovely Lady St. John, who was the female drawing his attention like no other. Newly married, the pair had difficulty keeping their eyes from automatically seeking the other's every few minutes.

After Alex captivated Caro with a mystical dream he believed was prompted by his travels to the Orient, she decided to share her recent dream with him. She delighted in holding his intense interest as she regaled him with the three items presented to her by the strange little lady in the voluminous black gown. That the proffered gifts were then stolen by Dick Turpin on Black Bess added to the story fun.

She failed to notice until her tale was told that his demeanor had changed. He was now asking her serious questions about the old lady's appearance—the color of her eyes, her height, her hair and how she sounded. His relaxed, carefree manner had shifted to a lowered brow and lips that formed a thin line. What was she to make of that, she wondered? Why should he care about her silly dream? Before she could question his unusual response, Charlotte rose from the table, signaling the ladies to leave the men to their port and cigars and gather for tea in the red drawing room.

By the time the men joined them, Caro no longer remembered her questions for Alex and struggled to keep her eyes open. She grew sleepier with every tick of the ornate ormolu clock holding court on the mantle. In her comfortable, plush chair beside the warm hearth, her thoughts kept shifting to William and far away from those around her.

"Are we boring you so soon, Caro?" Charlotte teased as she poured more tea for her guests.

Caro finished the yawn she attempted to hide behind her hand before she answered. "No, no! So sorry I am such a dullard. I am afraid our travel today has stolen my conversation. I believe I shall retire and hope it returns on the morrow."

"I have no doubt it will, my dear," Charlotte answered, her eyes sympathetic to the trials of travel by coach. "Perhaps Aunt Augusta would go up with you." She pointed to the older woman who was snoring in her chair, a cup and saucer balanced precariously on her lap as if riding a gentle wave with every breath. "I should hate the poor dear to hurt herself if that falls."

"In any event, should we not remove her tea?"

"Therein lies the difficulty. The moment you lift it from her lap, she will awake and scold you for taking her tea before she was finished."

"Oh my." Caro looked askance at the tea undulating on the old lady's lap and started to reach for it anyway.

"One moment, Caro." Violet rose from her place on a nearby sofa and moved to Aunt Augusta's other side. "I shall lift her tea from her lap, so she will yell at me. You approach her from your side and offer to walk up with her to retire."

"Brilliant suggestion, Violet." Charlotte grinned at her friend. "Those managing skills will serve you well when you marry."

"Are you speaking of me by any chance, my love?" Her husband appeared from behind the sofa, leaned down to give her a kiss on the top of her head, and then winked at Caro and Violet. "Some of us know when we have been beaten and simply do not fight it." He shook his head in sympathy at the elderly woman as she snorted in her sleep but did not awake and moved to join the men on the other side of the room.

Charlotte followed his progress with adoring eyes before turning back to her friends, "Well, shall we give it a go, ladies?"

Aunt Augusta performed her part as if rehearsed. The moment the cup and saucer left her lap, she was awake and jawing at Violet as if the girl had been a thief relieving her of her favorite pearls. Violet attempted a remorseful look, but the corners of her mouth turned up just enough to give her away to anyone really attending. Caro swooped in on her other side and commiserated with Aunt Augusta about cold tea and a long evening, ending with an offer to escort her up to her chamber since Caro was going to retire as well. No one was altogether sure if Aunt Augusta knew she was being managed or not, but she was safely headed to her bed, so it was deemed a smashing success.

It snowed overnight about six inches, so with a bed of ice beneath the snow for support, it was the perfect sleigh weather. Violet begged to skate on the pond about a mile from the manor, so plans for ice skating and sleigh riding unfolded in tandem. Those who wished to skate would be ferried to and from the pond by sleigh.

A warming house beside the frozen pond stood ready to house provisions and necessaries for the skaters. A party of young people and a few of the older children signed on to the outing with great enthusiasm. Violet and Caro took on the task of organizing, since Charlotte needed to stay behind to greet those guests expected in the afternoon.

The day was gorgeous—blue sky with only a hint of puffy white clouds in the distance. Gliding along at a steady clip with bells jingling on the sleigh through pristine grounds was wonderfully fun. Caro remembered sneaking kisses from William as a teen, snuggled together in the back of a sleigh right behind her parents who never bothered to look behind them. How she missed those exciting times. She sighed and told herself to be thankful for all the friends and family around her. Wherever William was, he might not be so lucky.

Violet decided a little music was in order and struck up a lively tune. Caro knew only a few of the words, so she enjoyed listening to her friend sing for the children seated behind them. Violet's lovely voice flowed over the party as lightly as sunshine over the sleigh.

Arriving at the pond a short time later, Caro was happy to see the groundskeepers had already scraped the snow from the ice and cleared a path to the warming house. Some wooden benches, borrowed from a summer house somewhere on the estate, now rested in conversational groupings that allowed the guests to watch the skaters. Lunch and hot drinks would be provided from the big house at appropriate times. It promised to be a fine day.

And it was, until the sleigh's third trip presented Cornelius Tremont. Caro busied herself with her "duties" as hostess until the red-faced man was beside himself at her obvious avoidance. Wishing to avert a scene, she consented to let him accompany her in a couple's skate around the pond's perimeter for about a half hour. That consoled him enough she did not fear he would suffer an apoplexy, but her would-be-fiancé woes were not so easily ended.

Shortly after luncheon, the skaters were back on the ice when jingles from the sleigh could be heard rounding the bend to the pond. Wondering who would be joining them, Caro motioned for Violet to meet them. A whoop from Violet made her doubly curious, so she skated to the closest exit and crunched her way toward the warming house.

"Halloo," a young man called to her, having just stepped out of the sleigh. Peering to see against the light, she recognized the size and shape of none other than Christopher Duncanby.

Violet rushed to greet him with a cheery hello and a huge smile, but the viscount only gave her a quick bow and a pat on the shoulder. Without hesitation, he made his way straight to Caro, kicking up the snow in a fresh path. She could feel her friend's disappointment. The blasted man was still bent on chasing her, when any fool could see Violet was pining for his attention. Short of throwing herself again at Lord Tremont as a diversionary tactic, she was at a loss as to what to do to avoid the viscount.

Afterward, Caro wondered if the universe had been listening to her plight. Louisa's oldest child crashed into the Fitzwilliam's youngest and the two set up a caterwaul that would have made their mothers cringe. It was exactly the distraction Caro needed to take her away from the all-too-friendly designs of both her suitors. Caro easily cornered the wounded cherubs and insisted they return to the house via sleigh for patching up and a good nap.

Violet's spirits quickly revived when Caro insisted Christopher stay and skate. While the baron sought refreshments inside the warming house, Caro jumped in the sleigh with her charges and escaped toward the big house unscathed. With a whimpering child on either side of her, she told them stories of similar scrapes when she was their age. By the time they arrived at the portico, all was well.

This managing business was a skill worth learning.

∞ ∞ ∞

The evening began much as the night before with a lovely

dinner, this time in the largest dining room because more guests had arrived. Due to order of precedence, Charlotte was unable to accommodate Caro's seating pleas entirely. Christopher Duncanby was seated across the table from her, where he proceeded to make calf's eyes at her every time she looked up. Really, it was quite disturbing.

Added to that, the baron insisted upon glaring at the viscount in such an overt manner, she feared Duncanby might call him out. Except the viscount missed most of it while mooning over her. Charlotte gave her consoling looks and Alex hid his grin, surely tipped off by Charlotte to the rivalry displayed so overtly through dinner. Violet attempted to keep the baron occupied by chattering in his ear, but she, too, was more concerned about where the viscount's attention lay.

At last, Charlotte stood, and it was time to retire to the music room where an evening's program would soon begin once the gentlemen finished their port. This room was larger than the sitting room they had occupied the night before. Huge fireplaces were at either end of the room and by the time everyone was seated for the performances, it would be much warmer.

At this point, however, the temperature was a little too cool for Caro in her swag-sleeved evening gown. Rather than send for a servant to retrieve a wrap, she decided to go herself. Stretching her legs was exactly what she needed, and she would relish a few minutes to herself to enjoy some quiet.

It occurred to Caro that Aunt Augusta, hunched in a chair by the door, might be chilled, too. The older woman was a handful for everyone, yet Caro had made some inroads with her the night before that she hoped to strengthen over the next few days. Striding to the doorway, Caro turned to ask the old lady if she might like a shawl brought to her while she retrieved her own. Having an ally like Aunt Augusta was never a bad thing.

The Grande Dame of the family answered in the negative, but a wicked grin spread across her face that made Caro's blood run cold. What was the woman thinking as she looked over Caro's shoulder that put such a mischievous gleam in her eyes?

She had her answer a heartbeat later when she turned and ran smack into Lord Tremont. The man grabbed her with an iron arm around her waist and pulled her into an open-mouthed kiss.

Shocked, Caro squirmed as his tongue thrust into her mouth, the sloppy kiss all but dripping from her lips. Forcing her hands between them she found his chest and shoved herself away from him, outrage having stolen her breath along with her words.

The baron grinned a wide, wet grin and proclaimed, "You'll have more o' that whenever you like, my little miss!" The revolting man stood there rocking to and fro on his heels, proud as punch of his kissing prowess. In answer to her indignation, he pointed innocently to the dab of mistletoe now dangling like last week's flowers from the lintel of the open door.

She knew that had not been there earlier in the day. No doubt the loathsome man had hung the elderly sprig there himself, waiting for an opportunity to catch her unawares. She had unwittingly walked right into his trap.

Mortified, Caro caught only a glimpse of the appalled and disconcerted faces in the room before she turned and ran. As her slippers hit the stairs, noise erupted from the music room as everyone rushed to share an opinion regarding the baron's audacious behavior. And hers. Blood raced to her brain making her face feel like it had been put to the flames.

Chapter 9

O nce in her room, Caro slammed the door shut and threw herself on the bed, letting the tears roll. Why must she put up with this sham of courtship when she did not want any of it?

While she had fallen in love with baby Lucy and desperately wanted a child of her own, she could only envision that happening with William as the father. No amount of cajoling, wheedling or entrapping would entice her to marry anyone else. She would savor being a spinster, an ape leader, or an old maid before she married anyone the likes of Cornelius Tremont. What an abominable man!

Christopher Duncanby was not much better. Oh, he was a true gentleman, and, in truth, there was not a thing wrong with him other than he was not William. The man was handsome, athletic, intelligent, and witty, but he did absolutely nothing for her when he took her hand and kissed it. Not an ounce of electricity skidded up her arm. Nothing.

If he felt something for her, it was not returned in any way. Why would anyone want to marry a person who felt not a modicum of attraction for them? Perhaps one day Christopher would figure out the woman he should be chasing was the charming, droll, darling named Violet Lowther.

Her supply of tears exhausted, Caro dragged herself from her bed, found her pitcher, and poured some lilac water into a dish. Wringing out a cloth, she gently sponged her face until the burning around her eyes subsided. She was a ninny to stay hidden up here for an entire evening. Experience had taught her she would be the topic on everyone's lips until she rejoined the party in the music room. The best way to get them to quit talking about her was to be present in the middle of the room. Why make it easy for the gossips to gossip?

She did her best to restore her hair, tucking in all the ends wrestled out by her pillow. Even though she smoothed the wrinkles out of her moss-green velvet gown, the poor bedraggled garment still looked sad. Even the paisley border of burgundy flowers around the hem drooped as if tired.

The tiny sleeves draped over her upper arms were not warm enough for a winter evening. If only she had remembered to carry her India shawl with her to dinner as planned! Yes, she was something of a mess, but the evening would soon be over, and she could not change out of this gown without a maid, anyway. That would take too long, so this one would have to do.

Caro pawed through her dresser for a shawl. Usually, Betsey laid out the creamy Kashmiri wrap with a moss and burgundy border that matched her gown. Of course the girl would have neglected to do that tonight. Finding it after disordering two drawers, she threw it over her shoulders and marched from her room.

Once in the hallway, she decided to take the servant stairs down the back of the house to avoid making an entrance into the open music room. This way she could slide in while someone was performing and hopefully not be the center of attention.

Passing nary a servant on the way, Caro congratulated herself for remembering to use the back stairs. As she swept out into the hallway of the main floor, however, she heard voices coming from a nearby sitting room. One belonged to Alexander St. John, but the other seemed unfamiliar at first, yet something about it registered with her.

She peered into the room to see if perhaps she could identify the second speaker but was surprised to see no one there.

Curious, she slipped in and traced the sound of the voices to a terrace that opened off the sitting room through double doors. Caro had spent many a sunny summer morning on that terrace, but now a sharp wind blew in, making her pull her shawl closer around her body.

"I cannot think what to make of it, Gylda." This was Alex speaking. "She described you to perfection, right down to your very blue eyes."

Who was with Alex? Wait, she recognized that raspy voice. It could not be the woman from her dream, could it? Astonished, Caro tiptoed into the room and worked her way around the edges in the shadows until only the drapes stood between her and the two on the terrace.

"How odd, my dearie. I do not believe I have laid eyes on the gel before."

Oh, my! It was, indeed, the same old lady, standing there in the same voluminous black gown from her dream. Stunned, all she could do was listen.

"Interesting, but what about the three items she describes that she says you gave her? Do they not point her to William Lowther in America? How would she find out he is actually there?"

William is in America? She was sure her heart had stopped beating, she was straining so hard to hear what they were saying.

"'Tis puzzlin' fer sure. Ye must remember that I am not the only one with powers in this world. Mayhap she possesses some she knows nothing of?"

"Are you saying Lady Caroline Wyckham is a witch?"

What? Surely, she had not heard them correctly. Caro cupped her hand behind her ear in a perfect copy of mostly deaf Aunt Augusta and leaned in to listen.

"I know not, laddie, but since that message did not come from me, it originated somewhere else, right?"

Alex seemed taken aback by the thought of Caro as a witch. He was not alone. Dumbfounded by the thought, Caro stood frozen to the spot as if under a spell.

"It would seem to me, Gylda, that William Lowther must be in trouble or Lady Caroline would not have received a message of any kind from him."

"Ye may be right about that. I was set to bring him home before Christmas, but that Abasi creature has played havoc with my time travelers in London for months now. Most distracting! Ye and Elena were fortunate ye escaped him the last time ye passed through. Duvall and his family led him on a merry chase and got away, but me and me travelers are now wary. The next time one of ye passes through London, ye may be trapped in the twenty-first century with no stone to get ye out. After all, I cannot be everywhere at once, now can I?"

At first, Caro's mind refused to process what she had just overheard. Witches? Time travel? William's absence? Her brain whirred into action and all the pieces fell into place. Well, at least the time travel part and William in America. Could she really be a witch and not know it? She would think on that later.

She must have made a sound as she gathered her thoughts because only a heartbeat passed before she detected she had been discovered. Instead of excusing herself or backing away she charged out the doors and confronted the pair. Her father had taught her that in awkward situations it was best to take charge and not look back.

"What in the world are you talking about, Alexander St. John?" She poked a finger in his chest and demanded an answer. "You just called me a witch!" She poked him again. "Why would you say that, and why would you not tell me William was in America if you believed him to be there?" She glared daggers into his face. "Well, explain yourself. And while you are at it, please introduce me to this person who happened to be in my dream not two nights ago."

Alex's eyebrows attempted to escape from the top of his head and his eyes flared as big as a pair of quizzing glasses. After fleeing the party a short time ago in dismay, her aggressive behavior surprised him. Did he admire her or fear her? She could not tell.

Recovering himself, he said, "I only put it all together tonight, Lady Caroline. To my mind, your tale of the dream was quite telling. I recognized whom you had met in your dream, so I called for my friend to come meet with me today." He stepped back, so the old woman was face to face with Caro. "May I introduce you to Olde Gylda of Hampshire? Gylda, this is Lady Caroline Wyckham, of whom I spoke moments ago."

The two women eyed one another with interest. Alex continued, "Gylda is a witch and directs time travelers who move about the world with the help of Guardian Stones."

Caro's mouth dropped open and then her eyes narrowed. Was he playing her for a fool to get out of explaining what really happened to William?

As if she had read Caro's mind, Olde Gylda stepped in to pick up the story. "He is telling you the truth, my dearie. 'Tis my belief ye have powers not yet tapped, or ye would not have dreamed of me or of the three items I gave ye." She paused to let Caro consider what she said. "Do ye know the meaning of them, perchance?"

Caro refused to be rushed. "What do you mean by time travelers? Where do these people go and why?"

A female voice interrupted from behind making Caro spin to find its owner.

"They are speaking of Guardians of the Stones—people who are assigned tasks to perform for mankind in worlds and times not of their own." It was Elena St. John, Alex's wife. "I am sorry to bother you, Alex. I wondered where you went and set out to find you."

Alex grinned at his wife as if happy to focus on someone other than the hornet in front of him. "You missed me, hmmm?"

"I did," she admitted with a shrug, sliding in next to her husband who tucked her under his arm to keep her warm. He gave her a kiss on the top of her head before he turned his attention back to Caro. Her struggle to understand all that had been said was apparently written on her face.

"I am a time traveler and a Guardian of the Stones, Lady Caroline. I met Elena in 1363 England and fell in love with her." Awe followed by a pang of jealousy shot through Caro as the two exchanged a smile that clearly showed their love for one another. "Someday we shall share our story with you, but right now, we must consider what to do for your William. He must be caught in the American Civil War, fifty years in the future, or you would not have had the dream you told to me."

Caro's eyes roamed from one face to the next as the three stood before her awaiting her answer. For a moment, the edges of her world went black, and her knees weakened, but then she dug down for her resolve to find William and stiffened her spine. If William was lost and needed to be found, who better to do so than she?

"I gave William a pocket watch with my miniature in it before he went to India. It bore the inscription, 'Yours for all time. Love, Caro.' In return, William gave me the watch his grandfather had given him. We exchanged timekeepers as our way to stay connected."

"Excellent. That would explain the watch, would it not?" Alex turned to Gylda who nodded in agreement. Alex continued, "The map probably appeared because William has been in America for the last two years working with Rick Duvall, another Guardian."

"You have known for two years where William was and never told me? How could you!"

"Now, Lady Caroline, you must admit that while we knew of each other, we had never talked to one another until last evening at dinner."

"Well, you knew Charlotte. You knew I was betrothed to William, and you knew his whereabouts were unknown to us. Furthermore, you cannot be oblivious to the fact my father keeps trying to marry me off to someone other than William." Caro's voice had risen with each sentence until she sounded more like a fishwife than a lady of the ton.

"Calm yerself, child," Gylda crooned, placing a hand on

Caro's forearm. Instantly, Caro felt her anger fall away. She looked hard into the woman's blue eyes and saw them twinkling like a twelve-year-old's. Who was this woman?

Gylda answered for Alex. "He cannot go about informin' everyone about Guardian business, now can he? Ye admitted ye are not sure we are tellin' ye the truth about time travel. Do ye think we would get very far tellin' others, or would they find comfy spots fer us in Bedlam?"

The old crone had a point.

"So do not blame the lad for keepin' the details to himself. He does not go time trippin' without my knowledge as 'tis."

Caro gave Alex a tentative smile of apology, but it was Elena who did her best to put Caro at ease.

"There is much to take in when first you learn of time travel. I was the last to know my good friend Ashley Duvall was a time traveler. Her father is the one your William traveled with the last two years. Guardians are lovely people who work hard to help others, so William was in good hands."

Hearing that, Caro determined she might as well tell them what little she knew.

"Violet thought the white strip of fabric was a bandage or perhaps a flag of surrender." Caro put forth the options with a quaver in her voice. "Which do you think it is?"

"In truth, Lady Caroline, it could be either." Alex looked to Olde Gylda, who agreed with his assessment. "Rick Duvall is a Guardian and a medic from the future." He watched her face as she absorbed his words. "His task was to travel 150 years back from his time to teach the doctors of the American Civil War how to save more lives. Your William was tapped as a Guardian to travel 50 years into the future to meet Duvall to learn everything possible from him. Why send him? Because the British will need William's new skills in India next year, and then after that at a place called Waterloo."

Caro stared at the three of them while her mind raced to catch up with that unbelievable explanation. William was alive. She understood that part. He was in America. He was learning medicine. She got that. It was the man from the future traveling 150 years back in time meeting up with William who was 50 years ahead in time that made her dizzy. How could it possibly be true?

What worried her most was the status of William's health. Was he well or not? If the strip were a bandage, did that not mean he was hurt? If it were a flag of surrender, to whom had he surrendered and would he not be a prisoner or killed as an enemy? Neither seemed to be a good thing.

While she sorted through all of this in her mind, she was aware the others continued to talk among themselves. Tuning in a few minutes later, she had the distinct impression they had decided to take an action of some sort without consulting her. She forced herself to follow their words.

"We must find him immediately, my dearie," Gylda said. "I have not lost a Guardian yet and I do not intend to start now. I cannot go at the moment because of troubles with Abasi, but I can keep him busy while ye find William and bring him home."

"If you are uncertain where he is, how am I to find him, Gylda?"

"I knows where he should be. He was in the same regiment as Duvall. When they parted, William was sent to Tennessee to join up with Union troops outside Knoxville, so he cannot be too far from there now. I suspect this lovely here is keepin' me from seein' him. Track him. If ye need more help, ye know how to call me."

"I shall do my best, Gylda," Alex promised. His attention shifted to his wife and his eyes softened to a loving glow. "I must tell you that Elena will not be traveling with me this time. She is with child." The last was said with a reverence that made Elena blush to the roots of her golden hair. Caro did not hear Gylda's response as Alex's words took root in her mind.

Stay here?

Wait! Where was he going?

Looking more closely at Gylda in the dark, she realized the old woman was holding a flat stone in her hands the size of a paver. *What is that?* she thought, her mind now racing. Alex gave his wife a long, lingering kiss and without taking his eyes off her, turned his body and put his hands on Gylda's shoulders. Whatever were they doing? Elena did not look disturbed, but Caro had a terrible premonition something dramatic was about to happen.

Olde Gylda's eyes were on the stone that appeared to have words inscribed on its surface and was calmly repeating a strange sounding phrase.

"*Ar goll mewn amser. Ar goll mewn amser. Ar goll mewn amser.*"

The old crone repeated the odd phrase in a soothing voice like an incantation. What was she doing? What did those words mean?

It had been chilly standing in the doorway of an open terrace, but now a wind ducked in from outside and swirled about the room. That wind surrounded Alex and Gylda but did not touch her or Elena. Fearing the other two were about to be blown away, she scrambled to stop them. Screaming, she grabbed Gylda's arm in one hand and Alex's in the other before pulling back against the wind with every ounce of strength she possessed.

Alex screaked at her.

Elena shrieked at her.

Olde Gylda screeched at her.

And then her world went black.

Chapter 10

Longstreet's Camp, December, 1863

W illiam had experienced moments of great frustration at various times in his life—anger, depression, loneliness—but as he dragged himself up for another day, he was so worn down, he felt nothing at all.

If he thought life in the Union Army was rough, despite often being treated with more respect than an officer, he was amazed how much worse everything was in its Confederate counterpart.

Doctors were scarce on the ground, and the needs of the men he now served overwhelmed his meager resources. Almost a thousand casualties from that last engagement at Bean's Station needed care. Only one other doctor on the other side of the camp existed to ease that load. So much death. So much damage to so many young men. Even basic medicine and bandages were in short supply.

Over the last two years, Duvall had kept him engaged in learning and the time had flown by. William's ability to deal with the injuries and illnesses in front of him had soared. But now, alone, and fearing he would never be found to return to his own time, William was all but numb to the world around him. Without Duvall's good cheer, experience, and support, William slid deeper into despair every day.

Sam and Jeb had set him up over the last three days to the

best of their ability. The two argued with each other incessantly over every detail whether it be which one would drive the wagon or which would seek provisions. The yellow flag with the green H was now flying over a confiscated wagon which was open for service once more. William cared nothing about any of it. He watched their bickering as if detached and in another world.

Well, in truth, that is where he spent much of his time if not tending a patient. He examined over and over in his mind how he had been sent here to begin with. Rick had years of experience dealing with Gylda. On the other hand, William's interaction with the witch had been limited to only a few minutes before she sent him to America. What to do next was beyond him.

Before he departed last summer, Duvall had been certain William's wait to go home would be short. His trusted friend had been wrong about that. So, minute by minute, hour by hour, William sank deeper into emotional quicksand. Fighting it made him only sink faster. Hence, the numbness that threatened to swallow him whole persisted.

Sam and Jeb had managed the hundreds of soldiers who had straggled to his wagon for help in those three days. Most were battle casualties, but many were those suffering the usual illnesses that plagued both sides in this war. William had methodically treated each, doing whatever possible but speaking rarely. Sitting under the night sky, he felt drained. Empty.

"Doc, you ain't eaten enuff to keep a fly alive." Squatting beside a small fire, Jeb shoved a tin-plate loaded with fried potatoes and a stringy piece of meat under William's nose. The pungent scent of wild animal and grease made his stomach revolt. "Eat this. We cain't be havin' you git sick or Longstreet'll have my neck and Sam's, too."

With no choice but to take the offered plate, William used a forefinger to poke at the fried potatoes on the tin in front of him. Perhaps if he moved them around sufficiently, Jeb would let him be. He had no stomach and no words for an argument. Jeb gave him a hard look when all the food was still present and accounted for minutes later. Disgusted, he shook his head, and walked away mumbling, "I ain't gonna shove it down yer gullet, no siree." William sat stone-faced and stared into the fire.

Sam arrived shortly thereafter, only to ramble on and on about a clean set of clothes bartered from a laundress friend named Evelyn. According to Sam the woman had followed the drum behind her husband, but her man had fallen in late September right before the beginning of the Knoxville Campaign. Why did Sam think he wanted to know all that? Did he want money from him? He should know William had not been with the Confederates long enough to accumulate any, so what was the point?

The barrage of words in his ear did garner one effect, though. Instead of silence, William was now fuming. Why would these men not go away? On the verge of telling Sam to cease his yammering and leave him alone before he stuffed a roll of bandages down his throat, it sunk in what the man was saying.

"So, Miz Evelyn wanted to give you her late husband's clothes since you are 'bout the same size he was."

William raised his head and glared at Sam. "Why would she do that?"

"Well, they ain't doin' nobody no good in her bags, and she ain't goin' home until we're in winter quarters." Sam did not appear to understand why William was questioning his good fortune. A change of clothes was unheard of for the bulk of the men. Laundresses who followed the soldiers only washed clothes for those with enough money or goods to trade with them.

This was the job many women performed to stay near their husbands in hopes of keeping them safe and healthy. Others, like Evelyn, had no money and no place to go when their spouses were killed. The job of laundress kept them fed until they could figure out a way to go home. Much to his surprise, other women literally joined in the fight as soldiers, dressing in uniform, fighting, and sometimes dying along-side the men. For every woman, life with a regiment was a hard, cruel life.

Sam dropped the bundle in William's lap and stomped off

in something of a huff, grumbling about beggars who shouldn't be so choosy. The ensuing silence soothed William's troubled soul. Only then could he focus on the clothing now in his lap.

Staring at the cleaned, pressed and folded uniform neatly stacked in front of him, he absently smoothed down the pocket flap of the heavy shirt on top. His fingers came to an abrupt halt. With his attention squarely on the shirt, he poked his finger through a hole hidden there by the flap. He knew in an instant it was a bullet hole—one that had gone straight through to the wearer's heart. Was this what had killed the woman's husband?

Shame shot through him. The laundress was giving him not only clean clothes, but her dead husband's uniform and all he could do was wallow in self-pity? What an ungrateful hunk of humanity he was. He sported not so much as a scrape on his person when so many others were not so lucky. Sure, he did his best each day to save men maimed and broken in horrible ways by the bullets and cannon ripping at them throughout battle. But had he only survived because he was a Guardian of the Stones?

He dropped his face into his hands and moaned. He needed to get himself together. If women like this Evelyn could keep going and face what was in front of them each day and still be generous enough to think of the needs of others, he could manage to get through it, too. If he could not go home to his own time, it was his job to do the best he could here in this one.

The touch of a gentle hand on his shoulder made him jump, but it was followed by a comforting pat and rub. His mother used to do the same thing to calm him when life got the best of him as a child. Wondering if he were imagining the sensation of someone caring about him, he looked up straight into the eyes of an angel.

Well, she appeared to be an angel to him. One with a cloud of soft, almost white-blonde hair that fluffed around her heart-shaped face. Blue eyes the color of a cloudless morning had concern written in them as if she cared about him. His heart stuttered for a moment before resuming its regular beat. Who was this?

"I meant no offense, Doc. I heard tell you was captured without your possessions and thought you might make use of my Henry's clothes." The angel smiled at him with a gentle smile that lit her face from within. "I know not ever'body is comfortable wearin' a dead man's clothes, but winter is upon us, and you need to stay warm." She paused for a moment and her smile widened. "I couldn't part with 'em 'til now." She gave him a one-sided grin. "I guess we is all a little selfish in our own ways. We need you alive, Doc, cuz lots of folks need yer help so's they kin stay alive."

Evelyn. This must be Evelyn. Sam had not told him she was a beauty. Perhaps he might have suspected that since brawny, young Sam frequented the camp followers for reasons beyond laundry. William warned both Jeb and Sam about spending time with these women every time he treated a patient with syphilis or gonorrhea. Sadly, he knew they did not listen.

Evelyn was watching his reaction carefully as though he should have responded by now. He was at a loss as to what she might have asked because he had been busy basking in her warmth.

"You feelin' sick er somethin', Doc?"

"Yes, ma'am," He jumped to his feet and then stood there like a big lummox—a big, inarticulate lummox. That was all he could spit-out? "Or something like that." William rallied himself to make some sense before this lovely creature decided he was a bedlamite.

Instantly, her cool hand was on his forehead assessing if he had a fever. "You look a might peaked, but you ain't fevered."

He laughed. It startled him because he had not heard himself laugh since Duvall left to go home. Recovering himself, he joked, "I thought I was the doctor here."

She smiled. "Well, a little laughter do make you look better." She waved her hand airily in the direction of his face. "Not so pasty white."

That made William snort. "Just what every man wants to hear from a lovely lady."

She grinned. "Yup, definitely better." She folded her arms across her chest which pushed her plump breasts higher, and he nearly lost his composure.

William flushed like an untried youth, heat rushing to his face as it was clear that each of them found the other attractive.

"And before you go thinkin' I am one of them camp women that gits passed 'round fer a man's comfort, let me assure you I am not."

Embarrassment heated William's face. Had he forgotten he was a gentleman? Evelyn was obviously a widow, not a camp whore. What should he say? Oddly, his training had not foreseen an instance where he needed to apologize to a lady for believing her a lightskirt when a part of him hoped he was wrong.

Wait, what was he thinking? One pretty face, and he was ready to forget Caro? No, he would not allow himself to even give that thought breath.

"Please forgive me, Mrs...?" He lifted an eyebrow and waited for her to fill in her married name, planning to bow over her hand as he had been taught.

Instead, Evelyn laughed a full-throated laugh that made him smile too. "My but you got purty manners, my English friend!" She fanned her face in mock heat at his awkward address before backhanding him across the chest. "I don't need no lover, Doc, but I shore kin use a friend."

Inexplicably, she plopped down beside the fire, reached up and gave his hand a yank, making him drop down beside her. She began explaining who she was and how she had come to be a laundress in the Confederate Army.

"The name is Perkins, Evelyn Perkins. You kin call me Evie if you like. Most people do since I don't always answer to Evelyn or Mrs. Perkins." As she babbled away, she warmed up William's plate of food and passed it to him. This time he popped a potato in his mouth and enjoyed the greasy piece as it slid down his throat. It even smelled better.

Was she an angel? No, probably not, but she made him laugh when he thought he would never laugh again. Here she was sitting by the fire chatting with him like she had known him since childhood, and he found himself smiling back at her. He did not want a lover, either, although he did find her more than the "purty little old gal" Sam had called her.

She was a slip of a thing, not much bigger than a child, yet there was a life force in her that spoke of a strength that had not been tested to its fullest even as a widow trailing an army. Dressed neat as a pin, her clothing still carried a whiff of lye soap.

He noted her boots needed to be replaced, worn through, no doubt, from all the miles she had trudged. Perhaps she might ride sometimes with him on the wagon, so she did not ruin her feet. What an odd thought. He had only met her moments ago, yet his soul knew the person she was.

Without Rick Duvall around he did need a friend. Sam and Jeb acted more like servants than friends in their role of care-takers of the doctor. Yes, William was sorely in need of a friend.

Maybe, just maybe, he had found one.

Chapter 11

C aro was completely confused when she popped open her eyes and everything was still black. Her first thought was that she had died. But something was jabbing into her back in several places, and the air smelled like woods with the heavy, moist air of night holding her in place.

Listening more intently she could hear the rustle of some small animal through undergrowth and the soughing of branches swaying in a slight breeze. A whooshing sound seemed to pass by periodically, but it was an unfamiliar sound she struggled to identify. Running a hand down her body she determined one other thing—she was wearing a silk ball gown. What was she doing outside, flat on her back in the middle of the night dressed for a ball?

Before her imagination rendered any scenario that put her in such a place, she became aware of others around her. Fearing she had been abducted, she sat up and drew her legs up to her chin, hugging her knees. Beside her was a man, also dressed in evening wear. Peering closely at him, her breath caught when she recognized Alexander St. John. He coughed and sat up. Clearing his throat, he straightened his cravat and grumbled, "As long as I live, I shall not get used to that blasted wind."

At the sound of his words her memory fluttered back. She had stepped into a whirlwind to save Alex and the old woman, and instead been sucked in along with them. Wait. Where was the old lady?

"'Tis about time ye both surfaced! I bin waitin' on ye way too long."

"Stuff it, Gylda," Alex moaned, sounding distinctly put out for the affable man Caro knew him to be. "You know we cannot travel as easily as you." He bounded to his feet with a groan, brushed off his pants, and jerked his waistcoat and jacket into place. His gentlemanly demeanor restored, he reached down to offer a hand to Caro to pull her to her feet. "I apologize for the untimely travel, Lady Caroline. If I am not mistaken, you did not intend to time travel with us, did you?"

Unsteady, standing beside him in her dancing slippers, Caro worked to regain her balance in more ways than one. Did Alex just say she had time traveled with them? Perhaps she needed to take a moment to compose herself before answering. She adjusted her bodice which had slipped lower than propriety allowed, smoothed small twigs from her skirts, and reached up to tame her hair. As she patted it, she realized it was a lost cause. Part of it lay tumbled down around her shoulders, and the other part felt like a bird's nest.

Taking a deep breath, she started to speak and then had no idea what she should say. The only thing that came to mind was no, so that is all she said. "No."

"Did you not hear us discussing time travel to return William to you?"

Caro shook her head.

An exasperated Alex responded, "I see." He rearranged his face into a more neutral mask before he continued. "I was planning to travel with only Gylda who would create a diversion here to move me through modern London without difficulty. When you grabbed my arm and Gylda's, you hitched a ride with us."

"I did not hear what was said, my lord. I only thought to save the two of you from a wind I believed was swirling you away from Lady St. John and me." Caro felt her face redden in embarrassment.

"Well, my dearie, ye learned a lesson, did ye not?" Gylda

chuckled, giving Caro a kindly smile. "I imagine ye will be listenin' more diligently in the future. But 'tis no matter now. Since ye are here and I've no time to return ye, ye shall go on to America with Alex. He will take good care of ye, will ye not?" She turned to a disgruntled Alex for confirmation, gave him a huge grin, displaying her few teeth to the fullest, and dispensed his marching orders. "Do not dally here, my boy. Abasi has men watchin' ever'where. Ye best be on yer way before day breaks or ye'll have trouble on yer hands."

"Might we change clothes before we go? I can outfit us in more appropriate garb if we can go undetected to my flat." Alex straightened a cuff as he waited for an answer.

Gylda gave each a once-over before searching the skies to assess how much time before daybreak was left. "Sadly, dearies, I think 'twill be daylight long before ye make it back here to pick up yer stone near the Westbourne Gate even if ye takes a taxi. That means Abasi will be waitin' for ye."

"Taxi? What is a taxi?" Caro envisioned words flying above her head like unknown birds. What were they saying?

"Ah, you have not had the opportunity to see what modern life looks like, have you, my lady?" That thought appeared to put Alex in a much better mood because he waggled his eyebrows in a tease. "Too bad we don't have time for that now. I'll explain later."

A roar overhead drowned out his last words. Shocked, Caro put her hands over her head thinking the world was crashing down around her.

Alex hooked her arm in his and shouted in her ear, "It is only an airplane, Lady Caroline. You need not fear."

Caro cringed and shook her head, wondering what an airplane was. He did not appear to be afraid, however, and as the noise diminished, she looked around to see all was well. Alex patted her on the back and reassured her she was fine.

"Ye must find clothes on t'other end, Alex. Ye best be off. I shall do what I can to divert Abasi, but 'twill no' be long before he is on to my tricks."

Alex nodded and turned to ask Caro if she were ready for the next portion of their journey. When he stepped back a moment later, Gylda was gone. Just gone. The old woman must really be a witch because no one else could have disappeared from view that fast.

Looking around the area, she still had no inkling where she was. They were standing at the edge of a thicket, with open space abounding on the other side. Stars still shined brightly in the night sky, but it did feel late, like the dark right before dawn.

Whoosh.

There was that sound again.

"What is making that noise, Alex?"

He raised a brow for further explanation, so she did her best to copy the sound.

"Ah, that would be a car going by in the street, Lady Caroline."

"A car? You mean a carriage, right?"

"No, I shall explain later, my dear. Right now, we'd better do as Olde Gylda bid us and leave the park."

"We are in a park? Which one?"

"Hyde Park."

"What? You mean my townhouse is only a few minutes away? Surely, we can get out of these clothes."

"Not exactly, Lady Caroline. We are a couple hundred years past our time. I do not know if your home is still standing. This is modern London. Welcome to the twenty-first century!"

His jovial response made Caro's legs buckle. If Alex had not reached out a hand to steady her, she likely would have fallen to the ground.

"Sorry. I forget you are not familiar with time travel yet. When we are safely where we need to go, I shall tell you more."

Caro had no words to answer him, so she nodded and braced her knees to hold herself up.

Alex put an arm around her waist to support her as he moved them quickly along a path through the dark trees. At one point, Caro thought she heard footsteps behind them. Alex must have thought so, too, because he dropped his arm from her waist, took hold of her wrist, and pulled her along at a faster pace. Who was this Abasi person Olde Gylda and Alex were so wont to avoid? Before she could ask Alex, he was calling for Gylda to deliver the stone.

But Gylda had already gone, had she not? She searched the path behind them as they burst into a small clearing. Alex dropped her hand and picked up a stone from the center of the area. Holding it in one hand, he called to Caro to come to him. She obeyed, sensing the unseen danger around them.

A whoosh on the other side of the trees was interrupted by a screech, then metal crunching, followed by running footsteps. Alex sucked in a breath, and she could feel his body tense. Before she could question him further, he folded her into his body spoon-style with one arm around her waist like a steel band. The other held the stone. He muttered, "Hold on tight and do not let go no matter what."

Terror shot through Caro, but it was too late to do anything other than what he said, so she clamped down on his arm with all her might.

"*Ar goll mewn amser. Ar goll mewn amser. Ar goll mewn amser.*"

She did not understand what Alex was saying, but it sounded like what she remembered Olde Gylda chanting right before the wind started. She had almost completed that thought when the wind whipped in from above, plastering her dress to her body and lashing her hair into her face. Forced to close her eyes, she took a deep breath and let herself be inhaled by the wind.

Chapter 12

Evelyn Perkins was a revelation. She was full of life and energy in everything she touched, usually chatting non-stop. Normally, William hated an incessantly chattering female. Now, not being in the company of any woman for more than a few minutes for two years, he simply enjoyed the sound of a non-male voice. He did not attempt to follow most of what she said. It was the trill of her voice and the softness of her appearance that pleased his senses.

William tried not to think too hard about his response to Evie. He was not ready to give up his old life or Caro. However, that little nagging voice deep within wondered if he would ever return to London, his own time, or his beloved Caro.

It was vaguely reassuring that he found another woman attractive. If he had to be stuck in America for the rest of his life, perhaps he might be able to find a wife and live out his days in something other than despair.

To compensate for his wayward thoughts, he yammered on about Caro during the free time he spent with Evie. Oddly, it did not seem to bother the girl at all. Fascinated with his stories of London's fancy balls with lords and ladies, she wanted to hear descriptions of the events as if he were a society reporter reciting the latest *on dits*. What did the ladies wear? What foods were served? What were his favorites? What was his life like on the estates that his family owned? It was a life she had difficulty imagining, but like a fairy tale, she found it spellbinding.

He avoided speaking of titles as much as possible, but Evie was delighted to find that Caro was really Lady Caroline, and he was Lord William. She loved calling him Will or Willie, both names he despised as a child, but coming from her they did not irritate him. Only when she teased him by addressing him as Lord Willie did he draw the line. Still, he enjoyed laughing along with her. Laughter felt good.

In short, theirs was an easy, friendly, comfortable relationship. Evie met up with him as often as she could considering her laundress obligations, but now she assisted him in some of the more complicated surgeries. She was indefatigable, a quick learner, and a fearless assistant. In the evenings, she joined Jeb, Sam, and him for the last meal of the day, but she returned to her own tent for the night. Sam reliably walked her back before returning to the hospital wagon to guard William until it was Jeb's watch.

Weather was becoming an issue as it was markedly colder each day. Plans to winter further south were not to be. Brief skirmishes with Union troops kept everyone on edge. As the army moved slowly toward Russellville, the days were long on travel and short on daylight. At those times he found himself dispensing help and medicine from the back of a moving wagon.

Today was one of the harder days for him once they were settled in camp. A young soldier, probably in his early twenties presented himself with a leg so gangrenous William had no choice but to remove it before it cost the young man his life. Evie remained a rock through the surgery, holding the young man's head and talking to him like the angel William had thought she was when he first laid eyes on her. The operation had gone as well as could be expected. He was able to leave a bit of a stump for the man, so he would be able to walk one day with the help of a prosthetic. That was the best he could do.

He finished giving instructions on the lad's care to his buddy who then helped Sam move the soldier back to his tent. William would like to have kept him in the hospital wagon, but it was filled with patients needing round the clock care. Unfortunately, there was nothing more in William's power to do for the man. At least he had been able to administer enough morphine to dull the pain during the surgery. Nonetheless, the young man's recovery loomed like a long road ahead before he would be able to return to any semblance of normal.

Once the army reached its winter quarters, the soldier would be sent home. The war was finished for him. William hoped the man would be able to work his farm again with his wife and children one day. He watched the ungainly procession of patient and buddy pass through the camp until they disappeared.

William turned back toward his wagon to clean up just as Evie tripped over a spot of uneven ground, lost her balance, and pitched forward. He was quick enough to reach out in time to keep her from slamming into the ground. Pulling her to her feet, he took a hard look at her. She did not look right to him at all. Her face was drained of color and her eyes were glassy.

"Glory be, Evie, you must be exhausted. Let Sam walk you back to your tent now. You need a break, don't you?"

Evie burst into tears, completely surprising William. She never cried. What was wrong?

"Damn and blast, Evie! Are you ill?"

By now the girl was sobbing in great gasps and cries, words to answer him well beyond her ability. He did the only thing he could think to do. He took her in his arms and let her cry. She clung to him like she feared he might run away, with her hands curled into the lapels of his coat and her body melded to his. She felt nothing like Caro who was taller and fit him like a glove, but her soft, female body reminded him it had been a long time since he had held a woman in his arms.

While he enjoyed the contact, even with tears wetting his jacket, he realized he did not feel particularly excited or aroused by her. He let her cry until she was finished, patting her back in a very paternal way until she was done.

Pulling back, he looked at her tear-stained face and

dragged a handkerchief from his pocket with which to mop up the wet. Evie took the cloth from him and blew her nose in it.

"I-I p-promise to warsh this and give it back to you tomorrow, Willie."

William snorted, "I am not worried about that, Evie. I want to know what made you cry. You have seen worse since you began assisting me, so I do not believe it was the surgery. What was it that tripped your tears today?"

Evie let out a shaky sigh. "I ain't sure. He was such a young man, and he'll be goin' home to his family maimed fer life. It made me think of my Henry and what our life'd be like if he'd come draggin' home without a leg. This war ain't fair, Willie, it jist ain't fair."

"No, Evie, there is nothing fair about it at all."

"At least her man will come home in time fer Christmas. Mine won't." That thought sent Evie's tears flowing again.

Good glory, Christmas. He had forgotten all about Christmas. It would be upon them in a matter of only a few days. What an insensitive nodcock he was to think only of himself and his work. This would mark Evie's first Christmas without her husband, and she was still far from home. Of course, she'd be bluedeviled with her emotions riding close to the surface.

"My dear girl, shame on me for not thinking about how these things affect you in your present situation. I worked you to the bone today. Skedaddle! Go to your tent and leave the rest to me. You have done more than enough for today."

"Nah, I am fine, Lord Willie," she snuffled, refusing to acknowledge the command in his tone. "I kin finish here if ya'll need me."

"No, Evie, you are not fine. Go take a rest. I bet laundry awaits you yet today, too. Am I right?"

Emitting a shaky sigh, she nodded. William hugged her tiny body and gave her a pat on the back before letting her go. "You are a very dear person, Mrs. Perkins. I insist you take care of yourself immediately and leave the laundry for another day. Doctor's orders."

Evie stepped back and eyed him speculatively. "You sure you ain't gonna be short-handed without me?"

"I can always make Sam or Jeb assist me, if I need the help." William grinned. "You are far easier on the eyes than either one of them. You know the soldiers much prefer looking in your pretty face than one of ours," he winked, "but I believe we can make do for the rest of the day."

Evie teetered for a moment unsure of what she should do.

"Off with you now." William teasingly shooed her toward her tent. Rarely had he met a person as giving as Evelyn Perkins. She never asked for anything for herself but gave freely of her time and her talent to him and the soldiers she helped. Who would take care of her sweet little self if he were fortunate enough to go home? That thought niggled at him as he realized he had not mentioned Caro to Evie all day. He would have to make up for that tonight when he bid Caro's pocket watch picture a goodnight.

"Maybe a nap would fix me right up," she replied, a huge yawn interrupting her thought. "I promise to do better tomorrow. Thanks, Doc Willie." Evie stepped closer, stood on her tiptoes, and gave him a kiss on his cheek. Not to be outdone, William hugged her tightly and kissed the top of her head before releasing her.

"Goodnight, dear girl."

Chapter 13

This time Caro recognized the drugged feeling pulsing through her when she awoke as a byproduct of time travel. Her head weighed a ton. Flopping like a rag doll when she sat up, it lolled on her chest as if too heavy to hold up. Alex mumbled something beside her, and she was relieved to know they had arrived together. Hating the thick haze hanging over her body and mind, she slapped herself in the face and gave her cheeks a solid rub. It helped a bit.

Scanning around her for familiar landmarks, she found none. They appeared to be in a valley with wooded hills on one side, a river at the base and terrain she would call mountains on the other. Rarely traveling beyond London except to a family or friend's estate, she had never heard of a valley like this one even in her schooling. Geography had not been a favorite subject, so perhaps this might be a part of England with which she was unfamiliar.

An overcast sky spread a gray pallor over the landscape. How much time had passed since leaving London? Caro dug under her gown in search of William's pocket watch pinned to her stays. Flipping it open, she read the time as six o'clock. That was not right because the sun's position was high in the sky even though her watch ticked on as if undisturbed.

If they had not time traveled and were still in England, where were they for the time in between dawn and now? Did that mean they really were fifty years into the future? How long did it take to make that time jump? Hours? Days? Weeks? How would she know? Were they actually in America? With those thoughts scrambling her brain, one stood out above all others. Where were they now?

Caro shivered and was happy to find her shawl still tied around her waist. Pulling it off she wrapped it around her shoulders, crossed it securely over her chest, and tied it behind her back. To keep her hands warm, she tucked them inside the folds. Huddled with her knees drawn up under her chin, the cold still crept in. Wherever they were, the weather was far more frigid than what they had left in London.

"I think I hit my head on a rock," Alex groaned, rubbing the spot which splayed his blond hair into halves like sheaves of golden wheat. Stumbling to his feet he shook himself like a wet dog. Meeting Caro's eyes, he asked, "How did you fare, Lady Caroline?"

"Please, Alex, call me Caro. I think it is a little late for formalities, and I do not believe we want others to know our true identities, do we?"

"Indeed, madam." He straightened his now beleaguered evening dress, jerking his cravat back to the center and stared at Caro. How was it he looked no worse for wear? Dratted man. A nerve ticked in his cheek, betraying his annoyance despite his words, "I am sorry you must go through all this travel. I do not imagine you are enjoying this as a way to spend an evening. Here, let me give you my jacket."

"Oh, do stop apologizing, Alex. You do not want me here, and I am nothing but a thorn in your side. I know that. Thus, I will not take your jacket. I am wrapped up quite like a cocoon in this very large shawl. I'm fine. My joining you was an accident as we established earlier, but I am determined to make the most of it. After all, locating William is a shared goal. I promise to do my best not to annoy you."

His mouth ticked up, this time in humor. "You do not mince words, do you?"

"No, to my mind, being indirect only adds to one's confusion." He helped Caro to her feet and steadied her with a hand on her waist.

"Then we shall get along well, I think."

"Hmm," she replied, giving him a sideways smile. "With that settled, do you have any idea where we might be?"

"Lost in time," he responded with a serious face.

"*What?* Lost in time?" Fear surged through her veins.

Alex smiled. "Let me explain. That chant that you heard from Gylda that I repeated over the stone in London is Welsh for *lost in time*."

"So, we *are* lost?" Now Caro was upset enough that her voice trembled.

"Not exactly. Olde Gylda places a new word at the front of her incantations for each mission."

Caro frowned, so he continued. "Each time a stone is called for a specific mission, the same incantation is used for each time jump. Gylda knows where she wants you to go, so when she sends a stone and the mission incantation is read aloud, it will take you where you need to go and eventually return you to your starting point. She used *lost* because that is how she sees William at this point—*lost*."

"Are we lost now or are we where we're supposed to be?"

He paused to gather his thoughts. "The last time Olde Gylda had contact with Duvall and your William, they were in Arkansas, but that was before Duvall left. Since then, she has had no luck in contacting William. This is troubling because Gylda is not used to losing her Guardian charges, you see. Normally, she knows their exact location and can travel to them at will. That is what has her so upset. She cannot hear William and fears he cannot hear her. What is keeping their communication from happening is part of why I am here."

"You sound as though William might be d-dead." She turned her head away so Alex would not see the tears that rushed to fill her eyes. Closing them tightly she resolved to banish those thoughts from her mind before they swamped her.

She sucked in a breath, stiffened her spine and faced Alex again. "Surely, I would know if that were so!"

"I am sure you are right, my dear." Alex gave her a comforting smile, though she saw pity in the depths of his eyes. "He is undoubtedly alive, but something is wrong, or Gylda would know precisely where to find him." Caro struggled to smile back, recognizing his attempt to placate her. She wanted none of his pity.

"As for where we are, Duvall told Gylda that William was to be sent to General Burnside in Tennessee, so she decided to put us down near a place called Knoxville."

Caro mulled that thought for a moment before replying, "So, we really are in America?"

"Yes, my la- . . .er, Caro." He cleared his throat. "I will not find it easy to address you by your given name."

Caro grinned. "You are such a gentleman, Alex! We shall manage nonetheless." She turned in a full circle examining their surroundings. If William were somewhere nearby, she was itching to be about the business of finding him. "Is Knoxville a city or a village? How are we to find William there?"

"Good questions. First, however, we must seek a change of clothing and shelter for the night. If we are successful with those things, we should have no trouble asking for help in determining William's whereabouts."

Caro giggled. "We do look a tad silly toddling about the countryside in a ball gown and evening wear, hmm? Just how are we to explain our odd manner of dress?"

"We'll think of something. Right now, I believe we shall have the most luck heading toward that copse of trees over there. Unless I am mistaken, a road lies in front of it."

Caro scanned the area one last time before nodding her agreement. Taking her by the arm, Alex turned them in the appropriate direction, and they set off wishing their shoes were not flimsy dancing slippers. The ground was cold, rocky, and slippery in places. Caro's feet had gone out from under her twice in the span of ten feet. Thankfully, Alex had righted her before she had fallen.

"Well, these are called slippers for a reason, aren't they?" she joked. Alex did not crack a smile at her quip. She caught her balance again and sighed. It would be a long walk to those trees.

To Caro an eternity passed before they reached the road. Alex had a death grip on her arm most of the way and had all but carried her from time to time. As he hurried her along, she had to remind him periodically that she was wearing a corset and could not keep up the pace he was setting. He had growled at her, but he slowed down. The bottom of her dress was wet up to her knees which made her even colder than before.

The temperature had not risen significantly along with the sun which still sent weak rays of light through heavy clouds. A crispness in the air made her think of Christmas back home. Would she ever see home again? A gust of wind froze a tear to her cheek, and she came close to losing her equanimity entirely. For now, she decided she had better push all thoughts of that to the back of her brain and concentrate on finding William.

What passed for a road when they reached it was not much more than a dirt trail in places without a hint of what lay in either direction. Foliage alongside the road had been trampled by horses and wagons at some point, but their tracks showed travel in both directions. Which way should they choose? Following the movement of the sun, they determined north and figured the road spread from east to west. Where would they find Knoxville? If they went the wrong way, they would lose precious time in their hunt for William.

Alex climbed a boulder on the tree side of the road to get a better view of the valley. Caro took advantage of the break and sat on a downed tree to examine the damage to her slippers. Having walked through the tender soles of her shoes in several places, she would be walking on bare feet before long. Well, new blisters would match those forming on the back of each heel as her slippers rubbed up and down with every step.

Checking the time on William's watch to see how long they had been walking, she prayed they would find help soon.

Her stomach gave an audible rumble, reminding her they had not eaten in ages. What she would not give for a restorative cup of tea and a luscious lemon tart!

Dear William, where are you? Was that her imagination or had the image of William just winked at her? She peered closer at the portrait. Nothing was different. Why would she have thought he winked when that was impossible?

Jumping down from his bird's eye view, Alex trotted over to her. Where was he getting the energy for that, she wondered? Without fortification her muscles were steps from refusing to move any further.

"I believe we should go east, Caro. Just beyond that rock formation, I think the roll of the hills is hiding a house or structure of some kind. Is not that smoke from a chimney wafting up into the sky?"

Caro peered closely at the sky and whether it was wishful thinking or reality, there did appear to be a trail of smoke floating skyward. "Yes, I think it is, Alex! Perhaps we can trade them something for food. I am a might peckish."

Alex, the beast, guffawed. "Only peckish, my dear? I am famished. Perchance we can wrangle something to eat, a bed for the night, and horses for tomorrow."

"That, sir, would be most welcome. How far away do you think the place is?"

"I should think not all that far." He winced at the condition of her feet and slippers as she put them back on. "We should be there by nightfall."

Not all that far turned out to be further than either had imagined. Night had fallen and the weather was turning meaner by the minute. Alex put his arm around Caro's shoulders which helped some, but both were frozen. The smell of snow in the air taunted them as they limped toward the hoped-for shelter. Fortunately, that cold ensured a steady stream of smoke continued to belch into the air for them to follow like a beacon.

Nearing the place set off from the road by a long lane, Caro made out a small, unpainted house with light seeping through a pair of wavy glass windows. A barn twice the size of the house loomed in the yard. The stench of the barnyard reached out to greet them with nary an animal in sight. In fact, if not for the light in the windows the place would appear deserted. Was it not the custom here for a dog or two to announce any visitors?

An aura surrounded the place that was eerily quiet as though all living things had gone into hiding. Nevertheless, she picked up her pace hoping to get inside and off her feet as quickly as possible. Alex slowed her down which surprised her. Did he not want inside as much as she did?

"I am sorry, but we cannot rush into this without a bit of surveillance first. We have no idea who lives here. It may be a harmless farmer, or it may be brigands of some sort, like soldiers who have deserted."

Caro's heart sank. What if they had walked all the way here and could not be helped in any way. "What must we do?"

They were standing beside the barn in the shadow thrown from a full moon. "First, we should take off all our jewelry. We may need the gems to barter for food or shelter. We don't want these people to know the extent of what we have with us."

Caro obeyed, pulling off her emerald earrings, her diamond and emerald necklace, and the emerald and gold bracelet with diamond accents. She had a gold ring with a sizable ruby on her right hand and a smaller gold band with several diamonds inset on her left. Alex took them from her but gave her back the small gold band. "Wear this turned around so that it looks like a plain band."

"If brigands robbed us, would they not have taken my ring, too?"

"I was thinking of you, my dear. As awkward as this is, we are without a chaperone. Your reputation will survive best if you pose as my wife. Otherwise, you are likely to be taken for a light-skirt traveling with a man to whom you are not married."

"No . . . oh, uh . . . I see," Caro stammered. "I had not thought of that, but you are right, I am sure." She dutifully slipped the ring onto the third finger of her left hand and turned the diamonds to the inside. "I shall seek Elena's forgiveness when we return."

Alex grinned at her flustered response. "You need not fear on that score, Caro. I am devoted to my lovely wife, and she to me."

Alex rid himself of the sparkling diamond stick pin tucked into his cravat and the signet ring on his pinky. He held out his hand to take the rest of her jewels, depositing them in the interior pocket of his jacket with a pat to flatten out the stash.

"Stay here," Alex commanded, "and I will learn what I can from spying on the occupants through a window. If there is more than one, I might glean a few things before we try to talk with them. In the meantime, you need to come up with a wonderful reason for the way we are dressed." He winked at her as she rolled her eyes, an involuntary shiver ending any debate regarding assignments.

"I understand. Please pay attention to the women in the house, Alex. I do not know how unfashionable my gown is or what I should be wearing to fit in with them."

"Just like a woman," Alex teased. "You may be wandering without food or shelter, years from your own time, but heaven forbid you be unfashionable."

"Go on with you! Men never understand these things," Caro whispered, only a bit annoyed. Did he not realize how ridiculous being clothed in styles fifty years out of date would look to another woman? She gave him a shove toward the house and scoured the area for anything to sit on while she waited. Her feet were too sore to hold her up much longer.

Spotting a wooden bucket by a water pump, she flipped it over and sat down gingerly, hoping it would hold her weight. When nothing squeaked, she relaxed onto it and plopped her feet out in front of her, hugely relieved to be off them.

She watched Alex prowl like a feral cat across the farmyard to the window with the brightest light. Shapes passed by the curtained opening now and then, but she was not able to discern much else. Hopefully, up close, Alex could see more than just shadows.

Once under the window, Alex bobbed around before finding a spot he liked. Minutes ticked by before he began his return creeping across the shadows in the yard. She lost track of him after only a moment. Then he popped up so suddenly in front of her she barely stifled a scream.

"W-what did you find out?" she breathed softly, calming herself with a hand over her chest as if that could ease her racing heart.

"Not enough to answer all our questions, I am afraid, but enough for the moment." Alex stepped to the lane and looked out toward the east. "The good news is we chose to walk in the right direction. From what I can tell from their conversation—it is an older man and his wife, I believe—both armies passed by here in the last week. The Confederates came through here first, followed by the Union army. We are east of Knoxville, so we saved ourselves some time by not going there first. It sounds as though the Confederates lost their hold on Knoxville and moved in this direction with the Union troops right behind them. William was assigned to a unit in the Union army, so he should not be that far from here."

Caro's hand gravitated to William's watch pinned beneath her clothes and clutched her treasure to her heart as if it held her life force. Alex lifted a brow at this, but Caro shook her head. "William gave his grandfather's timepiece into my keeping before he left. I will not be parted from it."

Alex started to argue and then reconsidered. "Keep it hidden under your clothing, and we shall hope it remains in your possession."

Caro's mind had moved beyond the watch. No one would be taking it from her. More importantly, were they truly close to William? "Wait. What is the bad news?" She held her breath waiting for him to answer.

"The farmyard is quiet because the Union troops stole their animals."

"Oh, no! That is what feels so wrong here."

"Indeed. It seems the Confederates bought a few chickens and a hog, but the Union took all the animals they wanted without paying a penny. That is all I found out because the woman got too close to the window, and I feared discovery. I thought it best not to press my luck."

"So, have you a plan for getting us inside, clothed and fed?"

"Perhaps." He bent to Caro's ear and explained what he thought should happen.

She nodded a time or two before grinning up at him. "You enjoy this hugger-mugger business, hmm? "

"'Tis my job, madam," Alex answered, tipping his nose in the air, mocking a superior attitude.

"Then certainly we shall succeed," Caro responded with equal temerity before her face fell and her lips quivered.

The smile on Alex's face dimmed as he noted Caro's change of expression. "We'll find him, dear girl. You shall see."

Afraid her voice would betray her, she nodded.

Alex and Caro set about making themselves even more bedraggled. She messed up her hair, so it looked like she had been dragged through a hedgerow backwards. He ripped the outside pocket on his jacket which helped to disguise any jewelry bulge from within. She tore a draped sleeve, so it hung down to her elbow and cringed as she dirtied her beautiful shawl. Smearing a little barn grime on their faces for added effect, they decided they were ready to meet the farmer and his wife.

Crossing the yard to the farmhouse door, Caro took a deep breath and prayed she could play the scene well enough to keep them from asking too many questions. More was at stake here than had been years ago when she, Violet and William had played their pranks on their families and friends.

Alex knocked loudly. They could feel the tension erupt from inside as the farmer peered out the window to see who was on his doorstep. His dark eyes got big as he spotted Alex and Caro. His wife ducked in below him to get an eyeful, too.

The door flew open with a bang as the farmer stood with feet spread apart and a very long gun pointed at the two of them.

Never having stared down the barrel of a rifle before, Caro was speechless. Alex, on the other hand, presented his usual gregarious demeanor.

Using his aristocratic intonations, he calmly addressed the pair. "So sorry to bother you, my good sir, and madam, but my wife and I are in need of your assistance."

He bowed to them with a flourish and Caro curtsied with a graceful dip, noting the woman's dress in detail as she did so. The silhouette was not as different as she had feared, just fuller skirts. Besides, 'twas obvious they had come from England, so it made sense styles would be different.

"I am afraid we have had a spot of bad luck." He paused for the couple to get a good look at them. "We encountered brigands upon the road who robbed us of our valuables at gunpoint. Our hired driver and outriders deserted us by fading into the night at the first opportunity. We were left beside the road with nary a cloak or hat, let alone a horse, as the outlaws drove away in our coach." He looked to his feet and Caro's before adding, "We are frozen to the bone having walked for miles in search of someone to help us."

Caro let out a sob as she moved a foot to show them the sad state of her slippers and was pleased that it sounded pathetic.

"Yer English, ain't ye?"

Caro was unsure if this was a question or an accusation and looked to Alex for direction.

"That we are, sir," Alex replied with a tip of his head. "We are in this country in search of my wife's brother and were expected at the hotel in Knoxville—." He turned to Caro and asked, "What is the name of the hotel again?" Alarm flared in her eyes, but seconds later the farmer's wife offered, "Lamar Hotel?"

"Yes, that one! Thank you." Alex bestowed the full force of his killer smile on the poor woman who almost fainted. "We were to meet friends there for dinner who might know of his whereabouts." Seeing that he had won over the wife, he lowered his head slightly and turned puppy dog eyes upon her. "Might you help us, madam?"

The farmer remained suspicious of the pair, but his wife ushered them inside with a snap of her white apron and a swish of her gray skirts. In only a matter of minutes, they were seated by the fire, wrapped in blankets, and enjoying a tasty stew.

Alex persuaded their hosts to let them sleep by the fire for the night. Caro was fine with that as she faded in and out of the conversation, her head sagging on her chest. The farmer's wife, Irene, produced some pillows and two more blankets and it was agreed to call it a night.

The last Caro remembered, Irene was promising to find fresh clothes for them to wear until they could regain their possessions or buy new. She spilled information as fast as her mouth could move. Her husband, Jeremiah, said not a word. Unable to keep up with the woman's drawl and her steady rate of speech, Caro was lulled to sleep, hoping the morrow would bring her closer yet to William.

Chapter 14

Awaking to the pungent scent of coffee and bacon, Caro wondered why she was sleeping in the kitchen. My goodness, what was Cook thinking to let her sleep on such a hard surface? Her face was likely smooshed out of shape. She had watched Cook prepare meals since she was a small child, but never would the dear woman have left her to sleep there.

With that question on her lips, she pried open her sleep-glazed eyes, only to be presented with the rough interior of a farmhouse. A thick timber beam formed the peak of the ceiling overhead with whitewashed walls beside her. The house appeared to be one big room with a bedroom curtained off at one end and a kitchen with a hearth at the other.

As if on cue, the aches and pains of yesterday rolled back into her brain with startling clarity. Wait, where is Alex? If that man had dumped her like unclaimed baggage so he could finish the mission faster without her, she would wring his neck—if she ever found him again. Surely, he would not leave her alone here with people she barely knew to wait for him while he found William, would he?

That frightening thought sent blood raging through her body which in turn overrode her weariness. Struggling to stand on her damaged feet, she shook out her hopelessly wrinkled gown and pushed back a tangle of hair that fuzzed out of her long braid. She had a job in front of her to just make herself presentable again. If she ever found William, would he even recognize her in such a disgraced state?

Turning to the hearth, the woman called Irene was busily frying bacon with one hand and checking on something in a Dutch oven with the other. Biscuits, perhaps? The scent made her stomach rumble.

"Something smells delicious," Caro remarked as she moved to look over Irene's shoulder.

"Nothin' here but ol' country fare. Not quite the spread someone like ya'll be accustomed to." The woman's words belied her expression of pride as she lifted the lid so Caro could glimpse the fluffy, golden brown biscuits within.

"Oh, my, those are exceptionally fine. Our family cook cannot begin to make biscuits like that." Caro glanced about the room. "Might you know the whereabouts of Al—my husband?" She braced herself for the response that he had left without telling anyone, but she was pleasantly surprised with the woman's answer.

"Oh, he went 'long with Jeremiah to tend to the animals."

Caro frowned. "I thought the Union troops took all your animals."

Irene grinned like a wicked cat, her toothy smile accented by sharp canines. "That is exactly what they wuz to b'lieve. After the Confederate troops come by and bought what they needed, they warned us the Feds were behind 'em ransackin' ever' small town and farm place 'long the way. My Jeremiah has never been one to wait to see what'd happen once informed o' trouble. He rounded up all our stock and hid 'em at an old farm place sev'ral miles from here. Left our youngest sons Jed and Isaac to mind 'em."

Standing tall, she smoothed out her apron. "Our oldest boy is fightin' with General Bragg. Leastways, we hope he still is. Haven't heard from him in a while." She shook off the wave of darkness crossing her face and chose to plaster a cheery expression there instead. "Anyways, Jeremiah set off to fetch eggs fer breakfast, and yer husband went with him."

"How very clever of you to save your animals!" Caro nodded her approval, much to the delight of Irene. "You saved yourselves much hardship as replacing them would be extremely difficult at the moment, I imagine."

"Ma'am, you got no idea how hard!" Irene was just warming up as she expertly flipped the bacon in her pan without sending grease flying everywhere. "Me and Jeremiah talked las' night about you, we did."

Caro's eyebrows flew up in concern over what that meant.

"Yessum, we don't think you should be runnin' 'round the country wearin' them fancy clothes like ya'll have on. My man said you'd be right wise to wear some of our boys' clothes and pretend to be a boy. Bein' female roun' a bunch o' soldiers in war time be askin' fer trouble."

Caro blushed to her roots. "Dear me, having never been near an army, I had not thought of that."

Irene's eyes roved over Caro's body ending with a warning shrug as she stared at the exposed decolletage provided by the evening gown. Caro felt like a lightskirt and tugged up the top of the bodice as high as it would go. Might she really be in danger? Having lived in London and traveled only to well-protected estates in the country, she had never been in the position of needing a guard. "Do you think I could pass for a youth?"

"Why shore ya could. We git ya flattened out on top with a bit o' bindin' and put ya in some baggy trousers all belted up and throw a beehive hat o'er all that hair and ya'll do jist fine."

Mulling that picture as it rolled around in her head, Caro replied, "You are more than generous, madam, to offer such assistance. How might we repay you for all your troubles?"

This time Irene's penetrating gaze landed on the ring finger of Caro's left hand. Before she could stop herself, she blurted, "'Tis all I have! I could not bear to lose my wedding ring when the brigands stopped us, so I stuffed it under my tongue and said nothing the entire time their guns were aimed at us."

Her heart was beating fast as she caught her breath and held it. Would Irene believe her story? The older woman thought it over with a dour face until interrupted by a commotion in the farmyard.

Rushing to a window to see what was happening, Caro spied Jeremiah carrying a bundle thrown over the back of a rugged red saddle horse. A moment later, she silently chortled at the sight of Alex coming into view atop a stout white pony with red splotches on its face and body. Wearing a light tan jacket with fringe on it, his long, evening-clad legs almost dragged on the ground. How amusing to catch sight of elegant Lord St. John like this! But why was he riding a pony?

Then Irene's scheme dashed through her brain, and she understood what she was seeing. Alex must have arranged to buy the horses from the couple, so they did not have to walk as they searched for William. He would have the larger horse, and she would pose as a lad riding the pony. Now it all made sense. What would he have used for payment, she wondered? Her ring? She would have to keep her lips sealed until she understood what he had in mind.

"So, the menfolk's back, is they?" Irene did not flinch a muscle, just sent a glance in the direction of the window as she spoke. "Would ya be so kind as to holler at 'em to hurry it up with them eggs? The bacon's ready, and we got to git the food on so ya'll can be on yer way."

Before Caro had a chance to comply, the door burst open, and Jeremiah strode in with his knapsack over his shoulder. He grinned at the disheveled Caro making her acutely aware of her appearance and swung the bag in her direction. "Here ya go, ma'am. Them's duds in there fer you and yer man to change into. Ye got to dig out the eggs that are ridin' along with 'em first for Reenie, though, so's she don't git mad at me." He winked at her and motioned for her to do as he asked.

Caro blushed her understanding. With careful fingers, she pulled out a dozen fresh eggs from the folds of the clothing and placed them in the bowl Irene handed her. Once the eggs were safely in Irene's hands, she insisted Caro and Alex go into the bedroom to change their clothes.

Caro's face heated as she contemplated changing her clothes with the help of Alex. There was no other place with any privacy, and she would feel foolish asking Alex to wait for her to change. Besides, she did need his help to get out of her gown.

Not meeting Alex's eyes, she made her way through the curtain to the small bedroom and waited for him to follow. She tossed the bag on the colorful quilt covering the big bed and pulled clothing from it. Which items were meant for which person was not difficult to discern.

"Jeremiah's sons are staying in the old place with the animals, so I bartered for this jacket and the clothes in the bag," Alex explained, keeping his voice low. Caro turned and looked him over head to toe and back again with a raised brow and enough intensity to make him flinch.

"You do not think your evening trousers are a bit much for the fringed cowhide jacket?"

"I plan to start a new fashion—daywear into evening—no need to change before the ball." Executing a sweeping bow with a wave of his hand from his new jacket to his tattered evening trousers, he extended his muddy dancing slipper to a point for her perusal.

"Very practical for travel. The *eau de barnyard* cologne is simply devastating, as well."

"Do you think so? It does have a certain *jenesais quoi.*"

As he modeled the ensemble for her doing a full turn, Caro could not contain her giggle which emerged as a snort. That made her laugh even harder, requiring Alex to quickly muffle the sound with a shirt thrust in her face until her shoulders quit shaking.

Much more relaxed than when she entered the bedroom, Caro felt him take a stance behind her and efficiently undo the tapes of her clothing. Taking care to apologize repeatedly to the absent Elena for being put in this position, she waited until Alex finished before asking him to please turn around. Except that he had anticipated her request and turned away by the time the words crossed her lips. He was a true gentleman.

She scrambled into her clothes as fast as she could. She decided to wear her thin chemise after testing the shirt's scratchy homespun fabric against her skin. Glad to be rid of her corset, she used one of its ribbons to attach William's watch to the bodice of her chemise. Carefully, she tore off the bottom of the garment and wrapped it around her breasts to strap them down as flat as possible. She had just enough to tie the sheer fabric into a tidy knot at the small of her back and tuck the ends under.

The cream-colored shirt was still several sizes too large for her, but when she rolled up the sleeves to her elbows it did not look too outlandish. The pair of dark brown trousers were almost slick, like they had been waxed. Sliding into them, they fit better than the shirt. She stuffed the excess from the chemise and the shirt tail into the pants and buttoned the fall. It seemed to erase her tiny waist which aided the illusion of being a boy.

Rolling up the pant legs far enough to avoid walking on them, she turned to find Alex stepping into different trousers. Oops, she'd better give him a little more time. Glaring at her bare feet she wondered if she should retain her silk stockings. It would be risky since any self-respecting boy would never wear them even if he froze his feet off going without.

"Were shoes or boots part of this bargain?" She was proud of herself for remembering to whisper this time.

"Yes, they were."

"Do you mind my asking how you paid for all this and the horses too?"

"It cost me my stick pin and your ruby ring."

Caro sighed. She had liked that ruby ring. "Where did you tell the men you had hidden those items when the brigands raided us?"

"My shoe. I told them I had tossed them in the toes of my shoes."

Caro's eyes jumped to Alex's ruined dancing slippers. They did not appear as destroyed as hers from their trek across the wilderness. Anything tucked in her shoes would have disappeared long ago through the gaping holes in the soles.

"Hmm, Reenie spotted my ring." She twisted it around again on her finger, so the gold band was the only thing showing. "I told her I had stuck it under my tongue and never spoke while the robbers were there."

"Good thinking. At least we will have our stories straight."

"Do you think she will find a way to get the ring off my finger?"

"I think she may try." Alex buttoned up a woolen vest over a muslin shirt and reached for the fringed outer jacket he had thrown over a chair while he changed.

"Yes, I agree. Do you have a plan for evading her, Alex?"

"Inspiration has not yet struck. And you?"

"No. You are the professional traveler here. You lead the way," Caro whispered with a sweet smile that told him he had better come up with something fast. Their credibility was at stake.

Caro stuffed her undergarments into the middle of her folded gown and shawl. She would not grieve the loss of her corset because the boy's clothing she wore was not only freeing but a great deal warmer. Her beautiful shawl, however, she would miss.

Once back in the main room, the food was ready and on the table. Unmatched chairs were pulled up for Caro and Alex. Reenie promised to dig out some socks and boots for each of them after breakfast. Caro's toes were freezing, but food had to be eaten here the moment it was ready, or it would be cold, so she did not complain.

The simple fare was as delicious as it looked. Lighter biscuits she had never eaten, and the fresh eggs had scrambled up into fluffy mounds that were perfectly complemented by the crunch of the bacon. Conversation was kept to a minimum. Apparently, when food was on the table the job was to eat it, not discuss it. She and Alex were happy to comply.

True to her word, Reenie dug out boots from the attic of the barn. Her sons slept there when home which made Caro wonder if they were walking away with the boys' best shoes.

However, if the family could get to Knoxville and sell the gem-stones, it would likely pay for more than one pair of boots. That meant now was not the time to worry about the sons.

Reenie was more than proud of the socks she had knitted herself. Caro was just happy they made her feet warm and cozy in the rough pair of brown lace-up boots that fit her best. That footwear likely had been passed down through the boys as they were well-worn, but the soles had been patched and seemed tight. Alex fared a bit better, snagging a newer pair of leather brogans that had to be a Sunday pair for one of the boys.

Alex already sported the cow skin jacket, but Caro needed something for outerwear, and a knitted scarf would be welcome as well. She elbowed Alex and let him know to ask for her. It was an unnecessary move. Reenie produced a wool vest and a suede jacket that fit her nicely, further concealing her female body.

The crowning glory, however, was the felt beehive hat. With her hair braided tightly and tucked up under the hat, she tugged the brim down firmly around her head. It should stay in place even in a stiff wind, but a string attached to either side se-cured it just in case. Pulling a neck scarf for each of them out of a knitting basket in her bedroom, Reenie proudly presented more of her handmade goods. She stepped back to assess her work and gave Caro a squinted once over.

"Yessir, I think you'll do real nice. If I ain't knowed ya wuz a woman, I'd not think so now."

"Do be careful, though, how ya move, darlin'. You swing them hips like usual and you won't like the looks comin' ya'lls way." Jeremiah took a few mincing steps imitating Caro, and they all laughed.

Somewhere along the way he had thawed considerably and was presently downright friendly. Just how many pieces of their stash of jewelry had Alex given him beyond the two he had admitted to trading? The man grinned like he had struck it rich.

As if he'd read her mind, Jeremiah produced a leather slouch hat and handed it to Alex, who looked properly surprised and very thankful for the gift. Or was it a gift?

Caro's eyes landed on her fake wedding ring and wondered if she would keep it or if it would go as payment for their new wardrobe. The ring had been given to her on her thirteenth birthday by her father and was something she would like to keep.

Thinking of her father, she was jolted by the realization that she was fifty years into the future. He would be dead by now. Would she ever return to her own time to talk to him again? No matter how hard she tried she could not keep the tears from spilling down her face. Embarrassed, she wiped them away with the back of her hand and marshalled her emotions back down.

As she looked up, Reenie's eyes were on her, but this time sympathy shone in them rather than want. She shook her head at Caro and smiled.

"No, sweet thing, I ain't goin' to take your weddin' ring. Seems yer man done settled up fair and square with mine. Do take care of each other. There's many a man out there'd rather shoot ya as look at ya. I hope ya'll find yer brother soon, cuz winter can git pretty mean 'round these parts." She shuffled across the room and plucked a cloth wrapped parcel off the table. "Here's the rest of the biscuits and some jerky for ya'll. Good luck and God bless."

The unexpected kindness melted Caro's heart into a puddle with tears continuing to run down her face. That made her want to hand over her ring and anything else to express her thanks. Alex stopped her when he caught her eye. With a slight shake of his head he made her realize it would be rude not to accept the offered graciousness.

Backs slapped and goodbyes said, Caro and Alex mounted their horses and set off into a stiff wind sweeping down from the mountains. Shivering despite her warmer clothes, Caro wondered if today she would find William. She tightened the chin strap on her hat and prayed.

Chapter 15

"I've never ridden anything but sidesaddle, Alex. This position feels so odd. I did not think a horse's back could be so wide."

Alex's eyes followed her for a moment before he smiled. "You cannot be used to riding astride, so I am sure you are right." Turning out of the lane, they headed northeast along the main road. "I assume you are an experienced horsewoman?"

"I adore horses. Riding is one of the pleasures afforded a duke's daughter nearly from birth on. I had a pony like this one, I am told, from the time I learned to sit up." She patted the little pony called Shorty over the red splotches on his neck, and he twitched his ears in appreciation. "One of the grooms would walk along-side me to be sure I stayed atop. After that, my mother insisted I be trained to a sidesaddle as soon as possible, so riding astride was never an option."

"Do you enjoy the country where your father's stables are? I understand his cattle are among the best." Looking up at Alex a good foot above her on Ryder, his much larger red roan, she was dwarfed by comparison as though she were a much younger person. She sat up a bit taller, not pleased to be so small.

"You hit upon his pride and joy, sir. I must admit I love riding neck or nothing across the meadows on a fine summer morning atop a prime goer. I think horses must be in our blood."

"No doubt, but what does your father say regarding your

behavior?"

Caro laughed. "Oh, he thinks I am a hoyden and sure to kill myself."

"Does he?" Bemusement shown in his eyes.

"Yes, but he knows I will not stop doing so, because I learned it from him!"

"Ah, yes, the perils of a headstrong daughter," Alex laughed. "I shall take note." Caro watched his thoughts drift to Elena and the child she was carrying. Would it be his heir or a daughter? Did he care which one? Was he a husband who would demand his wife give him a male child? She did not think so. Genuine love flowed between him and Elena.

Would Elena hate her for accompanying Alex? It had been an accident. In the end, whether unintended or not mattered little. The fact remained that she was detaining him from being with his wife, since she was not supposed to be along on his mission. She promised herself to be as easy a companion as possible and not do anything that would delay his return.

Glancing above, the clear blue sky should have harkened a beautiful day, but the weak sunlight shining down on her shoulders did little to warm her or the air around her. The trees lining both sides of the road smelled lovely and appeared to have needles like the Scots pine she knew from home, but they had different shapes. They bent to and fro, creating something of a wind tunnel with gusts whistling down the road.

Caro shivered as cold air shot inside her jacket prompting her to wrap the scarf more tightly around her neck to seal off its entry. "Please tell me what else you learned from Jeremiah, Alex. Where exactly are we in relation to the Union army? Might we reach William's camp today?"

"They are supposed to be wintering outside of Blaine's Crossing. That is a place not far from here that runs along the Holston River. This road, as sad as it is, should take us to within a few miles of their quarters. They were to go further north to a more secure location, but a battle a while back changed those plans. Now the two armies winter only a few miles apart, so they can keep an eye on each other."

"How does one approach an army to ask about William? They won't shoot at us on sight, will they?" She recalled Irene's warning to trust no one easily.

"Ah, I sincerely hope not." He grinned at Caro, raising one eyebrow for emphasis. "Jeremiah told me to expect to meet pickets or sentries as we get closer to the army's location."

"Will they stop us?" Sudden fear rushed through Caro, erupting in a shudder. "I would die if I were within moments of finding William and was stopped."

"I expect they will question us, but according to Jeremiah, civilians are not strangers to camp, but move in and out of the area with ease. Folks, including sutlers, are always trying to sell soldiers goods and relieve them of their army pay as quickly as they get it."

"Like peddlers?" Caro shifted uncomfortably in her saddle and marveled again at the great width of Shorty's back. Perhaps his name should be Tubby or Lumpy.

"Quite." Alex surveyed her appearance with a thoughtful expression. "Since you are dressed as a boy on a pony, we should not appear too threatening to any of them. Besides, I have no firearm at present—a fact I shall remedy at the first opportunity. Jeremiah and his sons had none to spare."

"Oh dear, that is unfortunate!"

Alex acknowledged her response with a grimace. "It does leave us unprotected." He kept a calm demeanor, but Caro read his concern in the set of his face.

"Where does one acquire a gun in the midst of a war?" The trees had given way to a valley that stretched beneath them with a river winding its way along the bottom. It was obvious to Caro from the terrain they had encountered yesterday and today, that there was no civilization, let alone a store, for miles in any direction. It was a beautiful, but lonely place.

"Good question." Alex skillfully moved his mount around a muddy patch in the middle of the road. He smiled as Caro's pony doggedly followed in his tracks as if being led. "Sutler wagons are like miniature trading posts around the perimeter of camps like the one we will visit. They float between camps, so there is no telling how they acquired their firearms, or if any are for sale, but they are likely our best bet."

"Alex, did Jeremiah tell you all this, or have you traveled here before?"

"My travels as Olde Gylda's assistant have taken me to many places throughout time. Remember, I met Elena in the fourteenth century."

"So she said! I find that hard to believe, but then, here I am." Caro shook her head as if she still could not quite believe where she was and what was in front of her. Was she dreaming?

"Indeed. I never know where Gylda will send me next, so I acquire history books whenever I visit the twenty-first century to study when not assigned a mission."

"You are a scholar?"

"Something like that. I keep a flat, as you might have guessed, near Hyde Park. I read what I can regarding time periods to which I might be sent, so I can fit in and avoid undue attention while there. It is a bit hit or miss since some of what those history books describe is entirely wrong. I know first-hand of what I speak and would love to correct the real scholars, but I cannot without giving myself away as a time traveler. They would not believe me anyway."

"I do not doubt it."

They rode in silence for a while, Caro mulling over all that Alex had just told her. One thing still bothered her. "I understand we are in the middle of a war between Confederate and Union soldiers, but I confess I did not glean from our conversation with Jeremiah and Reenie what it is they are fighting over. Might you explain the circumstances? Is it not unusual for a country to fight itself?"

Alex grinned. "If Scotland wished to separate from England, would we let them go?"

"Oh, I see. Is that what has happened here?"

"Well, it is an unresolved issue dividing them. In the

North, the Union is opposed to slavery, while in the South, the Confederates want it to continue. As America has added states and territories to its union, the question of slavery has loomed as a divisive issue. It reached a boiling point a couple of years ago when the Southern States seceded from the Union and formed their own government. The North is determined to stop them and keep their country whole."

"We abolished the slave trade in England years ago, did we not?"

"We did."

"Is that why Olde Gylda placed William with the Union?"

"Perhaps. More to the point, Gylda wanted him to learn medicine from Doc Duvall in preparation for where she will send him in the future. It is not his war to fight."

"Still, he could be killed in the fighting if he did not defend himself, right?"

"True, but Gylda would not send him there if she thought that a likelihood." Alex studied her worried face before adding, "You must not give over to those thoughts, Caro. We will find out what has happened to him soon enough."

Caro nodded, but she felt her brow furrow as she pondered Alex's explanation. Automatically, she reached up to smooth out the frown that formed there as her mother's words echoed in her head, "No man wants to marry a young woman wrinkled like an old one." Somehow that worry mattered little now. As she shifted uncomfortably on the pony's wide back, she thought of a more pressing concern.

"Alex? Alex! I cannot feel my legs any longer."

∞∞∞

"Hold it right there!"

Caro shrieked in surprise as a Union picket wheeled out from behind a thicket and pointed the end of his bayonet to within inches of Alex's throat. The high pitch of her scream hung in the air, and she cringed even more when she saw the rider flash a scowl at her before he focused his full attention on Alex.

It was clear within seconds neither she nor Alex had a weapon, so the man relaxed somewhat even though he still aimed his gun at Alex.

She tried to calm her frazzled nerves by copying her partner who had thrown both hands into the air, palms out. Alex looked composed with just the hint of a smile on his face, but Caro could read the tension in his body. He was not as relaxed as he appeared.

"Good afternoon, sir," Sitting tall in the saddle and using his crispest articulation, Alex addressed the man formally. Caro saw the rider's eyebrows hop up. Would their English manners and nationality be enough to get them through this unscathed? So far, they had benefited from it as it seemed to imply they were neither friend nor foe.

"State yer bid'ness," the man growled. He busied himself eyeballing every inch of both of them with eyes as black as pitch staring out from under heavy black brows and a mop of unruly hair. He was hatless and cold by the looks of him. Dressed in what appeared to be a uniform underneath a heavy jacket made of hide, the details of the rest of his face were hidden beneath a mass of thick black beard. The stench of dirt and unwashed body rushed out to accost them, and they were a dozen feet apart.

"Of course." Alex bowed his head a touch to signal deference before continuing. "My young friend and I are searching for his older brother who is reported to be a surgeon with your army. We were told to ask about him here."

The man's head hitched back for a moment as he thought about that. "Git separated by the war?" He barked his question in Caro's direction making her flinch. Once again, her words failed her, but she nodded with vigor which seemed to satisfy the man.

"How far might it be to the camp, if I may ask?" She knew Alex was trying to keep attention off her as the man turned back to glare at him as he answered.

"'Bout two miles up this here road." The man motioned off to their left with his free hand.

For the first time, Caro realized they had stopped at a crossroad hidden by a thicket when the picket accosted them from the left. The road to their right had been obscured from view as well. If not stopped by this man, would they have passed by the turn off? Perhaps providence was on their side after all.

The day had faded to a dingy gray with the sun having long ago taken refuge behind thick dark clouds. Her thoughts as the hours passed had been on William rather than the stunningly beautiful scenery around her. What would she say to him when they found him? What would he say to her? She had imagined one scenario after another, with each of them ending the same way—with William's arms around her.

They had stopped very few times during the day and only for necessities. Talk had ceased miles ago as they had sought solace in their own minds. Caro was so hungry, tired, and sore that only her determination to find William had kept her in the saddle. Alex looked no worse for wear than he had when they left Jeremiah and Irene. She could only imagine how truly wretched she would look when they finally found William.

"Hulloooo there!" a deep voice rolled out of the trail off to their right. Caro stared in amazement as a lone covered wagon clinked and clanked as it rumbled its way toward them. Her eyes found Alex's, and he mouthed the word *sutler* at her. She sat back relieved to know it was not more trouble heading their way.

A big grin formed on the picket's face. He hollered back a greeting of his own to the driver perched behind a pair of work horses that trudged along a rutted road. This man held a rifle across his lap atop a wagon that looked like something out of a gypsy caravan. Covered by a dirty-looking canvas, the wagon was made of unpainted wood. A crude sign that read "Ezra's Goods" was painted on a board propped up on the side.

"If it ain't ol' Rusty Guts himself! You been gone longer than a month o' Sundays, Ezra."

"But I come bearin' a load o' Bark Juice so quit yer bellyachin'."

This was said with no rancor whatsoever. It was obvious to Caro the two men knew each other well, but what language were they speaking? Caro searched Alex's face to discern if there was a problem, but he was smiling, too. The driver must have noticed her worried face because his next words were about her.

"You been tormentin' young'uns again, Lucas?" He winked at Caro which threw her completely. Did he know she was a female? Maybe her disguise wasn't as good as she had imagined.

"Nah, they's jist lookin' fer a doc, tha's all." Lucas spat and a long stream of brown juice shot from his mouth, hitting the ground with a splash.

Caro's stomach turned over with a thump. Bile rose in her throat.

"Is the little un sick?" The bear of a man showed a hint of concern as he eyed Caro again. Ezra was a grizzly old man with a heavy, graying beard and eyebrows so thick they shaded his face like a pair of awnings.

"No, sir." Alex pulled his forelock in greeting. "We are looking for my young friend's older brother. We think he's in this camp as a doctor."

The man missed nary a beat as he proclaimed, "Then we best quit jawin' and git on with it 'for it gits dark." Noting the picket still held them at bay, he hollered, "Git that pig sticker out o' the man's face, Lucas, and let 'em go. I'll keep an eye on 'em and sees they git to camp."

Lucas took no offense, only nodded and stepped back to clear the way. "You jist be shore to save me some bark juice, ya hear? And maybe some chawin' terbaccky."

"You got it, soldier. You got it." A belly laugh rumbled out of the old man as he slapped the reins on his big horses and the wagon waddled off over the rugged road. Caro and Alex were more than happy to fall in behind Ezra's wagon and leave Lucas watching their backsides until they disappeared.

Now that they were only a mile or two from the Union camp, Caro's fears unleashed themselves. What if William was not in this camp? Would they keep looking indefinitely or would Olde Gylda order them back to Woodworth? How were they to find him among the thousands of men in the area? Would she know if William was close by?

She closed her eyes and sent out feelers for him. For years, she had known anytime William was in a room the moment she walked in. She never had to look for him. All her senses were attuned to him, and it did not matter if it were a crush or not, she could look directly at him without a search. Did she still have that power?

"Are you quite all right, Caro?" Alex was staring at her through worried eyes. "Does your head hurt too?"

Caro took a deep breath and shook her head. "No, I was trying to use my senses to locate William."

"Ah, I see."

She could tell by his tone he really didn't. "I used to be able to sense his presence before I actually laid eyes on him. I-I thought I would see if I could do that now since we are close."

She expected him to laugh at her, but his response surprised her.

"I would not have thought that possible before I met Elena, but now I know that can be done." One side of his mouth quirked up. "You miss William a great deal, I think."

"Yes," she whispered. It could have passed for a one-word prayer. "Let us hope we find him soon."

Alex's blue eyes were full of sympathy when he asked a short time later, "Well, did you sense him?"

Caro's face fell. "No . . . I did not."

"There are hundreds, if not thousands, of men in this camp. Perhaps it will be easier for you to find him once inside the camp."

The lump in Caro's throat kept her from answering.

Chapter 16

The hum of the Union camp echoed in the evening air long before they could see it. As they made their way down to the camp nestled in the valley below, a sea of tents with a few crude buildings opened before them. Campfires glowed in all directions and smoke hung eerily above the area like fog. It was an impressive temporary city.

Someone had tipped off the arrival of the sutler because bodies were moving in their direction and gathering force as they merged like tributaries to a river. Dozens of soldiers as small as ants headed toward Ezra's wagon intent upon getting what they wanted before others could buy him out. The sight had Caro overwhelmed. Should she turn around and gallop away? She did not want to meet that many soldiers. Then she remembered she was on Shorty and sighed.

Ezra stopped the wagon and called to them, "Anything ye want afore that hoard descends on me? Won't be much of anythin' left once they git started."

Alex rode up next to the man and explained his need for a weapon or two.

"Yer in luck, sir. I got jist the thing yer lookin' fer. How 'bout a sawed-off shotgun fer you small enough to handle easy-like on horseback, and a pistol fer the young'un."

"That would serve," Alex responded, sounding greatly relieved.

"Ya'll got any money?" Ezra looked hard at Alex, assessing what he could charge them. The old man was a shrewd dealer, despite his charm. "I take 'bout any kind o' token ye got. Don't care if it's store, patriotic, or sutler. It's all the same to me."

"No tokens," Alex answered, "but we do have a valuable to offer in exchange."

"Ye do, huh? And what might that be?" Now Ezra's interest had been piqued. Caro hoped Alex was skilled at bargaining or they would lose all their jewels long before they found William.

During one of their stops, Alex had taken the time to remove some of the precious stones from their jewelry with a knife left behind in his borrowed trousers. The plan was to trade the single gems for needs like food or shelter. No sense in giving away a whole necklace for a loaf of bread, Alex had told her. She had to agree. It hurt to see beloved family jewels pried apart and their settings left like empty shells, but William was worth whatever it took. Alex had dropped the gold remains, looking as skeletal as old bones, into his boots for safekeeping.

Most of the loose stones were tucked into Alex's vest pocket. It was a secure place inside his jacket that was deep enough and lined with satin to prevent the small stones from escaping. As a precaution, he had given several of the diamonds to Caro. If they became separated, she would have a means to pay for her needs until he could find her again.

Hers were secreted inside William's pocket watch. She must remember to open it carefully tonight, so she did not spill them out of the special compartment when she said her goodnight to William. She prayed he would be there in person and her ritual would not be necessary.

"You look like a man who knows the value of his goods," Alex remarked in a jocular voice. "How much do you want for the guns and some ammunition?"

Adopting the same tone, the old man answered, "I'd have to compare my goods, son, with the value of whatever ye got to trade, if ye ain't got no coin."

"If we find our doctor, we may not need any weapons. It

will depend on how he's fixed, so we had better wait to see what is needed."

Now Ezra could see his sales slipping away and he didn't like that one bit. Before Caro could even wonder what tactic he would employ next, the man looked straight at her.

"Young man, would ye like to work fer yer supper and p'rhaps that weapon or two?"

Caro wanted to answer an unequivocal *no*, but she looked to Alex to see if she should do it.

He was quick to respond. "What are you offering, Ezra? You know we are here to find his brother—a doctor named William Lowther. Ever hear of him?"

"Nah, cain't say I have or haven't. Leastways, I don't know nobody by that name." He scratched his crotch so vigorously, Caro looked away wondering if he had lice. Cleanliness was not a concern for the picket they had met, and this man was no better. Ezra adjusted and collected himself before he continued, "If ya'll help me with sellin' my goods, I kin work with ye on the price of the guns I got fer ye."

"Why would you do that?" Alex squinted in confusion and Caro had the same question. No country peddler she had ever met would offer a deal that wasn't good for him.

"Sadly, my new friends, them soldiers is like to steal ever'thin' out from under me as not, with jist me doin' the dealin'. If I am in the back, they are in front sneakin' goods out and vicee-versee. Where I am told to park my wagon ain't called Robber's Row fer nuthin'."

Surveying the wagon, Caro could see how easy it would be to take advantage of one man.

"Why do you work by yourself then?" Alex had risen one brow as he threw the question Caro wanted answered, too, in the man's face.

"Had no choice this trip. My assistant got hisself throwed in jail over a card game gone bad last night in Rutledge." Ezra spat in disgust as he related his tale.

Caro was relieved to see it was not the disgusting stream

of tobacco juice like the picket had unleashed. This was just a plain old spit.

"If ya'll kin watch them soldiers fer me and keep 'em from swarmin' my store like angry bees, I kin help ye find yer man when the first rush is done." His eyes roved over their horses where saddle bags should be and added, "I kin feed ye, too." He sat back and eyed them speculatively. "Have we got a deal?" He reached under his seat, pulled out a short apron with several pockets that clinked with coins, and tied it around his waist like a storekeeper.

Both Alex and Caro had seen the size of the camp as they had come down the side of the valley. Not knowing how to find William in that mass of people, it seemed like an offer that made sense. Besides, the sun was sinking by the minute, and they were hungry as well.

Caro nodded to Alex that he should accept, and the two men shook hands on it.

The next hour or two was a blur for Caro. She manned the inside of the wagon, handing items out the back to Ezra as he called for them. At first, she had no idea where to look for the items he demanded with a shout, but the wagon was small and the requests fast and furious. In no time at all, she was tossing Ezra plugs of tobacco, decks of playing cards, peppermint sticks, cheese and butter, and the like with some skill. Bottles of alcohol she had to hand out as Ezra told her they were too precious to the men to risk breaking.

Alex's job involved roaming around the front and sides of the wagon as well as minding the horses. Physically imposing in his person, he also brandished a mean-looking, long-barreled handgun on loan from the sutler that forbade anyone to challenge him. The skies were black when Ezra decided he could not see well enough to keep doing business. His goods were mostly gone by then anyway. The three of them had functioned effectively as a team, leaving Ezra quite pleased with his take. Caro was relieved to be finished with clerking and now wanted to get on with finding William.

Ezra was in no such hurry. He was hungry and not of a mind to go off searching on an empty stomach for a man who may or may not be in the camp. It was obvious arguing would do no good.

The old man proved to be no slouch at giving orders for getting them through the meal. Alex was to set an iron grate with four spindly legs over the fire Ezra built. Caro was told to dig out some tin plates and forks from the jockey box attached to the side of the wagon. By the time the cast iron pan had a slab or two of ham frying along with some sizzling sliced potatoes, Caro had to admit that the food first was a good plan.

Seated around the fire on upside down buckets and an overturned wooden crate to keep off the wet ground, there was little talk as they gobbled up the food before it got cold. As the weight of the warm meal settled comfortably in her stomach, Caro's nerves settled down with it. A sense of well-being enveloped her. Everything would work out. She was sure of it.

Other campfires had sprouted like ant hills after a rain and now glowed throughout the valley, casting an eerie light over the area. A boy no older than ten slid like a wraith into the circle of their campfire and crouched on the ground next to Ezra. Alarmed, Caro wondered why a child so young was in a camp of soldiers like this one. He was fair-haired and blue-eyed with a chubbiness to his face that betrayed his age. Wearing a frayed uniform jacket rolled up on the sleeves over a thick shirt, the boy's lower half fared no better with shabby pants tucked into scuffed boots that looked two sizes too large.

"Ah, Jesse, my boy! Good to see ye, lad." Ezra slapped a hand in greeting on the boy's back that nearly knocked him forward into the fire.

"Hello, Mr. Ezra." The boy grinned as he recovered himself, and Caro could see he liked the man.

"I suppose ye have come fer that peppermint stick I promised ye?"

The boy nodded emphatically.

"Have ye brought me the information I asked ye fer?"

Again, the boy's head bobbed with rapidity as he dug a wad of paper out of his britches. Ezra produced a peppermint stick from inside his coat and passed it to Jesse in exchange for the papers. Her curiosity over the crumpled pages must have been more obvious than she had thought because Ezra noticed her interest immediately.

"Ain't nuthin' to worry 'bout," Ezra said, shaking his head at Caro. She felt her face flush at being caught with her nose where it didn't belong. "The boy here jist collects lists of supplies from the officers that tell me what to bring 'em from Rutledge when I come nixt time."

Caro was relieved it was not some scurrilous skulduggery. Ezra explained that Jesse was a drummer boy and had the run of the camp, delivering messages from one officer to the next and so on. Caro's heart started pounding when she realized this child might know something about the doctors assigned here. She opened her mouth to speak, but Ezra beat her to it.

"These here folks, Jesse, are lookin' fer a doctor called . . .?" Ezra's face scrunched as he tried to remember the name.

"William. William Lowther," Caro provided. Her voice was breathy with excitement, and she feared anyone who heard her would never believe she was a boy.

"Yes, William Lowther," Ezra repeated, giving her a questioning look. "Do ye know a man answerin' to that name?"

"Yep," the boy answered, closing his mouth over the peppermint stick while eyeing the two newcomers.

Caro's heart skipped a beat. *Could William really be only a short walk away?*

Ezra nudged the boy with an elbow to continue.

"He war here a whilst back, but he's gone now," he announced with finality, pulling his candy out of his mouth only long enough to spit out the words.

What? Caro sucked in a breath and held it.

Shooting a sharp glance at her, Alex asked, "Do you know where he went, Jesse?"

"Nope."

Caro released the air she held and felt her hopes shrivel along with her breath.

"Do ye know what happened to him, boy? This young man over here is his brother." Ezra poked a finger in Caro's direction as he spoke.

"Oh." The boy's head swung between Ezra and Alex before focusing on Caro, sizing her up for himself. Satisfied that the old man told the truth, he waved the peppermint stick at Ezra. "Why didn't ye say so, Mister Ezra?" He paused, shook his head, and spoke to Caro. "I like Doc Lowther. He's my friend, so's I didn't want to git him in no trouble if somebody come lookin' fer him that he don't wanna see." The boy's attention shifted to Alex, giving him a once-over with eyes that glowed in the firelight before adding, "Ya'll talk jist like him."

Her eyes now watering, Caro pictured William with Jesse and it eased the hurt to think of her beloved befriending the boy. Taking a deep breath, she blinked to hold back the tears that seemed determined to fall.

"So, where is he now, Jesse?" Alex prodded to get the boy, busy sucking his candy in long pulls, back on track.

"Still don't know, sir, cuz he got stoled by the Rebs when we fought over by Bean's Station."

Caro's heart sunk to her toes at those words. *Stolen? The Confederates had William? Would they hurt him?* She sent a frantic prayer to the heavens to watch over him until they could be reunited. The rest of the conversation with Jesse mushed in her ears except for tidbits that broke through. Meanwhile, her mind kept running to their next move, but pinning it down was near impossible because she had no idea where those Rebels were that had snatched William. Would Ezra know how to find them?

There was no time to ask him because Jesse was not their only visitor. As they got off duty, soldiers drifted by for the few remaining goods for sale in the sutler's wagon. Even Lucas presented himself shortly before the camp quieted down for the night. Ezra had turned red and fumbled for words, clearly having forgotten his promise to hold out tobacco and the vaunted bark juice, but Caro saved him. She had set aside those two items earlier as she worked inside the wagon.

Scrambling up to get them for Lucas, she heard the old man singing her praises. What would her father think if he were to see her now—in trade? Her smile turned sour as she thought of trying to support herself in America if she never found William or got back home again. This was a mighty tough life.

Chapter 17

Morning arrived too soon for Caro even though the plan was to begin their journey to the Confederate's camp. Reveille had jarred her from a sleep that featured William kissing her senseless. Flustered and warm, it took several minutes for her real senses to kick in and discover her fingers and toes were frozen stubs. She was forced to get up and move around to thaw them.

Ezra had offered Caro a place at his feet in the bed of the covered wagon where it was warmer, but she had been afraid to accept. If he had discovered her gender, things might have gone decidedly wrong.

At least around their campfire, she was safe with only Alex there to witness any problem if her hat came off and revealed her long hair while she slept. Thankfully, the hat was soft and not bothersome, and no one questioned that it kept her head warm. Besides, Ezra was guarding his profit with the bag of money and a pistol pressed to his person. If he had forgotten she was there and thought her an intruder, he likely would have shot her.

Their night huddled around the campfire was largely sleepless. In her wildest dreams she would never have imagined herself sleeping outdoors beside a fire in the middle of an army of Americans. It boggled the mind.

Alex had foraged for wood before bedding down, so every few hours he awoke to feed the fire that kept the two of them from freezing. It was an uncomfortable night in every way. Not only was the frozen ground hard beneath her hips, but her side next to the fire would get too hot while the other side froze. The two conditions kept her awake and flipping over and over most of the night. Despite her delicious dream, it was a relief when morning arrived, and it was time to get moving to find William.

While she washed her face with ice-cold water from a bucket, she became aware of eyes on her person. Her first thought was that someone had found her out, and a chill as cold as the water shot down her spine like an icicle dropping from a rooftop. She turned around to face a young man seemingly not much older than Jesse. He stood clutching an item in front of himself with a sheepish smile upon his face as if he were guilty of holding something not his.

"Yer Doc Lowther's little brother, ain't ye," he said with a certainty that surprised her. "I heard tell from Jesse that ye were here helpin' old Ezra sell off his load."

By now Alex had come to stand by Caro, so the young man nodded a hello and continued, "I'm Clay Davison. I war an aide to the doc and helped him when he needed an extra hand with a patient. He war real nice to me." He smiled and nodded at Caro before picking up his story. "When the Rebs grabbed him, I did not know what to do with his personal things. Nobody knowed where he come from nor who his people be. He never got no letters from home." Here he paused and swallowed like he was a schoolboy in trouble with the school master.

"When folks heard he was gone, they come round like jackals hopin' to git whatever he left. Doc never owned much other than his issued gear and an extry shirt." He hesitated before continuing with a note of apology in his voice. "Alls I kept war these letters in case somebody come round and wanted to know 'bout him."

He thrust out a small package tied up with brown string for Caro to take. She realized the moment he dropped the letters into her hand they were not from her. A shudder skittered through her. The paper was obviously of poor quality and the envelopes were the wrong size. If not her letters, whose letters had William saved?

Squinting at the paper, she saw something written upside-down across the face of the top envelope, but it was hard to read the pencil markings in the glare of the morning light. She turned the packet around and used a hand to shield the sun to see what was scribbled there. Her breath hitched as the letters of her own name popped into place. It took a moment for the meaning to register with her. William had written these letters to her.

To her relief, Alex sensed her heightened emotions and rescued her. "Thank you. That will mean a great deal to young Lowther here as well as to his family."

A sly look spread across Clay's face. "I don't think they's fer his fam'ly, sir. Ever' night Doc would take out his fob watch and stare at a picture of a purty lady tucked inside it." He shot Caro a sharp glance but did not slow his story, returning his gaze to Alex. "I think these letters war intended fer her." A frown puckered his face. "Don't know why he nivver sent 'em to her when the mail picked up. He jist said she war not where she could receive 'em right now, so he'd hold on to 'em fer a while. There ain't no address on 'em, so I could not send 'em, m'self."

Caro's eyes watered, and she dropped her gaze to the letters in her hands before tucking them securely inside her jacket. Turning away abruptly, she picked up a blanket at her feet rather than let the young soldier see the tears that filled her eyes.

"We are indebted to you, Clay, for returning them," Alex said. "The pretty lady is Doctor Lowther's betrothed. She will be most happy to receive these letters."

Clay grinned and looked pleased with himself, relieved to have responsibly disposed of them.

"We hope to find him alive and well in the Confederate camp in the next few days," Alex finished with a smile for the boy.

"I wish ye all luck, sir. If ye find him, will he come back here?" The young man's face held such hope as he asked that she hated to disappoint him. Again, Alex answered for her.

"No, he is needed back in England, so we intend to return him to his family there."

Clay's disappointment was visible, but he nodded his understanding.

"Davison!"

Clay jumped in response to the deep voice calling him from several tent rows away. His face scrunched up in guilt. "I-I gots to be goin' now. If ye find Doc, give him my best."

The same authoritative voice swore loudly in language that made Caro blush. The young man rolled his eyes at them in apology. Taking off at a run in the direction of the oaths, he turned and shouted over his shoulder, "So long!"

Caro held up a hand in farewell. She wanted nothing more than to find a private spot to read her letters from William, but she knew there would be no alone time this morning. Her right hand gripped the letters tucked over her heart inside her jacket as if she were able to read them with her fingertips. She looked up to find Alex grinning at her and answered him with a big smile of her own.

Ezra, mildly interested in their interaction with Clay, was now all business once again. He had a sale to make. They moved to the back of the sutler wagon where Ezra laid out the guns they had agreed upon. It was obvious when Caro picked up the long-barreled gun Alex had used to guard the wagon that it was too heavy for her. Ezra traded it out for a smaller version he called a Smith and Wesson revolver.

Revolvers were new to Caro and Alex. She was fascinated it was possible to shoot seven times before needing to reload with something Ezra called cartridges. What an amazing invention!

When presented with the sawed-off rifle as recommended, Alex was not impressed. He opted instead for the same long-nosed pistol he had used the day before. It, too, used cartridges and went by a name Ezra could not remember. "Le-fat-show or some Frenchie-soundin' name," he'd said. Caro smiled when she spotted the name Lefaucheux stamped next to M1854 on the underside of the barrel.

Ezra told them the gun was popular among the Rebs, so trading it later would not be a problem. The better of the two weapons, it was a solid choice for Alex, fit him well, and chambered six shots. At last, they held in their hands the weapons Alex was sure they needed, so Caro relaxed.

However, with a better gun in the mix as well as ammunition, the old man insisted on a new deal, so Alex was forced to part with a small diamond to secure it. After that, Ezra scrutinized the two of them more closely, and Caro feared he suspected their ruse. Still, he said not a word before he handed over the weapons. He promised to provide them with food and shelter in Rutledge to even out the trade.

The day was set to be a long one. Ezra would accompany them to the Confederate camp as promised, but he needed to return to Rutledge to reload his wagon with goods stored there. He confessed that he was only supposed to serve the Union soldiers, but due to a shortage of sutlers available in the area, he had contracted with the Confederates, too. Apparently, sutlers were more scarce than the commodities they sold.

Caro thought about the soldiers Ezra had described robbing him as he served them and knew it was a dangerous job not everyone would relish. Union officers probably knew he was two-timing them with the enemy, but with no waiting sutlers willing to fill the need, they were not about to boot him out.

In a hurry to be on the road, they breakfasted on coffee brewed over the open fire and some sweet biscuits from a tin can Ezra had stashed under a canvas in the back of the wagon. Caro's sweet tooth welcomed the hard, but tasty treat after two days with only plain fare.

She recoiled, however, at the horror of another day in the saddle as she mounted her pony and the pain shot through her hips and bottom. She would have to ignore the hurt since she had no choice but to spend all day in that position. Woozy at the thought of unabated pain, she focused on talking a blue streak to Shorty, who responded to the attention by lifting his head and swishing his tail.

They were trotting along after the sutler wagon on the road to Rutledge when Alex interrupted her thoughts.

"You now have a gun tucked into your belt and ammunition, and look the part of a young lad, but do you know how to use the revolver?" The corner of his mouth hitched up on one side as he observed her bouncing along beside him on Shorty.

"Of course I do," Caro answered matter-of-factly.

Surprise registered on Alex's face. "I would not have thought a duke's daughter would be taught that skill."

"Who said it was intentional?" Caro laughed up at him with a gleam in her eye. "My mother knew I was a complete hoyden in those days and chose not to know what William, Violet and I got up to every day during those long, hot summers."

"I see." She thought this time he really did see.

"As a young man of about thirteen, William was the one taught to shoot. He took to practicing in a pasture that ran between our properties. Violet and I could not simply sit there all day while he shot dirt clods, now could we?"

"No, I suppose not," Alex answered, with a chuckle.

"It was terrific fun until a big fat robin had the misfortune to fly into the path of William's shot." She thought about that for a moment and then gave Alex a discerning look. "At least that is what he told us at the time." Alex stifled a laugh. "We gave the poor thing a somber burial complete with words spoken over its tiny plot."

"Very appropriate, I'm sure." Alex grinned at her. "I trust, then, you will not accidentally shoot a foot off?"

"Actually, I already did that."

"What?" Alex frowned and waited for the explanation.

"Well, sort of." She snickered as the memory played out in her head. "William wanted to show me how to use the sight on the pistol and tried to take the loaded gun from me. It went off and shot the toe out of his boot. How it missed his toes is a mystery. Sheer luck, I guess. He was forced to ditch the boot and claim one had fallen into the river whilst he was swimming so his parents wouldn't find out."

"That sounds much like the scrapes of my own childhood," Alex said with a shake of his head. "Lord knows what we would have done with a revolver at our fingertips!"

"Indeed," she agreed with a giggle. "Violet was always the better shot, but I did learn how to shoot with some accuracy." She did not want to brag, but she was a decent shot. William had said so.

"We shall hope you do not have to test your skill any time soon." As they talked, they had slowed, so Alex gave his mount a gentle kick and moved ahead to catch up to the wagon. Shorty jogged along right behind without Caro needing to nudge him. She would not be left behind if the pony had anything to do with it.

Confident now in her ability to protect herself, Caro was happy to follow suit. Maybe her days running wild with the Lowther siblings were not a loss after all.

∞∞∞

Three full days stood between Caro and William. Three days of hard travel following the sutler wagon astride a pony as wide as a couch. Ezra was focused on his next commission, so stopping for anything in between was not in his sights. It would take one day from Blaine's Crossing to Rutledge where they would reload the wagon. Then two from Rutledge to Russellville where the Confederates were hunkered down for the winter.

The roads were rutted and non-existent in places, particularly close to the Holston River, so it was slow-going with a wagon. Caro had no disagreement with Ezra's plan to push on through with no breaks since each step brought her closer to William. She was, however, afraid she might never walk again after hours in the saddle with no relief.

Food was eaten on the move too. Caro got her first taste of hardtack and decided it should be her last. How soldiers were expected to live on such food was horrifying to her. Ezra did have some delicious ale to wash down those sheet iron crackers, though, and Caro rather liked the taste. The more she drank the less her bottom hurt. Alex finally put a stop to any refills after she swayed so dramatically that he pronounced her foxed and feared she would fall off her pony.

When their small party entered Rutledge, it was a toss-up which end of Caro hurt the most. Her head pounded and everything below it ached. Fortunately, as soon as they turned onto Marshall Street, they pulled up beside a tavern with the simple sign reading Tate and Co. Ezra hollered to them from the wagon that they would be staying the night in the inn attached to the tavern.

Relief pulsed through her as she all but fell off Shorty, her legs threatening to crumple beneath her weight. Alex took one look at her and promised to get her inside and settled before she cratered. Not only did the world around her spin, but as feeling returned to her bottom half, she realized just how saddle sore she was.

Ezra bolted inside to secure rooms for them while Alex and Caro guarded the wagon. He returned a few minutes later with a skeleton key he said was to a room on the second floor of the inn. The building was an L-shape, with the tavern on the Marshall Street side across from the courthouse and the inn side on the south skirting the road into town. The two businesses did not share an inside door.

Once again, Alex and Caro were to stay in one room with Ezra across the hall. At this point, Caro did not even mention the inconvenience, but accepted sharing a room as a matter of course. Alex was no threat to her, and she would have been more unhappy to be by herself in the unfamiliar surroundings.

Supper was to be in the tavern once they had settled in. The first thing Caro did upon entering their room was rid herself of the beehive hat crammed down on her head. After two days of continuous wear, she happily plucked out the few pins holding her braids, undid them, and massaged her head.

Sheer ecstasy.

As she ran her fingers through her hair in the absence of a brush, she did pause long enough to think about how far this was from her usual routine. New experiences doubled and tripled daily.

What would her friends and family think of a duke's daughter traveling half-way around the world without a chaperone, dressing as a lad, sleeping in the same bed with a man not her husband, selling goods from the back of a sutler wagon, and camping around a fire like a soldier?

A grin stole across her face as she scrutinized her reflection in the tiny mirror. My, what a difference a few days makes.

Nonetheless, she was not a complete heathen yet. She decided no matter how hungry she was, she was not going to put that dreadful hat back on to go round to the tavern for food. She certainly could not take it off as decorum required when eating a meal inside an establishment anyway, could she? So, when Alex suggested she might like to stay in the room and soak in a bath, Caro seriously could have kissed him. His eyes danced at her vociferous exclamations, but he recognized what she had not said —her mind and body were finished for the day. He left promising he would bring her something to eat when he returned for the night.

Caro had little memory of the rest of the evening. She soaked, she washed her hair, she thrilled over William's love letters, and she dreamed of William's arms around her. She might have eaten something, but she did not remember what when she arose the next morning, hungry, stiff, and sore, but in a much better frame of mind.

As it turned out, she need not have worried about wearing a hat through any dining experience inside this tavern. When she walked in, she saw that it was no fancy restaurant, just a large, open space with exposed wooden beams across the ceiling. A bar stood staunchly at one end and tables were arranged haphazardly around the room like someone had forgotten to return them to their proper place after cleaning underneath.

Seated for breakfast at a table by the entrance with her

hat jammed down over her brow once again, Caro endured Ezra's razzing about her saddle sores and absence from supper. She felt so much better she shrugged off the teasing with a hint of a smile. When she proved to be impervious to his ribbing, he left her alone.

The rest of the meal was eaten mostly in silence. Less talk meant more time to eat. She inhaled the fresh eggs, ham slices, and buttered biscuits at a pace that had Alex raising an eyebrow in amusement. She gulped a mouthful of biscuit and wondered if perhaps she already was a heathen.

Chapter 18

Two mornings later, Caro was not quite as fresh when she staggered to her feet after another uncomfortable, cold night around a small fire. The smoke had found her often during the night, leaving soot on her face that came off in her hand as she swiped her forehead. She must stink like a dirty fireplace. What she would not give to have a bath before getting to the Rebel camp!

The first day out from Rutledge had been uneventful enough. After loading up the wagon, they had kept a steady pace, crossing the Holston River at a low spot and camping on the Confederate side for the night. They were making progress, but it was slow-going and cold.

Last night the wind had blasted across the water and played havoc with their attempts to keep their fire stoked overnight. Cloud cover that had kept them a little warmer earlier in the day had cleared, leaving a night sky full of stars, but a distinct drop in temperature. Caro's toes had frozen inside her boots and her jacket might have been made of Swiss cheese since the cold seeped in from all directions. Ezra had helped by pulling out a few blankets for them, but it was still a night where morning could not come soon enough.

At least the scenery had been beautiful the entire journey. This morning was no different. Frost coated the grasses and the trees like gilding. With the mountains in the distance, she might have been living in a scene from a Caspar David Friedrich painting. It reminded her that Christmas was only a few days away. Would she ever get to return to the magic of the season at Woodworth? What were Charlotte and Violet doing now without her —other than enjoying clean bodies, stylish clothes, and warm rooms?

Caro sipped the hot coffee Ezra produced like it was a lifesaving substance. Its lovely aroma was divine. As the warmth spread through her body, she began to think she might live to see William after all.

"Today is the day we must be on alert," Ezra announced between slurps from his tin mug. "The Rebs is not as well-sprung as the Feds, if you take my meanin'. Shortages abound in ever'thin' supplied by the gov'ment—food, clothing, shelter. The need goes further than the money, so they's not above takin' any opportun'ty that presents itself to take what they wants from a sutler."

Upon hearing this, Caro and Alex gave Ezra their full attention.

"Do you want us to ride in front as look-outs or behind you as we have?" Alex asked. Caro could almost see the strategizing going on in his head about how best to protect them.

"Ye need to stay b'hind the wagon cuz the road ain't always clear, and we ain't wantin' to take no short cuts that turns out to be long cuts." He chuckled at his own joke but then turned serious. "Jist stay near and keep yer weapons loaded and at the ready."

Caro sneaked a glance at Alex to see if he agreed with Ezra's assessment and was worried when Alex's face showed true concern. For the first time in their journey, she realized they might be in real danger. She stood a little taller and took a deep breath. With no other option for reaching William, she would do whatever was necessary to get there in one piece.

∞∞∞

Three hours later, the wagon groaned and swayed ahead of them over some rough terrain when they emerged from heavy trees into a long stretch of open valley. Treeless rolling hills stretched into the distance weaving a track of road that dipped and rose in waves. They would be traveling without cover for quite some time.

This new landscape presented another problem. After telling herself for at least two hours that she needed to relieve herself, it was now a necessity. Nothing told the tale of her true sex like the fact she was unable to do so standing up.

"Alex!" Shorty's nose was only a couple of feet behind Alex's mount where it had stayed most of the way. Alex glanced at Caro over his shoulder, but he did not pull up.

She tried again. "Alex, you must stop for a moment!"

This time he reined in Ryder and allowed Caro to ride up beside him. His attention, however, was not on her, but on the wagon bouncing along ahead of them. It was clear he did not want to stop here at all.

"I must retire to the woods for a moment of privacy before we leave them," she said, emphasizing the word must as she spoke.

"Too much coffee?" he quizzed, one eyebrow rising as he looked her over. When Caro rolled her eyes and nodded, he added, "I wondered if you'd thought of that this morning."

"It was warm and delicious, and I could not help myself." She really wanted to say that it was none of his business how many cups of coffee she had drunk, but she knew he was right. With Ezra's warning still fresh in her head, it was a bad time to stop. Still, she could not very well relieve herself in plain sight of anyone who happened by. She might be dressed as a boy, but she was still a lady and had managed to avoid being discovered up until now. She needed the cover of the trees.

Alex had apparently arrived at the same conclusion and was half-way to the wagon calling Ezra's name by the time she finished speaking. Rolling the wagon to a stop, the sutler leaned in to hear what Alex had to say, and then only seconds later, he yelled gee-haw to his team and kept going.

Alex galloped back with a face black as thunder, pulling up beside her with a flourish.

"You must hurry, Caro. That stubborn old man won't stop to wait for you." He shook his head, still furious. "I told him you were suffering from quick-step and needed to squat in the woods. He ordered me to keep an eye on him and catch up as fast as we can."

"Quick-step?" Caro wondered what that was supposed to be.

"The runs!" Alex grinned when she caught her breath in horror.

"You did not tell him that!"

"You have a better idea?"

"You gave me no chance to think of one." Her face burned with humiliation. Then she remembered she was just supposed to be a lad and it did not hurt quite so much.

"You'd best get to it, my dear girl. Our friend is determined to make it to the Rebel's camp before sundown. He's vulnerable out there in the open without us behind him."

Caro slid off Shorty and threw the reins to Alex before running into the shelter of the trees.

As she secured her trousers a few minutes later, she heard Alex swear loudly and moments later shots rang out. Panic zapped through her as she thrashed her way back to the trail, earning scratches on her face and hands in the process. By the time she emerged from the woods, Alex was most of the way to the sutler wagon, galloping at full speed toward a disaster already well in the making.

They were not the only ones emerging from the woods. A band of four riders swooped from the shelter of a thicket to their right and were now descending upon the sutler and his wagon. Alex fired his revolver in the air as a warning to let them know he was coming for them.

In sheer terror, a shrill scream ripped from her when one of the riders shot back in Alex's direction. It missed and hit the ground on the far side of Alex sending a smattering of rocks into the air.

Ezra tried to outrun them, but that was impossible. He whipped his horses and shouted to them to run faster, but it only threatened to flip the wagon or break a wheel on the deeply rutted road.

The four were fast as lightning and knew exactly what they wanted from the sutler wagon. As Caro watched, one thief slipped inside the back of the wagon and started tossing out items to the other riders who stuffed them into bags attached to their saddle horns. His horse kept pace behind the wagon, dropping back only slightly without the rider.

Caro pulled out her gun and aimed, but everything was happening too fast for a clear shot, and they were quickly moving out of range. Should she gallop into the fray? Would she be killed in the wrong time period and never see William again? Her mind skittered between possible actions. Most importantly, she decided she could not sit here and let Alex or Ezra die because she hesitated. Her heels dug into the unsuspecting pony who jolted into a fast trot, entirely reluctant to gallop.

Alex and Caro's imminent arrival did not stop the attack. Ezra fired his sawed-off shotgun over his shoulder with one hand, not bothering to aim. Fortunately, it missed Alex, but did wing one of the attackers who yelped and swore and dropped back. It was enough for the others to realize they needed to make an exit before they got caught between Ezra and Alex, with Caro bringing up the rear.

The robber inside the wagon whistled to his horse to come closer. When the animal obliged, the man made a fearsome jump onto its back like a trick-rider at Astleys and took off toward his mates. With their loot flapping against their saddles, they wheeled and galloped off the way they had come.

It was over so fast Caro was not sure what had just happened. Shorty had balked at riding toward the fired shots, so all the action was over by the time she arrived at the wagon which had stopped with a lurch. Alex was at Ezra's side talking quietly to him. It was not until she got closer that she saw blood drip-ping from Ezra's shoulder and realized he had been hit.

She dived off Shorty, leaving him to comfort himself by nosing up beside Ryder. Climbing into the box of the wagon on the opposite side of Ezra, she assessed the damage. Alex pulled Ezra's coat down around his waist and ripped his sleeve open to get a good look at the wound. The bullet had torn into the muscle of his right arm near the shoulder.

"Did the shot pass through?" Caro asked as Alex picked carefully at the wound. William had told her once that if a ball was left in the bullet hole, or even a fragment of material from clothing, that it could turn bad and result in infection and death.

"I cannot tell for certain, but I think so." Blood was still flowing down Ezra's arm. "Until this can be washed and dressed properly, we won't know."

Ezra swore as Alex poked a finger a little deeper into the bullet hole. Caro was sure it was best to search for foreign ob-jects before trying to stanch the blood flow, but it looked brutal enough to make her stomach clench.

"Leave me be!" Ezra moaned. He caught his breath, pulled away from Alex, and let the pain subside for a moment. Then he directed his attention to Caro with the roll of his head. "There's bandages and medicine in the back in a small black kit, young Lowther. Dig it out and wrap one o' them bandages round this here arm, and it'll be jist hunkey dorey till we make the Rebs' camp." He winked at Caro despite his injury. "Maybe that big brother o' yers kin fix me up when we git there."

"Yes, sir!" Caro did not know what *hunkey dorey* meant, but Ezra was not fine. She could tell by his eyes that he was in real pain. Rather than make him move over to let her into the back of the wagon, she jumped down from the box and trotted around to the back and climbed in.

After a short search, she found the kit Ezra described and took it back to the box. Alex had pressed on the wound while she was looking for the kit, so by the time she produced it, the bleed-ing had slowed a bit.

Working together, Alex and Caro spread an ointment on the wound and dressed it with the white muslin bandages from the kit. It wasn't pretty, but it would have to do until they reached the camp.

Alex tied Shorty to the back of the wagon and rode beside them, scanning the area for any other trouble. Caro kept her place beside Ezra who let her take the reins while he sat beside her and shouted instructions in her ear. She had never driven a team before but had watched enough beaus driving their curricles to have some idea how to manage. She really did not need to do much beside slap the reins to start these horses. This was a route they knew well, so they plodded along with only mild guidance warranted.

The day wore on as days do when folks wish them gone. Ezra was in pain and weak from loss of blood. Every time he moaned, Caro reached over and put a hand on his arm. It seemed to quiet him immediately.

His color was not good, so she was relieved when his head dropped upon his chest, and he began to snore. She worried from time to time when they hit a bump that Ezra might fall off, so Alex used a length of cloth he found in the back to tie the old man's belt to the seat of the box.

As the sun moved lower in the sky, she noticed drops of sweat on Ezra's face. Reaching across, she put her hand over his forehead to check for a temperature. He might have been a pot boiling over coals he was so hot. She pulled up and hollered to Alex who rode over to check their patient for himself.

They shared a wordless moment as Alex's grim expression told her he agreed Ezra was running a high temperature. Did this mean the ball was still in his arm? Or maybe a piece of his shirt? She slapped the reins at the team and pitched the wagon into a faster pace, hoping either pickets or the camp would show up soon. They had no other option for help.

Would they find William in time to save the old man?

Chapter 19

"**I** do hope Lizzy is 'bout finished with Private Butler's laundry. I shouldn't be leavin' the child to git it done by herself. She's only just turned ten last week." Heavy with child, Martha Perry was stretched atop a raised camp bed while Doc Lowther checked her progress. They were inside a makeshift hut William had devised as a medical unit. Jeb and Sam had built a small fireplace at one end, so it was warmer inside than a tent would be. They were as prepared for the winter as they were going to be.

"Nivver you mind that, Miz Perry." Evy patted her hand and kept talking to her softly while William used his stethoscope to listen to the baby. "Ye got to worry 'bout gittin' this baby here afore ye go worryin' yerself sick 'bout Lizzy. She is a mighty capable youngin' and she will git the job done."

"She is a sweet child." Martha caught her breath as the baby kicked her stomach and made a ripple move across her belly as it repositioned itself. She thought for a moment before continuing, "So's Lulabelle. Little Nate keeps her a runnin' from dawn till dusk cuz he quit takin' a nap soon as he learned to walk."

"You have bin blessed, Miz Perry, with three beautiful children. It'll be four if we kin git this baby here right soon."

"Nathan's bin assigned as a picket stationed on the north side of the camp. Shore wish he were closer this week." Martha reached up and used her sleeve to wipe the sweat forming on her forehead. Sweat? It was so cold William's fingers were stiff, so he followed Martha's sleeve with his own hand, checking to see she was not running a fever.

He breathed a sigh of relief when she did not feel warm to the touch. Perhaps it was the exertion necessary to move her large, awkward body from one place to the next. He hoped so.

William leaned back and frowned, signaling to Evy with a small shake of his head that he thought all was not right. Evy got the message with a sharp intake of breath and then squeezed Martha's hand. She was the best of assistants at times like these —sympathetic, but practical and efficient in seeing to the needs of his patients.

He might not know in medical terms what was wrong, but his instincts told him to be on alert. The baby's heartbeat showed up the loudest in the wrong place. Did that mean the baby's head was not down where it should be this late in her pregnancy? Rick had told him that sometimes babies were born feet first or bottom first instead of head-first. How was he to know how the baby was sitting? It made him nervous. Mrs. Perry had complained of being kicked too low in the belly for a baby in the right position.

It was all worrisome. As he had explained to Evy, he had not delivered but two babies in his time in America. If things went terribly wrong during this delivery, Mrs. Perry would leave three children, perhaps four, and a husband behind. The mere thought so many lives depended on how successfully he delivered her, took his breath away.

The baby's heartbeat was too fast and not as steady as the others he'd heard in the past. Was that a problem? This was when he missed Duvall the most. The depth of his experience allowed him to meet a crisis like this without fear. Lost in his thoughts, it was a minute before he realized Mrs. Perry was talking to him.

"So sorry, ma'am. What did you say?"

"Doc Lowther, what is the thing called agin yer usin' to listen to the baby?"

"Ah, it is a stethoscope. They are new to most doctors—truly a useful tool. Would you like to listen?"

"Oh, my, kin I?" Her face flushed with pleasure as William removed the earpieces from his ears and hooked them in Martha's.

"Glory be!" The woman nearly shrieked loud enough for the sound to reach the Feds in their camp. "I had no idee you kin hear the babe's heart a beatin' like that!" Her eyes held William's for a moment in true amazement. "What will they think of nixt?"

William smiled at her and wondered the same thing. Duvall had given him some terrific medical tools. The only problem taking them back to his own time was some had not been invented yet. Might he sneak a few of them on his person? Would Olde Gylda let him?

He and Evy helped Martha to her feet just as Sam stepped into the hut. William was about to ask him to help Martha back to her tent when Evy piped up with her own request.

"Sam, darlin', would ye mind bein' a sweetheart and walkin' Miz Perry back to her quarters? She be needin' a nice, strong arm to lean on with her Nathan assigned on t'other side of the camp." She ended her appeal by delivering a dazzling smile at the man, and Sam was too smitten to say no. William grinned at the look on Sam's face as he set off a few minutes later with Mrs. Perry leaning heavily on his arm.

Pulling out his watch he checked the time. Hopefully, no other patients would head their way before they called it quits for the day. He wondered if Mrs. Perry would be back before dawn. Babies had a way of deciding on their own when they would make their appearance.

He glanced up to note Evy had followed the pair to the edge of the campsite saying her goodbyes. She turned back to William with a grin for him and a twinkle in her eye. He knew exactly what she meant.

"You are going to have to dispense that sugar with a twist

of lemon every now and then if you don't wish to encourage Sam's attention, Evy." He was only partly teasing. He had watched Sam fall deeper under Evy's spell every day. The man was willing to do anything for her, and she knew it. Part of William was jealous Evy gave Sam so much attention, and part of him was happy he himself was not her sole focus. She would be hard to resist, Caro or no Caro. The woman was simply a force of nature he was thankful to have helping him.

"Ah, shucks, Willy, who says I want to discourage him?" She gave him a saucy toss of her hair.

Well, this was new. Perhaps he did not know if Evy and Sam had come to an understanding in their relationship. All he managed in response was a raised eyebrow. His throat closed as he thought of Evy deserting him for Sam.

"Oh, don't look so forlorn, Lord Willy!" She sidled up to him, put an arm around his waist, and looked up at him wistfully. "Ye know there kin be nothin' 'tween us. Ye have yer Caro and I ain't a gonna git between the two of ye no matter what. Sam is a good man and I care fer him, too. I ain't got no fam'ly waitin' fer me at home. Sam? He has a big ole fam'ly awaitin' on him back in Arkansas. He says they'll all love me like one o' their own. How kin I say no to that?"

William threw an arm around Evy and hugged her hard. "You cannot, my dear, you cannot." He smiled down at the tiny woman with the huge blue eyes and even bigger heart. "You are my best friend, Evy. Just try not to leave me too soon, hmm? What would I do without you?" He leaned down and gave her a heartfelt kiss on her forehead.

∞∞∞

Dusk was rolling in as Alex and Caro found their way into camp, directed by a grim-faced Ezra. Awake now, the jovial man of their acquaintance was gone. In his place was a man with a raging fever who clearly felt horrible. Nonetheless, he did his best to stay conscious by sheer force of will in order to get them situated in the sutler's spot on the edge of the encampment.

Alex cornered the first officer he found, explained their dilemma, and insisted the man post guards around the sutler wagon while they took Ezra to see Doc Lowther. Ezra might object, but Alex offered a young Corporal Tanner first-look at the merchandise and a discount if they stayed until Ezra was able to manage. That seemed to be a deal the officer was happy with. Alex promised Caro he would handle Ezra if there was an issue.

A weight lifted from Caro as the corporal gave them directions for where to find Doc Lowther. The officer was acquainted with the man and confirmed he was, indeed, in the camp. Caro could barely breathe, and her heart banged in her head so loudly she was sure she might pass out from excitement alone.

They followed Corporal Tanner's directions and wove their way through the seemingly endless rows of tents and crude buildings that made up the camp. Ezra was semi-insensible at this point and Caro thought Alex may as well have dragged him. His feet had quit moving a few rows back. She made Alex stop, so she could slide under Ezra's other arm and slip her arm around his waist. The poor man quit moaning and his color was better.

Soldiers hollered hellos to Ezra when they saw him, but he was not able to respond. At least they helped by pointing them in the right direction when asked. Caro finally spotted the yellow banner with an H in the middle of it and was relieved they were almost there.

Rounding the last tent into the open space below the banner, they saw a man with his arm around a woman giving her a kiss on her forehead. Caro halted and almost knocked all three of them to the ground. She did not want to intrude on a private moment.

The man stood profile to them. He was a big man, tall and powerfully built. His mop of unkempt dark hair on the top of his head balanced a bushy beard jutting from his chin. The Confederate uniform, if it could be called that, fitted him poorly as if it had been thrown together piece by piece.

The first thing that rolled through Caro's mind as her attention turned to the woman facing her, was she appeared to be a Pocket Venus. Indeed, she was a tiny thing, trim and prim in a black gown with a white apron over it. Her white-blonde hair was pulled back from her heart-shaped face to reveal beautiful blue eyes that looked up at the man with warmth and admiration.

Wanting to get Ezra settled, Alex was quick to clear his throat and ask in a loud voice, "Do either of you know where we might find Doctor—"

"—Lowther, Doctor William Lowther," Caro finished for him, her high-pitched voice demanding attention.

The man started. He turned to face them and squinted as Caro's crisp clear voice—her British enunciation sharp as a briar—echoed in the cool evening air.

"Caro?" He swallowed. "Caro, is it you under that hat?" His face was a mask as he stared at her, but his voice trembled some.

Caro examined the man's face more closely. His bushy beard disguised the lower part of his face, but those eyes. Gray eyes. Those were familiar. But this man was with the little beauty, was he not? If this were William, who was this woman?

Her response floored Caro when the girl sprang to life like she had been poked with a stick. "Caro! Is this your Caro?" she repeated multiple times, her attention swiveling from one to the other. When the man didn't move, excitement overtook the girl who rushed at Caro so fast she flinched in alarm. The woman grabbed Caro's hand and pumped it as hard as a man ten times her size. The force of it knocked Caro's hat off and her auburn braid swung down around her shoulders. "Willy bin missin' you so bad, Miss Caro."

Ezra, who had been unable to form words for a while, managed to mutter, "I knowed that war no lad!" But no one paid him any mind.

Caro stared as if her face had frozen in a guise of surprise. It did not stop the bumble bee of a woman who buzzed around her tugging on her arms and talking nonstop in a narrative Caro could not follow. Without her consent or even her legs moving, she somehow found herself face-to-face with the man whose name was Willy or Lord Willy? Nothing about him seemed like her William except the color of his eyes.

This man was huge. When she had last stood beside William, he was only an inch or two taller than she. This virile man towered over her with shoulders at least twice as wide as she remembered. No boyish face on this one. Lines around his eyes were deep. Her William had an easy smile, like he was slightly amused much of the time. The look prominent in the slate-gray eyes looking back at her told Caro this man had seen things he wished he had not. No. This could not be her William.

And then he smiled.

Chapter 20

Caro's heart stuttered along with her breath. This was William's smile. His teeth were William's teeth. Perhaps not as white as she remembered, but the bottom tooth that lapped a bit over the next tooth at the center was exactly William's.

The woman held William's upper arm with one hand and Caro's with the other as if she had thrown them at each other. Maybe she had. She was grinning up at each of them in turn.

"Good glory, you two! Ain't ye gonna hug each other?"

Words appeared to fail both Caro and William until at last William reached out and pulled Caro into his arms and held her tightly as if she were the greatest prize on earth.

William was undone. Never expecting to meet his beautiful Caro in America in 1863, how was it possible she had found him? And here she was in his arms! He would never let her go again, he promised himself.

Gone were the trappings of her station in life as a duke's daughter—no beautiful gown, no elaborate hairstyle, no fancy coach. Here she stood before him in much the way she had when they were kids playing the days away with his sister Violet. Her hair smelled as it had then of sweat, dirt and the outdoors. Her clothes were filthy with mud half-way up to her knees, and they hung from her slim body as if she were a clothes rack. He grinned as he pulled a twig from the back of her jacket thinking she must have slept on the ground. What had happened to send her to him like this?

Fear shot through him. Had someone died?

She might have read his mind because she spoke directly into his ear, "Do not worry, William. No one has died. I got caught up in Olde Gylda's spell and accidentally transported through time. It has been an adventure."

"What? Who? How?" Why could he not form a sentence? Had he heard her say she had met Olde Gylda? She must know about time travel then, or she would not be here in his arms. It was too much to take in, so when words failed him, he held her wrapped in his arms until she squirmed, requiring air.

Olde Gylda had much to answer for if the old crone showed her face here again. But wait. How would they get home if Gylda did not allow it? He had been trying for months to leave and it had not happened. Would she show herself here with Caro? Hope zinged through him this time. Could they possibly be going home together? Or, if not, would Caro be allowed to stay with him in this time? So many questions.

"I hate to interrupt this happy reunion, but I believe Ezra has passed out again." Alex held the man like he was a giant sack of potatoes in need of being set down.

"Oh, Alex, I am so sorry I forgot you!" Caro trilled. She wheeled and pulled William by the arm to stand before Alex. "William, may I make known to you Alexander St. John. Alex, this is William."

Forcing himself to examine the man in front of him, William squinted, for to his surprise he recognized Alex. "You are Addington's heir, are you not?"

Alex's blue eyes lit up. "Yes, he's my father. I wondered if you would remember me from our schooldays at Eton."

William nodded but did not let go of Caro, holding her snug to his side as if afraid she might suddenly disappear.

Alex continued, "We encountered each other one other place a couple of years ago, but I don't believe you recognized me, and I was in no condition to speak."

William frowned in confusion and waited for the explanation.

"I was the soldier you were attending when Olde Gylda found you in India. Thank you for saving my life."

Caro and William stared first at Alex and then at each other, stunned into silence as they absorbed this new detail.

"That said," Alex cleared his throat and his tone changed, "my arms are about to give out and this man needs attention."

Snapped back to reality, William shook off his astonishment at Alex's revelation. He would have to think on that later. Reluctantly, he relinquished his grip on Caro and stepped away, assuming his doctor voice as he added, "I must tend him, my dear. 'Tis my duty." She pulled her eyes from Alex, nodded at William, and hurried to Ezra to check his temperature.

"He is still hot with fever," she explained to William, fighting the urge to move back into the shelter of his arms. An abbreviated version of the tale of their harrowing attack by bandits was told to William as he listened attentively and eyed the man. Caro was quick to get to the point. "He needs medicine we do not have, and his bullet wound requires attention."

While they were talking, the ever thoughtful and efficient Evy had moved into the hospital tent and prepared a bed for Ezra. She was just finishing her task of laying out the bandages, medicines, and a variety of implements she thought William might need, when they brought Ezra in.

"Evy, you are a true angel." William turned to Caro and made the introduction. "This is my dearest friend, Mrs. Evelyn Perkins. I think you, Evy, figured out that this is my betrothed, Lady Caroline Wyckham."

Evy's smile was radiant, making Caro look at her as if the woman might indeed be an angel. Caro acknowledged Evy with a tip of her head, but was unprepared for a curtsy, such as it was, from the girl. Evy may have needed practice in the social niceties, but he could see Caro was impressed with the way the young woman knew her business as his assistant.

In no time at all, the old man's wound was cleaned and

wrapped, and medicine dispensed. Tucked up in the bed in much better shape than he had been earlier, Ezra's snores rattled the makeshift walls of the hospital. Heat from the fireplace nearby kept him toasty-warm and comfortable despite the cold outside. The deathly pallor that had been his upon arrival was gone, leaving William to believe the man would survive to sell his goods another day.

Caro was still fussing at Ezra's side, more wilted flower than world adventurer. She was badly in need of rest and all he could think of was taking her to his tent and if nothing else, simply holding her while she slept. Would anyone here object if he rescued her? He did not think so.

Sam appeared out of the dark into the circle of firelight just outside the ramshackle hospital's open doorway toting a Dutch oven with a rag wrapped around the handle. Evy greeted him with an excited hello and ran to him, giving the man a peck on the cheek before introducing him to Alex and Caro. Sam's face split into a wide grin upon meeting Caro, and William realized the man was happy and relieved Caro would now be the center of William's attention and not Evy.

The group made quick work of devouring the potato and carrot stew Sam brought with him. It was very tasty considering the severely limited resources of the Confederate cooks. Soldiers like Sam were encouraged to forage outside the camp for whatever they could find because supplies issued to them were incomplete.

No telling where he had scrounged for these vegetables instead of using the desiccated ones the men called "decimated" vegetables. Those were dried vegetables that could almost be identified when added to water. Fresh vegetables were a real treat, and Sam enjoyed the accolades of the others but would not reveal his source for obtaining them. There were some things one did not share.

While Alex and Evy kept the conversation moving, and Sam told ribald stories for their entertainment, William slipped away saying he had business needing his attention. He came back a while later minus his bushy beard.

"Well, glory be, Miss Caro, would ye look at yer man?" Evy teased. "We ain't seen that purty face afore! Handsome devil, ain't he?" Her eyes sparkled as she grinned at her friend.

A flush stole its way up William's neck and onto his face, turning his freshly shaved skin a beet red. Caro blushed, too, when he looked at her. Their eyes held and two years' worth of pent-up feelings zapped between them.

Their absorption in each other seemed to mark the end of the evening for everyone else as they all found reasons to leave Caro and William alone. Evy and Sam bade them goodnight and walked back to their quarters, hand in hand. For once, it was not on William's mind if hours of laundry lay ahead for Evy before turning in. Vying for her time and attention was now a thing of the past.

Alex departed, too, announcing he had better check on the sutler wagon and sleep there tonight to make sure it was not stripped of its bounty before Ezra was back on his feet. He did not ask Caro what her plans were for the night and said nothing to William other than goodnight before he strode off in the direction of the wagon.

That left Caro and William alone for the first time in a very long time.

They turned to face one another and as their eyes collided, so many emotions vied for attention neither knew precisely what to say. Apart for so long, they found they had nothing and everything to say to each other. Where to start? Finally, he let the first question that entered his head pop out his mouth without further thought.

"How on earth are you here, Caro? I still believe I must be seeing things every time I look at you."

Caro's shy smile widened in relief. "'Tis the same for me. I was beginning to believe I would never see you again, William."

"And while you are explaining that, how did you come to be traveling with Viscount Huntington and a sutler for a chaperone?" He heard the reprimand and the tinge of jealousy in his voice and wished he had kept his mouth shut. Caro stiffened.

"This might look scandalous, William, but please let me explain." The hurt in her voice as she answered made him feel even worse.

"I am sorry. That did not come out the right way." He sent her his best disarming, sideways grin and tried again. "It's just that I do not understand how you came to be here."

Never able to resist that smile, she sensed his sincerity and nodded. "First, I must tell you that Alex is married to a lovely lady named Elena. She is a time traveler, too, and would have come along except that she is with child."

William let out a breath he had not realized he'd been holding. "That is good to hear." He reached for her hand at the same moment she reached for his. It made them both smile and sigh and begin to relax.

William moved to seat her on a log rolled close to the fire and eased down next to her. The night was cooling rapidly, so it felt good to settle near the flames, but better yet, to be together, side by side. William slipped an arm around Caro and pulled her close before stretching out his long legs to within inches of the fire.

Caro flinched at the contact, surprising him. Then he recollected he had never had his arm around her like this before. The rules of courtship in London seemed ridiculous here in the Confederate camp. It was hard for him to even imagine the world of the *haute ton* in which he had grown up. So many rules and so many ways to offend.

"You have not answered my question, my dear," William said as he squeezed her hand. "How did you find me?" Another thought struck him. "You are not a Guardian of the Stones, are you?"

"No, I am not. As I said, William, my traveling here is the result of a complete accident. Alex would love to have had my very neck for tagging along."

William scrunched his face in puzzlement. "An accident?"

"Yes, we were all at Woodworth at dinner, you see."

"Ah, a Woodworth Christmas! I remember those." Nostalgia rushed through William at the thought of an English Christmas. He pictured all of it in his mind's eye—Yule logs, parties, bounteous food, and mistletoe—especially mistletoe. "Would it not be wonderful to be there right now, sitting at dinner with our families and friends?"

"Mmmm." Caro sighed, staring into the fire as if picturing that scene, then took a breath and continued. "I was seated beside the viscount, having just been introduced to him before going in to dinner. Did you know he is Charlotte's cousin?" That was news to William. "Always off on a world adventure in previous years this was his first Christmas at Woodworth. As we chatted throughout the meal, he shared a mystical story from his world travels, so I told him of my strange dream from our night in Stilton. He was most interested in my story which I thought unusual."

His eyes followed Caro's every move as she talked. He had not forgotten how beautiful she was, yet the flesh and blood woman in front of him bewitched him as never before. Was it possible this was the same Caro he had known his whole life? The duke's daughter? The one always immaculately dressed and coiffed since making her come-out?

This Caro's green eyes sparkled in the firelight like shards of cut glass. Her flaming hair had escaped all attempts to tame it, and her creamy skin glowed with rosy youth and vitality. She was so . . . *alive.* The dauntless spirit flowing from her enraptured him. He longed to pull her into his arms and kiss her, yet he knew to bide his time. She was skittish as a colt.

"What was the dream about?" He was pleased his voice did not betray his tumultuous emotions but sounded calm—almost normal.

"Well, that is just it. How was I to know then that the old woman with the young eyes wrapped in a voluminous black gown was someone I would come to know?"

William's heart stopped while he sucked in a breath and his eyes widened. "Are you telling me you dreamed of Olde Gylda of Hampshire before you met her?"

"I am."

"Damnation!" William raked a hand through his hair. That old witch was full of surprises. "How can that be?"

"I am sure I have no idea. We had stopped for the night at The Bell in Stilton, and at dinner Violet told us the tale of—"

"—Dick Turpin!" William filled in as Caro's eyebrows shot up. Why was he so pleased with himself for filling in that detail?

"How did you know that?" Caro appeared less pleased to have her story interrupted. Those stunning eyes sparked a warning he had seen directed his way throughout most of his childhood. It hadn't stopped him then either.

"I told her that tale years ago to scare her silly on a fearsome, stormy night when we were both in leading strings. Violet had been too scared to sleep for weeks," he recalled, "until she realized she could tell it to others and scare them. The poor housemaids ran around thereafter with dark smudges under their eyes."

"Oh, well, she told it exceedingly well." Caro sat up a bit straighter and, as if miffed, shifted slightly away from him.

William hid his grin at her pique with a swipe of his hand over his mouth. She might not look the Caro of old in her boy's clothing, but she behaved the same way he remembered. "Please, do continue." He slid a leg over to rub up against hers, daring her to move away again. She did not.

"That night I dreamed Violet and I were driving a coach waylaid by Olde Gylda who was standing in the middle of the road like a highway robber. She held out three items she wanted me to take."

As if on cue and with complete disregard for those flashing emerald eyes, William could not resist prodding her. "What were they?"

"I am trying to tell you," Caro said, with a laugh of exasperation at his cheeky behavior.

When William obliged with a quirk of one brow and motioned with an exaggerated lordly roll of his hand for her to continue, she did.

His machinations made her struggle to keep a straight face. "A pocket watch dangled from one hand, and a white strip of fabric flowed from the other, with a map labeled America held between them. Before I could take the items from her, Dick Turpin swooped in riding Black Bess and stole all three."

"Oh, no!"

"Oh, yes," Caro chortled, by now enjoying his attention, knowing full-well he was teasing her as he listened. It had been their pattern of behavior since they were ten and twelve. "It was an unusual dream to be sure, but I thought it extremely odd when Alex asked many questions about what I thought it might mean."

William nodded his understanding and then Caro started to say something else but detoured, beginning again. Her face clouded, and he could see whatever she had begun to say was not pleasant. It made his grin turn to a frown. What was she not telling him?

"I had gone up to my room to retrieve a shawl and took a shortcut down the service stairs to rejoin the party."

When had Caro ever used the service stairs if not in trouble? She clearly had skipped something. Should he be concerned?

"Before I got back to the others, I heard voices in the morning room and recognized them as belonging to Alex and the woman from my dream."

"The devil you say! What a shock to have your dream become reality."

"Shocking? Indeed! Minutes later I had learned of time travel, Guardians of the Stones, and that Elena, Lady St. John was from 1363." William grimaced. Were these revelations what had bothered her a moment ago? Certainly, they were mind-numbing.

"While I was coming to terms with all of that in my head, I had paid no attention to Alex and Olde Gylda and did not understand they were preparing to time travel. When a burst of wind whipped through the garden door, I thought it would knock over the old lady and maybe even Alex, so I grabbed ahold of them."

William threw his head back with a groan. "You got swept up in the whirlwind."

"I did. We landed in London, but not the London you and I know. We had to hurry through Hyde Park because Alex and Gylda were worried about being seen by an enemy of the Guardians, and then we traveled again, arriving here . . ." she paused for effect, pinning her eyes on William, ". . .in evening wear."

A snort erupted from William who then tried to maintain a straight face.

"Grin if you must but yes, formal evening wear." By now Caro did not even try to hide her amusement, just sighed and shook her head. "It was the height of ridiculousness to arrive in America in wartime in formal evening clothes. My dance slippers turned to mush immediately. I might have frozen to death in my silk gown. And, I had to give up my lovely Kashmiri shawl in trade for these outrageous clothes." She self-consciously re-arranged her shirt collar before rolling her eyes up at William. "I cannot begin to tell you how much has happened in the four days we have searched for you."

William's heart melted at the stirring look in the depths of those lush green eyes. Just as he had hoped and without even realizing it, Caro had relaxed into the playful rhythms of their old relationship as they had talked. Feeling more secure and unwilling to wait a moment longer, William scooped her up, dropped her onto his lap, and folded her into his arms. She merely squeaked from surprise but did not fight him.

Her front was rosy-cheek warm from the fire, but her back side required that he rub warmth into it. At least that is what he told himself. His body sang with happiness, enjoying Caro's familiar scent and the newfound feel of her body clasped to his. He breathed into her ear, "I am so sorry for all you've been through, my love, but so happy you have come."

To his delight, she nuzzled her nose into his neck, ran a hand through his hair, and stroked his back. His tongue sampled the tiny bit of skin revealed where her shirt buttoned at the neck. She tasted of home and something entirely Caro. He wanted to devour her and never let her go, but a little voice in the back of his head reminded him not to rush his fences.

Reluctantly, he leaned back and decided to break the spell he had just woven by asking the questions niggling at him since Duvall's departure. "Why has Gylda not come for me herself? I have been trying to go home now for months, and she has not answered my call. Do you know why Alex was sent to search for me?"

William was gratified to see Caro blink twice before her brain caught up with his questions. Perhaps he wasn't rushing those fences as fast as he'd thought.

She shook her head and cleared her throat, taking a moment to recover. She licked her lips, sending him into paroxysms of regret for interrupting himself as she adopted a business-like tone to answer. "Ah, that is an interesting question. For some reason, Olde Gylda cannot hear you. She could tell us you were supposed to be in Tennessee, but she could not send you a stone to travel home because she cannot connect with you or see your exact location. Something is running interference." She stopped for a moment to catch her breath. "Alex thinks it is our time pieces because when Gylda has been able to see you another Guardian was with you."

Now it was William's turn to force his thoughts from the delectable dimple by Caro's luscious mouth to the answer she had just given to his question. Backtracking to consider her words, William pulled out the pocket watch Caro had given him, and Caro pulled out the pocket watch William had given her that had once been his grandfather's. William's eyes widened at the sight of the loose diamonds as she opened it to his portrait, but he said nothing as she scooted them to the side.

Holding the time pieces open next to each other, they were not sure what to expect. What would interference look like? No special signal was visible to either. The hands did not spin, no fire arced between them, no special warmth could be felt—nothing. The fire only popped and sizzled at their feet like fires always did.

Disappointed that something dramatic had not happened, William started to pull away, but as he did so, an unseen force resisted the separation. Had that been his imagination? He tugged harder.

"Do you feel that?" Caro's eyes were huge as her attention riveted on William.

"Yes," he answered, wonder shining in his eyes.

William's hands laced with Caro's around the watches, now securely held face-to-face in their palms, as they silently vowed to one another never to be parted again.

"This proves we belong together, Caroline Wyckham." William's grey eyes drilled into the depths of hers. "I love you."

Tears glistened in Caro's eyes. "And I love you, William Lowther."

Chapter 21

Caro was never exactly sure how they had moved from beside the fire to within William's tent. All she remembered was the moment his lips touched hers. After that, she was lost. Time disappeared, distance disappeared, awkwardness disappeared—all like smoke from the campfire into the nighttime air. Their two-year separation might never have happened.

Safe from prying eyes inside the dark of William's tent, they rediscovered their love for each other in a way neither had dreamed possible in their former lives. Fear of discovery for a kiss stolen in the garden during a ball failed to exist here. No father appeared to pronounce or deny his consent to court his daughter. No chaperone needed to clear her throat or shake a finger if propriety was not followed.

This Caro was not bound by rules. Somewhere along the way on this trip she had ceased to be concerned with what others thought of her. She had become her own person. This new iteration thought for herself, made decisions for herself, and exuded a resilience that was boundless. She had learned to be successful outside of the duke's shadow as someone other than her father's daughter. People responded to her and appeared to like her for who she was.

She gave nary a thought to keeping her distance from William for propriety's sake. She wanted him, and he wanted her and that was all that mattered. Had he been successful in India? How had he come to be in America as a doctor? None of it mattered other than she was interested in his story because it was his story.

What fascinated her the most was that underneath the very altered exterior of William, she found the genuine goodness of the man she loved essentially unchanged. Whatever made up William was still there even though the outward man was nearly unrecognizable. Now his tenderness and the way he held her in his arms made her feel safe for the first time in days and cherished as never before.

∞∞∞

Holding Caro in his arms, William was thankful he had chosen to build himself a thick mattress of leaves and soft grasses to replace the narrow cot provided by the army. Since the camp would be here for weeks it had made sense to work for whatever creature comfort he could muster. The cot would have been too narrow for the two of them, and he was loath to let her go for even a moment. Tucked between heavy blankets atop the soft bed was akin to cuddling in a nest for two.

The poor darling was exhausted and despite her best efforts, she had fallen asleep as she had relaxed in his arms. He smiled to himself as he stroked her hair from her face and pulled her closer to his body. She snuggled her nose into his neck and mewed in her sleep like a kitten as he petted her. He promised himself he would keep her warm tonight as she slept. They would deal with whatever the morrow brought when the sun rose.

What an amazing world he lived in. He had never dreamed of time travel as a lad growing up, yet here he was living in America fifty years into the future. To have Caro with him defied all the rules.

Over the last two years he had often wondered if he were

foolish to wait for this girl who had been in his life since childhood. How was he to know if what they shared in his time was puppy love, as her father had called it, or the real thing? He had puzzled over this world of the future. How would he be certain she was still waiting for him back in his own time? Maybe she had given up and was betrothed to someone else. All those fears had taunted him daily.

Today, none of it mattered because he had never found anyone he loved as much as Caro. Not even Evy, with all her winsome charm and warmth, had moved him to break his vow to Caro.

He loved Caroline Wyckham. Any other woman would have been a compromise—a union for convenience-sake. His eyes filled with so much emotion they nearly overflowed, and his heart rejoiced that he had chosen wisely to wait for the beautiful woman in his embrace.

He wanted so much from Caro—a home, a family, a life together. Things another woman might have provided, but only Caro filled the role of lover. Just when and how they had changed from compatible friends who enjoyed each other's company to a couple drawn to each other physically as well as emotionally, he could not say. He had always been her protector, but he protected Violet, too.

Perhaps it was the first evening after her come-out when Caro had overheard some young women in the retiring room describe her in devastating terms. She supposedly was spoiled, ugly, and arrogant, and the speaker was most upset that Lord William Lowther seemed to be attached to a shrew like Lady Caroline Wyckham.

Always sensitive to her status as a duke's daughter, Caro had tried so hard to be congenial to all she met that this condemnation from a nameless girl cut her defenses down to her knees. Violet was off dancing the night away with a new beau which left William the one she had run to for comfort. Caro was too proud to let her adversaries see they had made her cry, so he had ushered her out the garden doors and found a quiet spot behind a pagoda for her to regain her composure. Was it there his protective instincts changed into something markedly different?

His actions that night were certainly not without risk. If they were caught without a chaperone in the dark of night away from the terrace, he would be forced to marry Caro, or her reputation would be in tatters. According to rules of the ton, she would be ruined. In spite of that, it was a risk he was willing to take without giving it any real thought. After all, they had grown up defying all the proprieties without causing true harm. This was just one more indiscretion in a long line of escapades he and Caro had survived. Wasn't it?

As it turned out, it was something much more. It was a life-changing moment. That was clear to him now. He had not expected to be emotionally swept away when he took a tearful Caro in his arms and pulled her close to comfort her. She was not Violet. No brotherly desire to dry her tears and return her to the ball existed in him. Instead, his body registered the rightness of her body stretched next to his. All instincts told him to keep her there and kiss her. Not just a kind kiss of consolation for her upset, but a kiss-her-senseless kind of kiss. His body had decided he needed to possess this woman, not as a friend, but as a lover.

Somehow Caro was not shocked by his kiss when he capitulated and let his lips find hers. Her tears dried, allowing the moment to settle into a cloud of desire that engulfed the two like a sudden rainstorm, drenching them in feelings that were new and exciting, but absolutely right. Neither had looked back.

At first, Violet had thought the two of them had lost their minds. Likely, she feared the fun they shared growing up as a threesome would never happen again. When William reminded her that Caro would be her sister forever if he married her, Violet agreed it was a match and life appeared to fall out as it should.

That is until his interview with the duke. He had dressed fit for a dandy and strutted into the duke's library believing her father, who had always treated him well, would be deliriously happy about William's engagement to Caro. After all, he had spent as much time in the duke's home as his own, growing up on a family estate that was side-by-side with the duke's family seat. He could not have been more wrong. The duke had quizzed him on his plans for the future. Would he be able to support a wife in the style to which Caro was accustomed? Where would they live? What were his yearly funds? He had stammered like a youth half his age. The duke eviscerated him, leaving him skinned like a beardless lad rather than a man-about-town.

Truthfully, he had not stopped to think about any of that. Nor had he talked with his own father before going to present his offer for Caro to the duke. Money had never been lacking in his world. He had never wanted for anything. The Lowthers were not on par with the duke financially, but their family name was an old and honorable one. He was a second son who would not inherit, but his grandmother had left him a charming estate near London that would suit their needs, as well as a townhouse on the edge of Mayfair. Not lofty, but substantial for a young man of the ton. His father would provide a suitable portion, so he had not thought it a concern. Besides, Caro had a huge dowery, so he failed to understand why money mattered. What a young fool he must have looked to the duke!

He had never been a carouser, even in his Oxford days. Oh, he had taken part in the usual young man's game about town as a university student, but he had no taste for gambling or the nasty head resulting from a night of too much brandy. Perhaps he was just a dull blade, or perhaps his sights had only been set on Caro. Whatever the case, he had been shocked by the set-down he had received. He'd had no choice but to seek his fortune in India, since the duke had made it clear he would accept nothing but the best for his daughter.

Looking back, perhaps his life had spun out as it should have. He was not the cavalier lad of two years ago. Life since then had been a harrowing journey for him spanning an improbable fifty years on two continents. He had been forced to grow in ways that would have been impossible without the refusal of his suit by the duke. He was no longer a naive youth. He and Duvall had done their best to serve the needs of the soldiers they had cared for, but the job was immense and too many had died. It was a man's job he filled now. Would the duke refuse his suit again?

He did not think so. Caro's unexplained disappearance from Woodworth would not go unnoticed by the other guests. He must return with her and claim her as his so some other suitor did not slip in and steal her. This time his offer for her hand would not rest on the duke's consent. He would have her for his wife—the duke be damned! She would marry no other.

He leaned back to examine Caro's sleeping face. Would she argue with William's plans for the two of them? No, he was sure of her this time. Her response to him was unmistakable. The duke would have no choice but to accept him as a son-in-law.

Having exhausted himself with the struggles of his life thus far, William took a deep breath and relaxed into a shallow sleep. Deep sleep had not been his since landing in America with a war in progress.

Caro awoke in the middle of the night feeling warm and happy. She identified the arm thrown over her waist as William's without opening her eyes. Her senses were already attuned to him. She burrowed her nose into his shoulder and enjoyed the scent distinctive of him. My, how she had missed that simple thing.

She had drifted back to sleep when she awoke with a start. Was something wrong? Were they under attack? Then she heard what had awakened her.

"Doc? Doc Lowther? Are you awake, sir?" A voice sounded in a loud whisper just outside the tent entrance.

William was already alert and rubbing her back. "It's all right, Caro. It is only Billy Clark from Evy's side of the camp. Someone is likely in need of a doctor. Illness does not wait for morning, so it happens more frequently than I'd like," he said. "You need not rise. Rest easy for there is nothing for you to worry about."

By now Caro was wide awake and sure she would not be going back to sleep any time soon, judging from the alarm pounding through her blood. She sat up, blushed as she buttoned up her shirt, and reached for her jacket. Wild horses would not keep her from accompanying William to death's door. She would be keeping William within her sight for a very long time, she decided.

"Whatever it is, William, I shall help you if I can. I do not believe sleep will come again without you beside me."

William started to argue but her angst was palpable. Knowing Caro as he did, he was convinced she would not change her mind, and he was not ready for a struggle of any kind that would put her off for even a moment.

"Well then, let's see what Billy's about, shall we?" He pulled back the tent flap and allowed Caro to emerge first. Billy caught his breath and started to apologize for getting the wrong tent when William came out from behind her. Then he stood there looking back and forth between the two with his mouth hanging open. Had no one warned him about Caro? Perhaps not, judging from his shocked expression. Probably her appearance threw the poor lad, since her hair flowed down around her waist, and yet she still wore the work clothes of a boy. It was an incongruous sight forcing William to squelch the urge to laugh. Caro would not appreciate that right now.

"So, Billy, I presume this is not a social visit at this time of night," William began, checking his pocket watch for the hour. "I see it is nearly 3 a.m." He sent a wordless apology Caro's way, but her eyes were glued to Billy. "What, or should I say, who, is in need of doctoring?"

Billy Clark recovered himself and stood a bit taller, now ready to announce the purpose of his visit. "Miz Perry is hav—"

"Ah, Miz Perry's babe has decided to make its appearance, huh?"

Relieved he did not have to explain any further, Billy did have one last request before he was free to be on his way. "Miz Evy says to tell you that you'd best hurry. She said you would know what she meant." His brows formed a vee in the moonlight, and William understood his concern.

"I know exactly what she means, Billy. I have it from here. Go on now and go back to your bed. I will tend to Miz Perry."

"Thank ye, sir." The boy saluted and took off without another word. His job was done, but William's had only just begun.

Caro had found his lantern in the dark and was looking for a means to light it. He surprised her with a match pulled from a canister and torn from its brick of twelve. He struck it and lit the lantern wick. Caro was stunned by this action and was ready to demand an explanation when he held up a hand and said, "Not now, my dear, we haven't time."

Caro's mouth clamped shut and her eyes widened. Concern for Martha replaced her confusion. She nodded, following him out of his tent and to the larger medical tent where Ezra slept. "What can I do to help, William?"

"Find some warm blankets in the trunk to the right of the door. No telling what they might have where she is. She must not be well enough for them to bring her here, so we must take what we can there. I need to assemble some equipment before we go." He gritted his teeth and hoped she did not sense his fear.

As calmly as he was able, he collected his bag and grabbed odds and ends from drawers in small chests that smelled of chemicals. The weight of Caro's eyes was on him. Evy's message told him all was not well with Miz Perry. His heart pounded in his ears as he tried to envision delivering a baby that did not present itself to the world in the appropriate way. Would he be able to deal with the delivery so that both mother and child survived? Hell and damnation, doctoring was hard. He prayed he was up to the task.

Caro caught his arm as he reached for his stethoscope —the one through which Miz Perry had listened to her baby's heartbeat. He turned to see what had prompted her action only to find her face next to his, much closer to him than he imagined.

"How bad is it, William?" He grunted in surprise at her question. How did she know? "Your actions and your face tell the tale of your worry."

He sighed. "I have only delivered two babies. This one promises to come out the wrong way." Caro grimaced. "I do not know if I can safely deliver both mother and child."

"I see."

He believed she really did understand. Suddenly, hope spurted through him. If he impossibly had Caro by his side, all else seemed possible. Relief swept over him. Having gathered what he needed, he motioned for her to follow, and they made their way through the sleeping camp to Evy's side of the encampment.

Chapter 22

Caro spotted their destination when light flickered through the tents long before they reached Evy's location. The Perrys had a larger space than normal, having strung several smaller tents together to form a rather odd-looking conglomeration. Nathan Perry had constructed a ramshackle fireplace on one end that puffed smoke from its top. At least they would be warmer this winter than most.

Well-wishers and onlookers had begun to gather round the tent, knowing that Martha was having her baby. From the expressions on some of the women's faces, word had spread that this would be a difficult delivery. No one needed an explanation for that. Several women had taken it upon themselves to corral the Perry children whose faces expressed worry and anxiety about their mama's condition.

William had told Caro about the family as they made their way across the encampment. Once there it was easy to spot Lizzie holding little Nate who was sucking his thumb with one hand and rubbing his eyes with the other. The girl might have been a matron the way she clasped the shoulders of her little sister standing in front of her. Lulabelle responded to the authority in the touch of her older sister. There was no doubt in Caro's mind who would be in charge should the event go awry. All were huddled around a popping and spitting campfire that set their somber faces in a rather ghastly glow. It made Caro shudder because it looked like a scene from hell.

A collective sigh arose when William was spotted, and he was ushered into the tent with the crowd making way as if he were a king. She supposed in this world he was better than a king. Determined to stand by William no matter what, she followed him inside and braced herself for what they would find.

Miz Perry was stretched out on a table that had been set up near the fire, the hump of her baby rising like a mountain from her midsection. One glance at the woman's twisted face told Caro how much pain she was experiencing. Sweat ran off her brow faster than Evy could mop it up. The woman's entire body was wet. Standing at her head and working with a calm efficiency, Evy spoke kind, encouraging words to her friend. Hearing William enter, she looked up long enough for relief to swamp her.

Caro stood clutching the blankets she had brought from the makeshift hospital wondering if there was anything she should do to help. Evy moved as if she'd read her mind and took the blankets from Caro, tossing them to a corner away from the table.

"Miz Caro? Might you be so kind as to stand where I was and mop Miz Martha's brow?"

Caro felt a grin stretch across her face which was enough to make Evy's eyes dance. "I should be delighted to do so, Evy." At least she would not be a third thumb in the way.

William was all business checking out his patient. As he lifted the sheet covering Martha's privates, the color in his face fled. What on earth was he seeing that made him pale to a pasty white?

"Is that what I think I'm seeing, Evy?" Caro barely heard his words above the wail coming from Martha as a contraction took her. "It appears to be a bottom and not a baby's head. Am I right?" Full of emotion, William's voice quavered as he spoke, sounding like a death knell.

Evy nodded slowly and rolled her eyes mournfully at William.

Oh, no, Caro thought, will Martha and her baby die? It happened all too often in her day, but did it happen fifty years in the future, too? She shook her head to clear it. Of course, it did. Look where they were! William had no idea what to do to save either of them or he would be doing it. Baby's coming bottom first rarely lived, especially away from those experienced in delivering them. Caro's heart threatened to burst as she thought of those three children outside waiting for their mother to deliver a new baby.

Without thinking, Caro dropped the cloth she had been using to wipe Martha's brow and stroked the woman's cheeks. Laying her palms across the flushed face, Caro pulled gently in an upward pattern. Martha screamed as her body struggled to do what apparently it could not. But then something in Martha changed as Caro kept stroking her. Some of the tension released itself, and the woman calmed and stayed calm even as the next contraction arrived.

Caro noted Evy and William had shocked expressions on their faces, too, as they witnessed the change, so it wasn't her imagination.

"I might have known you have the touch, Missy!" The familiar voice crackled from the doorway as none other than Olde Gylda swept into the room. "That explains a great deal to me." Alex was right behind her but took up a post by the door without a greeting.

Why were they here at Martha's bedside? Were they ready to travel back home? They couldn't go now! Would that mean they would be left here if they did not? Alarm spread through Caro in an instant, but when she realized Martha intuited her unease and stiffened, she forced herself to drop the thought from her mind. Oddly, Martha relaxed, too.

With a nod of satisfaction, Gylda watched Caro's hands smooth over Martha's face and arms, calming her. "And yer hands have a bit o' magic in 'em, too, don't they?"

Caught off guard, Caro was unable to form a response. She did not understand why Martha was responding to her either.

But magic? Her jaw flapped twice and still nothing came out.

William had no difficulty responding. "So now you choose to appear, Olde Gylda? It's been months, you know! As you can see, we've no time for a chat."

Gylda ignored William as if he had not spoken and eyed the situation from several angles. Evy's eyes were huge as she watched the old woman move around the table, poking and prodding Martha as she lay there. Martha seemed oblivious to the actions, moaning only slightly as Caro kept up her strokes across the woman's body.

Having satisfied her curiosity, Gylda started to speak when another contraction bit into Martha. Her enlarged stomach clenched as if a giant's hand squeezed it. Evy emitted a gasp that she tried to squash, resulting in an empathetic squeak. Caro grabbed Martha's arms and held her, trying her best to share the woman's pain to keep her from hurting so much.

Untroubled by all their reactions, Gylda placed both hands on Martha's stomach and the clench released itself as if she had swatted that giant's hand away. As those muscles relaxed, Gylda's hands began to turn slowly in a circle as she pushed on the woman's hump. Caro realized with a shock what Olde Gylda was attempting to do. Was she actually turning the baby around in the womb?

William checked between Martha's raised knees to see if anything was happening. The awe present on Evy's face as she stared over his shoulder confirmed something, indeed, had taken place.

The room seemed not to breathe until Gylda completed a few more strokes over Martha and looked up at them. "That should do it, dearies. Lady Caro can take it from here." She whirled and started for the door as everyone spoke at once.

It was Martha that caught everyone's attention as another contraction took center stage. This time the squeeze that gripped her was much different from the last one. She followed it through its course from start to finish with only a small moan as Caro kept up her stroking.

William's head swiveled between Gylda and Martha. "You cannot leave now! Thank you for your assistance, but you can see we cannot go with you yet." He was so appalled his words came out in a staccato. "You. Must. wait!"

His admonishment was met with a cackle from the old witch who waved a hand airily in his direction. It was Alex who stepped in and reported what they had come to say. "We must leave now, William. There is trouble in London to deal with or no travelers like you will remain safe."

Caro uttered only one word, "Abasi?"

"Yes. The man is a terror."

Olde Gylda had reached the door and was ready to stroll out of the room when William all but yelled, "How are we to get home?"

Gylda stopped, turned with a grin that showed all the gaps in her mouth of few teeth, and replied, "I kin hear ye now, kind sir. All ye have to do is call."

Caro had a question of her own. "How do we find our way in London?"

Before she could answer, dismay passed over Olde Gylda's face making her flinch as if she heard something no one else did. She grabbed Alex and pulled him from the doorway of the tented room. Alex's voice was heard hollering, "I'll meet you in London!"

And they were gone.

This time Martha let out a shriek that made the foundations of the tent shake. As William resumed his role as doctor, the top of a baby's head poked its way through the birth canal, its dark hair making Evy cry out in amazement.

"She did it! Whatever that old woman did with her hands, it worked!"

Caro pressed lightly on Martha's stomach and the rest of the baby presented itself to the world. The next few minutes were chaos as the new baby, a boy, was cleaned, wrapped, and handed to Martha.

Nathan arrived shortly after and cried when he saw his wife and child looking pristine, swaddled, and draped in a clean bed . . . and healthy. One of the women had sent her husband to replace Nathan on guard duty, with a warning that his wife might not survive the birth. He was so overcome to find them alive and well, all he could say was his wife's name. Soon everyone was teary, too, but with joy.

Nathan's best friend, Thaddeus Newell from North Carolina, poked his nose in and yelled "Congratulations!" in such a loud voice everyone shushed him at the same time in fear of waking the new baby. He made up for it by passing out tin mugs all round for those present to toast the birth of the baby with a cup of his spectacular brandied eggnog.

"I was savin' it fer Christmas Eve, but since that's tomorrow night, this is close enough. My ma sent me the bottle of brandy and I foraged fer the eggs. Miz Congreve graciously donated the sugar." Thad bowed and accepted the general acclaim for his tasty wartime treat.

Nathan toasted to baby William, named after Doc Lowther, as well as Evy, Caro and "the old woman." Good cheer abounded as everyone told personal accounts of where they were and what they saw happen. All agreed it was a truly happy evening akin to an early Christmas Eve.

Baby William did his part and slept right through all the noise after Martha skillfully filled his little belly. Her three children gathered around their mother, tenderly kissing the baby's cheeks, and petting him with freshly washed clean hands. How lovely that scene played out instead of the one that might have been. The thought sent a chill down Caro's spine. Lucy's little face came to mind even though she'd lost her mother in an accident. Babies and children needed their mothers. That much she knew. She shook off that shade and focused on the coming trip home.

Christmas was only one day away. How shocking! If they left at first light, would they possibly get back to Woodworth before Christmas Day? How wonderful to be there with her family and friends, but to be there with William defied all her expectations. Would they be able to find Alex in London? What if they ran into this Abasi person Alex had told her about? At least she had William to help navigate their travel home.

She relaxed with a sigh that William interpreted as a sign it was time to leave the party. He shooed all the visitors out the door on "doctor's orders," leaving only Martha and her family in the tent. Evy, Caro, and William gathered their possessions and said goodnight to the happy family. William checked the time to find it was only a few minutes past 4 a.m. That should give them plenty of time to leave unseen before dawn. But how to say good-bye to Evy?

His heart ached as his attention turned to the little woman beside him whose unbound long hair shined a bright silver in the moonlight. The remnants of their earlier campfire still popped and sizzled in the fire pit outside the tent.

Evy paused long enough to cast a hard look at William and Caro. "I ain't got no idee what happened in there tonight, but you two belong together." When William darted a glance at Caro and started to reply, she cut him off. "No, Willy, don't ye say nuthin. I knowed ye warn't fer me, and I knowed ye wouldn't be stayin' here long. This here country ain't yourn." Her eyes burned brightly in the firelight and Caro choked up at the emotion she saw there. She stole a look at William who looked torn in two.

"What I saw in that tent with Miz Martha was magic, pure and simple. I do not know who ye are and I don't need to know. You, Miz Caro, got that magic in yer hands jist like the old woman said. And you, Willy, ye got the gift of fixin' up wounded like nobody I ever seen. The two of ye are special and I know ye cannot stay, even though it's likely goin' to break my heart to say goodbye."

William grabbed the tiny woman and hugged her hard. Tears had begun to slide down Evy's face and William was no better. Earlier, it might have been awkward to embrace in front of Caro, but now all three recognized their time together was over.

"Will ye be gone by mornin'?" Evy whispered in William's ear.

"I think so, Evy. We have to go back to our lives in London."

Evy rolled her eyes at Caro and back to William. "We all knows there's more to it than that, Willy. I heared the old lady and yer friend Alex." She shook her head with an air of finality. "If ye got to go, then ye got to go. Me and Sam'll be jist fine here. Ye taught me plenty in the time ye've been here and I won't fergit none of it."

William took Evy's hands in his and made her look at him despite the tears stealing down her cheeks. "Leave it to you, dear girl, to make my departure as easy as possible. That's what you do, isn't it? Your gift is to make the lives of everyone around you better than when you found them." Was he mistaken or had the young woman begun to glow with simply his praise? It took so little to please Evy.

"Aw, shucks. That—"

"No, do not belittle your gift in any way, Evy." He shot a glance at Caro, addressing her, but looking at Evy. "I would have been dead, Caro, if this little angel had not come into my life to save me. I had all but given up going home or ever seeing you again. I could not eat. I could not sleep. I was finished. Then this dear one arrived to pick me up, dust me off, and make me rejoin the living. She made me food, found me clean clothes, and then became the best assistant any doctor ever had."

"Them shore is purty words, Lord Willy. I thank ye fer 'em. I will hold 'em dear fer the rest of my days." She grinned and gave William a last hug and a kiss on the cheek before turning to Caro. "I's ever so happy to have met ye, Miz Caro. It makes partin' much easier knowin' yer there to take care of this man. He needs takin' care of, ye know!" Evy winked at William who gave her a lop-sided grin.

She gave Caro a hug and whispered in her ear, "Don't fergit to take care of yerself too." She kissed Caro on the cheek, lifting herself to her toes to do so. "Well, Sam will be waitin' fer me. He don't sleep so good 'til I git there, and he sees I'm beside him."

William raised his eyebrows at this new revelation, making Evy laugh. "Oh, don't look so surprised. Me and Sam have bin married fer a week. I jist didn't want to tell ye cuz ye didn't want to know that!"

"Why you little devil, you!" William let out a big guffaw that probably woke up several rows of tents. Evy and Caro did their best to shush him, but all three were giggling. "I'm sorry I won't be seeing that man of yours again. Give Sam my best, Evy. I wish you two a long, wonderful life with lots of children. Now skedaddle, you little sneak!"

She did.

He would remember Evy's eyes from that moment dancing with laughter and full of mischief as she confessed. That image of his best friend in America would remain burned into his brain for the rest of his life. Somehow it was just the right note to go out on. She turned back only once to say, "I'll make sure that old rascal Ezra is back on his feet in no time. Maybe someday Sam and me'll see y'all in London!" She didn't wait for a response but whirled on her heels and disappeared into the night.

Chapter 23

Everything was different this time when Caro awoke from the whirlwind delivering them from Tennessee. On the bright side, she felt the comforting reality of William's arms around her. She knew him by the scent that was distinctly his. With Alex and Olde Gylda absent, at least she would not be confronting any new threat alone. That was a relief.

On the flip side, she had expected Hyde Park to be as quiet as the first time she had passed through. This time when the travel-wind subsided, a loud drone of noise accosted her senses before she even had time to open her eyes. What is this? She sneaked a peek at William who had yet to rouse. With no help from that quarter, she decided to play dead until she was sure nothing harmful had come their way. Better to be safe than sorry on that score.

With her eyes jammed shut, she reached out with her senses to evaluate the dangers that might abound around her. She was aghast at the cacophony of sounds that met her. Loud and unrelenting, the noise made her want to cover her ears and pretend she heard none of it.

Shrieks, music, and laughter, along with the hiss and whine of mechanized works blended into a terrifying whole. Seeking to calm herself, she focused upon one sound at a time before moving on to the next. As she did so, she identified those discordant sounds as far less threatening than she first imagined.

The music playing sounded like nothing she had ever heard before. It blared as if an orchestra was at her fingertips, yet her senses told her she was at a distance from the source.

Moans and crunches of machinery screeched and groaned, too, like something from Merlin's Mechanical Museum. She had been twelve when her father had taken her to see the magnificent creations of the mechanical genius of John Joseph Merlin. She had never forgotten the sounds and sights of that day. What amazing inventions might be here to make such sounds?

A thrum of people noise drifted to her on the wings of a cold breeze. Having survived many a rout, she had no difficulty knowing what hundreds of people talking and laughing together sounded like. These people noises were punctuated by diabolical shrieks and gut-wrenching screams that pierced the air. Were those emitting the sounds happy, horrified, or scared?

Taken in pieces, she thought they must have landed in the middle of a fair of some sort. Were they beside the Thames at a Frost Fair? No, wait. Would London still have that fair and in Hyde Park? Perhaps this was a similar festival for Christmas? After her careful examination, it wasn't quite so scary to hear.

More intense right now was the smell of food wafting her way, sharpening a hunger pang as it registered in her body. Different from her usual fare, she was unable to pin down the new scent. The odor was meat mixed with sweet in ways unfamiliar to her. Might she still be dreaming? If not, where had they landed and who might be responsible for all these sights, sounds and scents?

Opening one eye at a time, she stared at William's chest for a moment, right into a button on his overcoat that read CSA —Confederate States of America. What an excellent reminder that her experiences in America had not been a dream. She reached out and gently placed a finger over the letters.

William's subconscious must have sensed her looking at him because his body jerked sharply and his grip on her tightened. She struggled to sit up, but hearing the noise around them, he pushed her down, hovering over her in a protective position.

She giggled at his behavior but enjoyed it just the same. "I think everything is not as threatening as it sounds, William," she managed to spit out. No sooner had she voiced that thought than a woman's shriek rose above the noise, lasting seconds before a resounding crunch replaced it.

"My God, what on earth is that horrible sound? Have we landed in Hell?"

Caro grinned at his unfettered response to the noises of the night she had been assessing for some time now. "It makes me think of something from Astley's Theatre or a night at Vauxhall. For all the shrieks and cries, people are talking and laughing too. I cannot think all this is something to be feared."

Relaxing his grip as he listened to her explanation, he moved aside and helped her sit up. Together they turned toward the crux of the sound and experienced identical shock upon seeing what was in front of them on the far side of the Serpentine.

"Are you seeing what I am seeing?" William blurted.

A long pause ensued while Caro tried to make sense of what her eyes told her was there. When she finally answered, her response was so breathy she might have been someone else. "If you are seeing lights sparkle and shine in the colors of the rainbow, giant spinning machines, and an enormous wheel turning round with people's feet dangling below. . . then yes."

William's eyes met Caro's, and they stared blank-faced at one another. "Duvall never described anything like this. I know not what to think of it all."

Caro decided if they both saw the same thing then it was not a dream and must be true. Still. . .

William got his feet under himself and then pulled Caro up. They stood with their arms tucked securely around each other's waist and their eyes glued to the whirling, spinning, whooping sight in front of them.

The colored lights lit up the night sky, allowing clouds to be visible hanging above the scene in an unearthly glow. Entrancing in its beauty, Caro wanted to see the sights up close. Looking around them, families were making their way toward the action with children skipping in their excitement to get there. It must be safe if people were taking their children along. This was Hyde Park, after all. Who would put something terrifying in the midst of a park?

"Shall we?" She tugged William's jacket, and he cautiously followed her as she dragged him by the hand to a nearby walkway where they fell in among those heading for the entrance.

The evening was crisp, but not as cold as what they had left in Tennessee. The Londoners around them were dressed for winter in short jackets, but many were hatless with just a scarf around the neck. Others wore knit caps, some with tassels bobbing along behind their heads.

A little girl darted in front of Caro wearing a hat decorated like a cat's head with ears and a pink nose on the crown and whiskers off the brim. It was adorable on the cherub who was swiftly caught by her parents and scolded for running off. Caro smiled at them, and they smiled back. No, not scary at all.

After a few minutes, Caro realized not a single long skirt was in sight—men, women, and children all wore breeches or pants. Looking down at her lad's attire, she was happy not to be lugging a gown around to draw unwanted attention to the two of them.

The mood of the crowd walking toward the lights was full of laughter and good cheer. A few folks even sang along to the music coming from an unknown location. Their excitement was contagious, making Caro want to skip along with the little girl.

The entrance was a giant arch proclaiming Winter Wonderland with traditional winter pictures painted on the sides of the structure. A huge calendar marking off the days until Christmas stood alongside it showing the day as December 23rd. Caro punched William and pointed to it. He grinned when he realized they still had time before Christmas to get to Woodworth.

Once they walked underneath the arch an entire world opened-up for them. A row of tents on either side featured shops of all kinds in a festive marketplace. Crowds huddled over merchandise ranging from silly fun to beautiful paintings. The Frost Fair on the Thames had been something like this, but there was so much more here than anything she had ever imagined. The sights and sounds were spectacular.

Groups of boys hollered at each other as they zigged and zagged through the crowd on the way to some unknown destination. Parents carried small children on their shoulders, so they did not get lost in the throng. Some small ones cooed in delight from their great height above the fray. Others pouted and cried. Food was sold and eaten everywhere. People ate meat from sticks or nibbled at treats sold in flimsy bowls they then crumpled and tossed into rubbish bins. Oddly, people sucked on sticks that poked out of large cups. She would have to investigate that.

Caro had difficulty taking all of it in. The colored lights on every structure everywhere were heavenly as far as she was concerned. They appeared to be made of bits of colored glass strung together on a rope. Small wires were visible in the middle of some of them, but how they glowed was beyond her. Perhaps William would know. Maybe it was magic? The effect was mesmerizing.

Before she could vocalize that question to William, he suddenly stopped. She was nearly jerked off her feet, and the people behind them bumped soundly into their backs. After suitable apologies were put forth, William pulled her beside a post and pointed a finger at the big box atop it. Caro's jaw dropped as she understood his reason for stopping. An orchestra and voices blasted from the box as if held prisoner inside with only the sound allowed to escape.

As they stood amazed at what they heard, one song ended, and another began. This song sounded nothing like the first with drums much more apparent and an instrument she did not readily identify. How could one little box hold two orchestras? She did not understand.

About that time, William dragged her by the hand to another box further down the lane where the same song played from the second box. Wait, what? Looking ahead, she spied more boxes, some on taller poles, some hooked to tents and other structures.

"'Tis the world of the future, Caro!" Excitement lit William's face as brightly as all the colored lights glowing around them.

"I have no words for this, William. It is amazing." Caro caught a couple nearby snickering at them and decided they must look ridiculous to those around them. She grabbed William's arm and forced him to walk toward a nearby booth with her.

"I fear we shall stick out like the bumpkins we are, William, and Abasi will easily find us."

William rolled his eyes down to hers in apology. "Of course, you are right. This is a place I never dreamed of seeing. I want to find out how everything works, but we have no time to do so, do we?"

The last two words were said with such a hopeful expression Caro had a hard time not smiling at him. His attention had already drifted to the speakers again as his mind struggled to figure out how they worked.

A man tapped William on the shoulder from behind, making him squawk in surprise.

"Sorry, mate. Would you mind moving aside, so I can get to the electrical box behind you?"

Neither she nor William had any idea what the man was talking about, but since he was dressed like a workman with tools hanging from his belt, they obliged by moving a few steps away. The same pole that held a black box at the top, also held a metal box chest height that was about a foot squared with a lock attached to the side of it. He and Caro gawked as the man unlocked and opened the box to reveal a row of switches.

William pointed out to Caro that black cords left this box and ran in different directions to the boxes atop the poles. The man pulled a switch down and the music from the box above them stopped. Caro and William looked at each other with eyebrows raised. How did the switch control the box? The man flipped a couple more switches and the sound once again played above their heads as well as from several more boxes nearby. Did the black cords make them play?

Now William was really intrigued. Caro thought he would gladly have gotten into the box and flipped all the switches just to determine what each would do. That dream ended with a click when the worker reattached the lock. Removing the key, one of dozens held on a loop, he shoved the mass of metal into his pocket where it created a noticeable bulge in his jacket.

"Sorry to disturb you. Sometimes this sound system just needs a reset to work right. Happy Christmas to you." The man tipped his cap at them and went on his way.

William stared at all the boxes with his jaw hanging open and his mind obviously whirling. If she wanted to see more than a black box, she'd better get him moving along or the night would be gone. Time for a change of subject. "Do you think Alex can find us here or should we be waiting where we dropped from the wind?"

Reluctantly, William pulled his eyes from the boxes to meet hers. "That I do not know." He grimaced and scanned the area as if Alex or Gylda might decide to appear without warning. "From what I was told of Olde Gylda, she will have no difficulty finding us anywhere we happen to be now because our watches are in sync. After all, she sent us a stone to get this far with no trouble."

"That she did. But what if Alex is by himself? How can *he* locate us?"

"That could present a problem." William scrunched his face in thought as his eyes roamed over the extraordinary world in front of him. "Still, Caro, when will we ever have the chance to see all of these wonders if we leave here now?"

"Oh, thank you, William!" Relief flooded Caro as she threw her arms around him and hugged him hard. Duty was one thing. Going home was another but spending time here with William was pure joy. "I hoped we might stay for a bit. There is something about these lights that makes me feel wonderful. I want to sing and dance like a child to this remarkable music and enjoy every little thing." She watched a girl beside them bounce along with a tune, the tassels on her hat bobbing in time to the beat. Caro was not the only one wanting to dance and that made her happy.

William grinned at her and gave her a kiss on her cheek. No one around them seemed to notice at all, so he hugged her tightly to his side and kissed her again. Caro laughed aloud at his bravery. There was freedom in the anonymity of the crowd.

Arm in arm they strolled along the walkways. Stopping to view merchandise in each booth, they enjoyed being a part of the mob that stretched like a giant ant hill through the marketplace.

They found themselves inside a tent filled with colorful hats and scarfs for the season piled on tables and displayed on racks around the walls of the space. Saleswomen wearing red nightcaps with fluffy white balls on the tips were showing their wares to dozens of people pawing through the items on the tables.

Caro nabbed a knitted hat with a ball tassel the moment the young woman next to her dropped the item back on the table. It was perfect and Caro fell in love with it. Everyone outside was wearing something like this, even the dancing girl, and it appeared to be the latest style. She wanted to be stylish, too.

The hat was attached to a matching long scarf with fringed ends and a pair of gloves. The set was a Christmas green that suited her and turned her eyes the same color.

William took the knitted scarf from Caro and wrapped it around her which prompted a saleslady to ask if they would like to make a purchase.

"Not at the moment, Miss, but perhaps later as the evening gets cooler." Caro spoke using her practiced hauteur as a member of the ton and the girl, hearing the aristocratic bell-tones in her voice, nodded, and whirled away to wait on someone else. Apparently, her clothes were not as off-putting as she had thought. She did wish she had money, though, because she wanted to keep the scarf and its accompanying gloves and hat.

With Caro still casting longing looks back at the knit shop, William pointed them in the direction of an open-air structure with a gaily decorated rooftop. "Are those people ice skating? The Serpentine is behind us, and I don't remember a pond there."

"I love ice skating!" Caro paused and pushed her lip out in a pout. "But it makes me think of the Christmas we are missing at Woodworth."

William gave her hand a squeeze and kissed her cheek before whispering in her ear, "We'll get there. You'll see." Caro kissed him back and for a few minutes forgot they were in the middle of a crowd of strangers.

Later, when they walked around the corner, they saw dozens of people circling the arena on ice skates vastly different from the ones William and Caro were used to. The only similarity was the single blade on the bottom of the shoe.

William noted that people at the door waiting to enter paid a man with what appeared to be shiny metal tokens not unlike the ones the sutlers and soldiers used for trade. Reaching into his pocket, he pulled out several tokens left from his time with the Confederates and bounced them in his hand. Would the man accept them? In Tennessee the sutler had taken a wide variety of tokens.

Either Caro had noticed the same thing, or she was a mind reader. "We can give it a go, you know. If he won't accept them, we have lost nothing for trying."

She was right. William pulled her toward the door where they waited in line and watched the doorman do his job by rote. When they stepped up for their turn, William dropped his tokens into the man's out-stretched hand without hesitation.

It almost worked.

The man was just about to drop their tokens in a pot when something must have alerted him to the difference. He opened his hand and stared at the metal coins they had given him. Then he turned them over and examined their backs before lifting them to the lamp above his head to read the inscriptions on them.

Dressed otherwise in a nondescript way, the man wore a red, white, and green vest loudly proclaiming him a worker at the festival. When he looked up, he directed his attention to William and then to Caro, taking in every aspect of their clothing and manner. He shook his head with exaggerated finality and motioned for them to leave, even reaching around Caro to take the tokens from the young couple behind them.

Embarrassed, William and Caro stepped out of line and walked quickly away. It was then Caro said, "He did not return the tokens to you, did he?"

Abruptly stopping, William turned and stared back at the man. Deep in conversation with another worker, the attendant was closely examining William's tokens. The two turned as if the eyes upon them had beckoned and stared at William and Caro for a fraction of a second before smirking at them. The doorman flipped one of the sutler tokens in the air before catching it and placing it in his jacket pocket. His toothy grin sent a cold chill down William's spine and Caro shivered. Had they made a big mistake? Who were those men?

William urged Caro into the moving crowd where they let themselves be carried down the lane with an ever-growing horde of people. Could they not disappear into the masses to avoid being found? Surely, Abasi's men would not be looking for them here, would they?

"They know what we look like now, Caro." William whispered into her ear as if someone might overhear.

"I know." Caro's green eyes flashed in annoyance. "Do you think they are connected to the man named Abasi?"

William shook his head in frustration. "Perhaps. Maybe they are simply fascinated with those unusual tokens."

"Or perhaps not," Caro replied, her tone indicating her dismay. "If we had some money, we might be able to buy something different and get rid of these clothes to throw them off." While a few people had taken note of their unusual clothing, most had not given them any attention at all. Caro had even seen a teen-aged boy with a beehive hat like hers.

"True, but how can we do that? Besides, who would want to buy these clothes?"

"Well, someone might." Caro sent a scowl at him that softened into a smug look when an idea replaced it. "Do you not remember I have diamonds in my pocket watch?"

"Ah, yes! I remember. But how did you come to carry loose diamonds in my grandfather's timepiece?" A myriad of expressions rolled over William's face before settling into concern. "Why were you carrying around expensive gems in the first place? If discovered, they might have put you in great danger."

Caro laughed at his consternation. She was proud to have survived her visit to America as an independent woman. "It is a tad unusual, is it not?" She fought a giggle that wanted to bubble up as she thought of her accidental visit to America. "If you recall, Alex and I landed in America dressed for dinner, so I was wearing my usual evening jewels, as was Alex. We had no money, only our jewelry, so Alex pried the stones out of their settings. We used them in trade for the clothes I am wearing now as well as for the horses we needed to reach you. Alex did most of the dealing, so he carried the loose gems on his person, but he gave me several of the diamonds to use in trade in case we became separated."

William nodded as she talked. "That makes sense. He was wise to think of that."

"Well, like you, Alex is a gentleman. It is his job." She knew speaking of Alex made William jealous, but the thought of teasing him was irresistible. To her surprise, he gave her a raised eyebrow and refused to take the bait.

"So, do you want to try to trade one of the stones for money? Do you think anyone here would buy one?" That was it? All he would say?

A stab of disappointment hit her. She had been expecting a much bigger response than she got. He had been jealous of Alex before. Looking closer, she realized a frown marred William's face, advertising he was not in a playful mood. Was the token incident bothering him? Did he know something more than she about Abasi?

If they were not to be victims, she reasoned, they would have to look out for themselves. If that meant wearing more suitable clothes to not stand out in the crowd, so be it. They would deal with food once they had money to spend. "Well, I think we should try. Did we not pass a jewelry shop walking through the marketplace?"

"We did. That would be the obvious place to start." He sucked in a deep breath, tipping his nose in the air. "Besides, all the food smells are making me hungry. You must be too." A family walked by with plates heaped with delicious smelling food as they headed toward a seating area. William's eyes followed those plates and Caro's stomach complained.

Ah, there was her opening. She knew what would make him smile. "Was that chicken I smelled? Bratwurst? You know my stomach is unruly if it is not dealt with at first rumble." William grinned at her, knowing the truth of her statement having grown up with her. She continued, "Did I tell you how embarrassed I was when out shopping on Bond Street with my cousin Louisa a few weeks past? My, it seems a lifetime ago."

Caro proceeded to entertain William with the story of the little man in the jewelry shop who was beside himself when Louisa could not make up her mind what she should buy for her husband for Christmas.

William thought it a smashing good story and teased Caro with ever-growing rumbling sounds that mimicked her audacious stomach the entire time they searched for the jewelry shop.

William's smile was back in place.

Chapter 24

They found the shop Caro remembered close to the entrance with a sign out-front proclaiming *Holidaze Jewelry.* Strolling in they were surprised to discover only a handful of people inside. The little marketplace held a variety of items from earrings and hair ornaments displayed on individual cards on one side to gemstone necklaces and bracelets on the other. The few patrons already there were on the earring side being tended to by a dark-haired woman who looked bored with her job.

Caro noted the man in a suit and tie behind a small counter on the more expensive side rolled his eyes when she and William headed in his direction. Not quite the reception she was accustomed to receiving upon entering a jewelry store. What would dear Mr. Kelty think? With a practiced eye she itemized the gemstone jewelry on display and found them of moderate value, with one or two pieces appearing to be quite valuable.

She ignored the man's snobby attitude and asked to view some of the diamond jewelry on display. Having been caught eyeballing them with obvious disdain, he hesitated and perked up the moment he heard her speak. He adjusted his tie, sat up a little straighter and shoved a plate of half-eaten sausage under the counter. Caro realized her cut-glass accent told him she was not from a poor family more effectively than any manner of dress ever could.

Shaking off his first impression, or so it seemed to Caro, he smiled and obliged her request by pulling out a tray of sparkling diamonds for her perusal. She assessed the pieces one at a time, looking for the price of each item on the little tag attached to it. William sucked in a breath beside her in response to the sky-high prices he was seeing displayed on those tags. She was having a similar reaction but trying hard not to let it show.

"Do you create the designs yourself? The settings are lovely." Caro gave the man her most charming smile. She had him. His eyes softened, and he began a run-down of each piece. She listened carefully, oohing and aahing over every item.

William stood behind her, letting her know with a wink it was her show. She loved that about William. When she took the lead, he was happy to support her. Not many men of her acquaintance would do so without argument.

"I wonder if you might be interested in a loose diamond I have?" Her smile widened when the man's eyebrows shot up. "Would you like to see it?"

She knew he would be churlish to say no at this point when she had listened to him so dutifully. It might have been the very last thing he wanted to do, but he reluctantly agreed, making her tuck her chin to hide her smile.

The man's attention was instantly alerted when she pulled out her pocket watch. The time piece once belonging to William's grandfather spoke of old wealth. It truly was a beautiful keepsake that looked as grand and as expensive as it was old.

When she opened it, she revealed several stunning diamonds that reflected the lights and shot rainbows around the room. She casually dropped one onto the swatch of black velvet in front of the man. His expression told her he was caught as surely as a fish on a line. Now all she had to do was reel him in.

The saleswoman, having finished with her customers, crossed the empty store to take up residence behind the man as he sat on a stool to examine the diamond. With his jeweler's loop in one hand and delicate pincers holding her diamond with the other, he stared into the stone with the hint of a smile on his face.

"What is the verdict, Arthur?" The woman flaunted a sizable diamond on her left ring finger as she placed her hand on the jeweler's shoulder. Were they husband and wife?

The man did not miss a beat. He just handed her the loop and let her examine it for herself. If she tried for a poker face, she failed. Her eyes bulged as she caught her partner's eye when she handed the loop back. It was obvious they knew the value of the diamond they held.

"Why do you wish to sell this diamond, if I may ask?" Suspicion seized Arthur who now wanted to know if he was about to buy a stolen gem.

Caro gathered her wits and launched into her story. "The truth is we are traveling, and someone took our belongings while we were resting on the other side of the park." The woman gasped with alarm, but Arthur didn't bat an eye while he waited for Caro to continue. "My friend had warned me of things like this happening while visiting a big city and told me to keep a gemstone or two in my pocket watch just in case. He said no matter what else happened, the stones could be sold to at least get us home."

William stayed mum but gave the woman puppy dog eyes and a sad, sideways grin that seemed to convince her they needed help.

"We can buy the stone, can't we, love?" The woman leaned down and whispered something in his ear. He responded by giving her hand a squeeze.

"How much do you want for the stone?" Arthur lifted his eyes from the blinding reflection of the near perfect diamond in his hand to meet and hold Caro's.

How should she answer that question? She looked over her shoulder at William who had read the tags of the diamonds as they looked at them earlier. He took his cue.

"We do not want to part with the stones at all since they have been in the family for. . ." He clicked his tongue before catching his breath to continue. ". . .centuries. However, if we do not sell one tonight, we shall have no place to sleep and nothing to eat."

The woman nudged her partner and messaged him with a look to make the deal.

The man sighed and for a moment Caro thought he might turn them down. The fingers of one hand pinched the end of his nose before sliding down and circling around his mouth. "Your diamond is actually worth more than I have in cash here in the store. Most customers buying a diamond of this quality pay for it with a credit card. That will not help you, so the best I can offer you is three hundred pounds." He raised his chin with a take-it-or-leave-it thrust.

Caro understood credit, even if a credit card was meaningless to her. She suspected the stone was worth about four thousand pounds compared with the gems she had just viewed. They did not need that much to get home. The deal would be a win for both parties. Still, she was compelled to bargain a little for bargaining's sake.

"Are you sure you do not have three-hundred and fifty pounds?" Caro watched a smile break out on the woman's face.

"Say it's a deal, Arthur! I'll get the money from the safe." She did not wait for her partner's approval, but it was clear he was happy with the sale, too.

A short time later, now flush with money in their pockets, Caro and William followed the smell of roasting meat wafting their way. Caro, however, had other plans the moment she spied the shop they had visited earlier with the wonderful, knitted goods. She dragged William inside and shrieked in happiness when she spied her green scarf, hat, and gloves still on the table. She snatched them up before anyone else could.

The saleswoman who had waited on them earlier moved in to make the sale, commenting that it must be "cooler out," and Caro's prizes were soon bagged and in her hand.

They slipped out of the booth and blended into the walkway once more until William stopped again beside one of the black boxes. This time his interest was on the long cord that draped off the box and traveled above their heads to other poles.

"I am still puzzled over how this works, Caro. These cords must have something to do with how the music comes out of those boxes, but where is the original sound coming from? That's what I do not understand." He pointed to a cord strung between the box and a nearby tent. "Cords like this are attached to all the boxes we've seen, including the metal one with the switches."

As he reached out to touch one for a closer look, a voice behind him grumbled in his ear. "I know, the sound ain't as pure as it ought ta be. Them speakers are a bit of rubbish, by the way, but prob'ly not a big deal for the masses out here."

William spun around and looked at the man, somewhat younger than he, and felt as guilty as a kid caught sneaking a tart from Cook's tray.

"Sorry!" the man said, throwing back his long, stringy hair with a swish of his head. "I didn't mean to startle you." He eyed William's clothes and asked, "Are you a rocker?" His breathy excitement implied he hoped so.

Neither Caro nor William managed a response to that as they understood not a word past the apology.

A second, long-haired man with a knitted cap pulled down over his ears moved in behind the first and said, "Don't mind Pete here. He lives for classic rock music and your vintage clothes are exactly what he's been trying to find for our band. Do you mind my asking where you got them?" His eyes danced over their clothes in a covetous way, until Caro felt the need to put her arms around herself like a shield.

"I see."

She didn't think William saw anything, but at least he was responding, so she nodded like she also understood what they said. William continued, "These come from America. Tennessee to be precise, so I don't believe you can find them just anywhere."

That was a real understatement. Caro smiled and ducked her head so as not to offend anyone.

"No wonder we ain't seen nothin' like 'em here." The first

man nodded like William was royalty. "If you ever want to sell any of that, let me know. I'll text you my info if you give me yours." He pulled an object out of his pocket the size of a large cheroot case and started tapping on it.

William eyed that as if it were alive, but patted his own chest, copying the move, and said, "Mine is not with me."

The man named Pete raised an eyebrow at him as if he didn't believe that possible. The second man once again rose to the moment. "Afraid business will take the fun out of your visit, huh?"

That sounded like a reasonable explanation, so both Caro and William nodded vigorously. Another thought passed through Caro's mind about the same time the same thought must have passed through William's. She grinned and nodded at him, prompting him to speak. "We might have a deal for you."

Ten minutes and lots of grins and giggles later, the two men left them wearing Caro's and William's jackets as well as their hats. Caro now wore a dark blue, puffy jacket that was light as air but unbelievably warm. William's jacket, dubbed a "pea coat" by its former owner, delighted William when he stuck his hands in the pockets and found a pair of warm gloves. The man's cap was now pulled low over William's ears.

Caro lost no time in digging out her purchased accessories and happily put on all three items. She bobbed her head repeatedly to feel the ball tassel bounce on the back of her head. William laughed at her delight but was pleased she was so happy with such a small purchase. She had never required expensive things to make her happy. That boded well if she were to accompany him in his role as a Guardian of the Stones traveling through time. It was not a life full of creature comforts.

Satisfied that Abasi and his underlings would have a harder time finding them now, they linked arms and strolled into the huge tent labeled *Bavarian Great Hall.* What they saw inside amazed them.

Long tables were set up the length of the room like a Bavarian beer hall. Dancers and musicians were on the stage entertaining the crowd wearing traditional Bavarian dress. Best of all, people were cheerfully sloshing giant mugs of ale in toasts to each other as they sang along, and food was plentiful. Sausages and sauerkraut abounded. Apple strudels with cinnamon tempted their noses. After their long day of travel, this was a slice of heaven.

They waited through the line for food with William watching closely those in front of him as they paid for their dinners. He was relieved the bills the jeweler had given him were small enough to be common for the cashier to handle, and they got through that part easily.

Caro found them a spot at one of the tables where they devoured their healthy plates of schweinebraten with side dishes of spaetzle and red cabbage with shocking speed. Neither spoke as they took in the gaiety of their surroundings. Fortunately, the noise was such they were not required to talk to those around them. Their only task was to raise their mug of ale and smile when the time came in the songs for toasts. And those came often. It was lovely.

Food and drink had its effect on them. Caro yawned and William's eyes drooped as they left the long hall, stomachs more than satisfied. All the ale she had drunk had Caro searching the area for a women's retiring room of some kind. She was growing in need of one with each step.

They were swept along the lane with a crowd even bigger than before when Caro noticed a line of women going in and out of a small building. Next to it men filed in and out of a similar building. Could that be the place she needed? She tugged on William's arm and motioned for him to use the men's while she waited in line with the women.

William did not want to separate from Caro for a moment, yet he could not expect her to wait. They were not in the woods or a soldier's camp any longer. Civilized society did not let you relieve yourself anywhere you chose. He scanned the area and found no problems, so he let her go.

William was waiting for her when she made her way out

of the little building a short time later. Her face glowed with excitement as she told William of the amazing little throne that took refuse away with the push of a small handle. He smiled at her account, but mostly he was just relieved she was back on his arm unscathed.

Turning to leave, they came within two steps of the token taker from the ice pavilion. He did not see them because he was busy scanning the crowd with squinty eyes.

Without warning William pulled Caro in the opposite direction and hauled her off the main walkway into the middle of a crowded side lane. Before she could speak, he whispered in her ear, "The token taker from the ice pavilion was back there." He tossed his head gently in the direction he wanted her to look. Caro sneaked a glance over his shoulder. "I don't think he saw us, but he looks like he's tracking someone." He paused. "Maybe us!"

She shivered and slid further under William's arm as they hurried as fast as they could away from the man. What a blessing they had dealt their jackets and hats to those two musicians. That would help. Guilt washed over him as he wondered if Alex were waiting for them on the other side of the park. It was probably past time to go.

When the people ahead of them disappeared behind a barrier and a worker asked William and Caro for their tokens, Caro realized they had not been attending. *What? Where are we?*

William appeared just as befuddled. To add to their chagrin, a couple behind them offered them their tokens, saying they had changed their minds about the ride and were leaving. What did they mean "changed their minds?" A ride? What was that?

The worker took the tokens from the couple and pushed William and Caro through. Totally confused, embarrassed, and at a complete loss as to what was happening, they simply followed the people ahead of them down a path where other workers loaded people into little carts attached to one another.

What?

With no exit in sight, their only option was to allow the attendants to direct them into one of the carts and fasten them into the seat with a belt and a metal bar.

"Do they think we are children? Why are we strapped in?" William was clearly offended. Then the whole row of carts took off with a solid jerk that pitched them forward and then slapped them back. Maybe the belt was not such a bad thing.

Seconds later their band of little carts was chugging its way up a very steep incline on what appeared to be a metal rail. When Caro rolled her eyes up at him, he read the fear harbored there. He pulled her close, just as the entire row of carts dropped like a rock over the top of the incline.

Caro screamed.

William screamed.

Everyone screamed, and the little band flew up and down and around at breathtaking speed for what seemed to William to be a lifetime. Traveling by whirlwind had nothing on this experience.

When the carts finally rolled to a jerky stop, William forced his left hand to release itself from the bar he had gripped in white-knuckle fashion for the duration. His grip around Caro's waist had been just as tight. When his eyes landed on her face, he feared she was hurt because her eyes were pinched shut and a tear-track streaked down her cheeks.

Mortified, he started to apologize to her. "Caro?" He shook her. The poor thing must be undone. Lord knows, he was. "Caro ... darling ..." His heart still banged in his ears as it struggled to regain a steady rhythm.

As for Caro, her eyes popped open, and she cried, "Might we go again?"

Shock silenced him for a moment before he regained himself. Damn and blast! The woman was full of surprises. He found he had nothing to say.

She chattered about the beastly thing called the *Arctic Coaster* the whole time they exited the area. He gathered she was elated with the experience as she laughed about her weak knees getting out of the cart, the way her heart pounded, and her desire to do it all again.

Amazing.

In no way did William want to repeat those few minutes. He had not shut his eyes and had seen the lights fly by as they defied gravity and good sense among screaming people. No. They would not be going again. Remembering Caro's story of shopping with Louisa, he decided a diversion was necessary instead.

Frantically searching for anything to pique her attention, William spotted shops nearby and tugged Caro away from the coaster toward the tents with a banner above reading *Yuletide Market.* Whatever she might desire here would be purchased no matter the expense.

Thankfully, shopping was always a diversion for Caro, and it wasn't long before she was sorting through a stack of blankets made of the "softest fabric ever." They were not expensive and would cover only one person.

The young lady headed their way to wait on them held one of those cheroot cases to her ear. He had seen others holding them as they walked about. When the girl talked into the object, a different voice could be heard coming out of it. He tried not to stare. He knew what it was now.

Rick Duvall had explained a cell phone to him, but he had never thought he would see one up close. Now he understood that it was a cell phone one of the musicians had pulled out earlier. Caro was oblivious, lost in her blanket search. He would enjoy regaling her with what cell phones could do once they were alone.

The girl ended her conversation, shoved the contraption into her pocket and announced to Caro that the blankets she was digging through were travel blankets meant for cars. Caro nodded sagely at that, as if she knew all about cars. Maybe she did. Alex might have shown her when they passed through the first time. William felt jealousy sting him as he thought about the time Caro had spent alone with Alex. He did his best to shake it off. Alex was only helping them, and Caro could not have found him without Alex's help.

Caro selected a blanket that matched the green of her

scarf, but with pink flowers bordering it. William cared not which one he chose, but he pulled out one with a picture of a caribou woven into it and proclaimed it his choice. His mind was full of worry about the ice pavilion worker as well as Alex. By the time they took their finds to the cashier, he had decided it was definitely time for them to leave the festival.

Caro had other plans.

"Look, William! It's a Galloper! I remember it from Merlin's Museum. See the horses going round and round and up and down? Please can we take a spin on it? Please?"

His resolve crumbling, William was about to grant her wish. Her joy in finding one treat after another at the festival was infectious. Then she surprised him again with a punch in the arm.

In seconds, her expression of delight inverted into one of terror. William followed her eyes to the front of a huge tent with a sign flashing *Zeppos Circus* in colored lights. Just off to the side of the entrance his gaze landed on the two workers from the ice pavilion in close conversation with the two musicians with whom they had traded clothing. Lots of hands were gesturing in ways William was certain were not friendly.

He sought Caro's eyes and the two said not a word to each other, but nearly ran in the opposite direction for the closest exit. They did not breathe easier until the noise and the lights were far behind them as they strode toward the Serpentine and the quiet, dark side of the park.

Would Alex be waiting for them? William certainly hoped so since he feared those men were somehow connected to the man called Abasi.

Chapter 25

William and Caro exited the Winter Wonderland festival at Brook Street where the temptation to walk straight to her home was supreme for Caro. Then William reminded her the townhouse was probably long gone, and if by chance it were still a home, she would not know anyone living there. As she let William pull her along the north side of the park, that realization hit Caro hard.

She was torn between some of the amazing things she had seen at the fair and a bone-deep desire to return to her own time. Would she be able to handle the lifetime of time travel demanded of William as a Guardian of the Stones? Would she be a wife patiently waiting at home for him, or would she be a wife at his side doing everything possible to help him in his travels? She never dreamed she would be confronted by choices like these. Who would?

She heard cars swishing by on the road next to them, just as before when traveling through here days ago with Alex and Olde Gylda. The festival lights must go dark overnight, she mused, or she would have seen them earlier, too. Would Alex come for them in the dark? He would not want people to see them swirling away in a whirlwind. That much she was sure of.

They were not the only ones leaving the festival. There was some solace that any nefarious person looking their way would have a hard time spotting them amidst all the people around them. The chatter from families on the crowded walk was different this time. Small children were tired and emitted cranky cries when they were told to quit dragging their feet. One father gave up and swooped two small bodies up into his arms to quiet them with a hug and a kiss before perching each on a hip.

That made Caro smile. Would William be that kind of father? What would he have done with dear baby Lucy if she had kept her longer? Giving him a sideways glance, she saw he was smiling at the man, too. Ah, yes! He did not disappoint.

Her satisfied sigh caught William's attention and his eyes met hers. "Are you well? We should be on the other side of the Serpentine shortly. It will be quieter there."

"I am fine!" She answered a little too quickly and added, "I will, however, be more than happy to sit down somewhere."

"Agreed! This evening has been exhilarating and exhausting, all at the same time." William squeezed her hand in commiseration.

"Do you think Alex will be waiting where we landed? He said he would find us, but I don't suppose he meant he would find us in the middle of a festival."

"No, he is familiar with the modern world, but I don't think even he was counting on that distraction."

According to signs in the park, closing time for the festival was at midnight. It was too dark along the walk to read the time on her watch—it was probably wrong anyway— but she thought it must be late because the crowds leaving were only getting thicker.

A park sign pointed them toward the Serpentine, but the area appeared unfamiliar to them. Four pools of water with a walkway between them like a cross loomed up in the night. This was new. She and William split off from the rest of the crowd as if guided by one mind and followed the center walkway to the darker side of the pools. They suspected Alex would not come where others were gathered. This part of the park was Kensington Gardens in her day. Was it still?

Once past the four pools, William found a walkway buried

in heavy growth along the far side of the Serpentine. Even this time of year it spoke of a natural wooded area. It would be lovely in summer, Caro mused. Perhaps she would visit again since time travelers apparently had to pass through here on their way to assignments. She had been oblivious to where she had landed with Alex and Gylda. This area was similar from what she recalled, but she had paid it little mind and simply followed along like a puppy trying hard not to be a bother to them.

A few steps later, William and Caro walked into a round clearing that featured a statue rising out of the dark to above their heads. In its center, silhouetted in what was left of light from the festival, was the figure of a young boy playing a pipe and dancing to his tune. Looking closer in the dark, Caro made out animal shapes carved into the pedestal like squirrels, mice, and rabbits. There were fanciful things, too, like fairies.

"Who is this supposed to be, do you think?" Caro rather liked the fairy part.

"The sign over here says Peter Pan. I believe it's based on a story by someone named J.M. Barrie. I'm not familiar with the work. Are you?"

"Never heard of it, but with rabbits and fairies and such, I suspect the story is a children's tale."

"I'm sure you're right."

William busied himself reading the rest of the signage, but Caro had more important plans having noticed steps wending halfway around the base of the statue. They called to her as the perfect place to sit. Her feet were tired, and her body was crying out for rest. Without warning, she collapsed on the stairs with an ugh and a sigh. Stretching out, she took the strain off her over-worked feet before curling up like a cat.

William chuckled and lowered himself to the steps beside her. As he thrust his legs out in front and crossed them at the ankle, he took a hard look around. "This should be an appropriate place to wait. We are not completely out in the open since we are hidden by the surrounding bushes and trees."

"Good, because I do not think my feet are going to carry

me another step." Caro pulled the bag with their last purchases from William's hand and dug out her new blanket, sighing as she rubbed the soft material against her face. "I had no idea I was so tired." She folded and rolled the blanket into a pillow shape and placed her head upon it so that she was nearly lying down.

"My poor darling! You have had no chance to sleep, have you?"

"Me?" Caro thrust a finger at him. "What about you? I just watched if you recall. You were the one delivering a baby." That prompted a grin from William that turned crooked a moment later.

"I was going to say that seems like worlds away and long ago, but in fact, it was a world away and long ago."

Caro laughed at his word play, but then her face changed to a more serious expression, too. "This time travel has been the most interesting, exciting, learning experience I ever could have imagined, William. Shopping on Bond Street and playing with Louisa's children cannot compare, much as I love both."

"No, I don't suppose they can." William scooped Caro up and placed her on his lap so her head rested on his shoulder. He chuckled when he realized her blanket was still rolled under her head. With one hand he shook out his caribou blanket and covered them both as best he could. "We have not had a chance to talk much, have we?"

"No," Caro yawned. "It's been too busy. You know, landing in a war halfway around the world, tracking you down in camps full of soldiers, working for a sutler, driving off thieves at gunpoint, helping you deliver a baby, comforting the sick. Just another day in the life of a woman betrothed to a time traveling Guardian of the Stones."

"So it is, my sweet, so it is." His hand came up to stroke her cheek. "But I wonder if it is the life you would choose, if given a choice." His words became breathy by the time he uttered the word choice. She knew what that meant: William was fighting with his sense of honor.

"Are you asking me not to choose you, William?" She held

her breath and waited for his answer.

"I don't want to, Caro, but you must admit this is not the life we would have had if we had married two years ago."

"No, it isn't, but it is the life we have." She pushed herself up on one arm to look straight into William's eyes. "Let me make one thing clear, William Lowther. I have no life without you in it. Wherever you are, there I shall be too. I choose you."

William's eyes softened at her words. "You will not miss the balls and routs of the *haute ton?* Perhaps other Christmases at Woodworth?"

"I am three and twenty, as you well know. I have had years of those balls and routs. Countless rules to follow or my reputation ruined? Lovely! Sniping mothers and their equally vicious daughters vying for the attention of every eligible man? Oh, what fun!" She rolled her eyes at William. "Frankly, I care not if I ever attend one again."

"Our future will not follow the same path as others born to our rank." She could hear the relief begin to color his voice. He reached out and held her cheek in his hand. "You are sure you wish to give up the comforts of a privileged life?"

"Very sure. This life is much more exciting. Besides, I love you, or have you forgotten?"

"I have not and thank God! I do not know if I could survive this Guardian life without you in it." Sitting up, he took Caro's hands and made sure she faced him. "I promise you, my darling Caro, that you have my love forever, no matter what world we find ourselves in."

"And I promise you the same." Those vows put conversation aside in favor of a long, sweet kiss.

Coming up for breath, Caro had one request. "We can tell Violet, can we not? I cannot imagine keeping something like time travel from her."

"Knowing my sister, she will have figured it out already and be angling for ways to join us!"

Caro giggled. "Of course she will. She is a force to be reckoned with, is she not?" She sighed, thinking of her friend. "We have been a threesome for as long as I can remember."

"Hmmm, perhaps, but I can think of one facet of our lives she will never be invited to join, can't you?"

Those words and an answering murmur were the only sounds coming from that circle in the woods for quite some time.

Chapter 26

Caro's dream of dancing with William on Christmas Eve at Woodworth was rudely interrupted by her maid shaking her shoulder in a grip that hurt.

"Ouch, you needn't hurt me, Betsey. I'm awake, I assure you!" Then Caro opened her eyes and discovered she was not at home in her room. She wasn't even in a room at all. She was facing two men she had never seen before as she sat upon the steps beneath Peter Pan in the middle of Kensington Gardens. To make matters worse, William was nowhere in sight.

"Calm down, lady. Ain't nobody goin' to hurt you." This was said by the bigger of the two men, and if appearances counted, the bully of the two. He did not take his hands off her, but at least his fingers no longer dug into her arm. Dressed in matching black pants and jacket, it was the knit cap pulled down low on his face that made him look sinister. His black eyes squinted out an unmistakable warning to her to behave. . . or else.

"My dear young lady, I am s-s-so very happy to meet you!"

Her head whipped around to find a new speaker staring at her with a huge grin on his face. He wore a knee-length jacket made of black wool that hung open over what appeared to be a suit in a style unfamiliar to her. The long, burgundy scarf wrapped around his neck matched his red nose. He stamped his feet and moved side to side to keep warm.

Caro and William had fallen asleep as they sat waiting for Alex to find them. Now she had no idea if Alex had taken William and left her, or if William had awakened and wandered off looking for Alex. Her brain refused to process all that was passing through it in addition to what was happening in real time so soon after waking up. She felt completely at a loss as to what to say or do. And she was only just beginning to realize how very cold she was.

Unfortunately, the man with the big grin knew precisely what he wanted to do with her. "Come along, my dear, come along. We have much to discuss-s-s, you and I."

The two men pulled her to her feet, each holding an arm, as they began walking her out of the clearing.

"Stop! Leave my fiancé alone! Get your hands off her. Now!"

Caro's head whipped around to find William standing with his hands on his hips on the other side of the clearing. Her captors froze at the sound of his authoritative voice. Taking advantage of their momentary surprise, Caro broke their hold on her and ran toward William. They grabbed her again in only a couple of steps, but what really caught her attention and made her freeze was the double-click coming from William's direction. She knew that sound. A gun cocking to fire was distinctive. It reverberated in the early morning air.

Caro looked up from her struggle with the two men in time to see two more men dressed in black step from behind William with guns cocked and aimed at his head. The man with the big grin was no longer smiling. His expression had turned deadly serious.

"Please to be nice, dear s-s-sir. I only wish to talk with you and the lady, but not here. Here is too cold, yes-s-s?"

Who were these men? What had William and Caro done in one London evening that would make anyone want to abduct them at gunpoint? Then she remembered the man Alex called Abasi. Was this that man? He did match the description Alex had given and it was the same description William reported getting from Duvall. It was highly unlikely another man made the same hissing "s" sounds as this one. It must be.

The man waited for the two newcomers to poke William in the back and force him to move across the clearing to face off with their boss. His expression changed back to the big grin as William met his gaze.

"Pray let me introduce my-s-s-self to you. My name is Abasi, but you can call me Abasi." He laughed at his own joke as he bent his head at William and then to Caro. Caro winced. William squinted and his mouth formed a flat line across his face.

"I have been trying to capture a visitor like you for quite s-s-some time, you s-s-see." He shook a finger at them as if they were naughty children. "There is much to discuss-s-s, dear friends, s-s-so let us take a car to my hous-s-se where we can be private, yes-s-s?"

Abasi did not wait for a reply but turned on a heel and nearly sprinted toward a park exit. Caro and William had no choice but to follow at the prodding of the three assistants. A multitude of questions for William burned in Caro's brain. Now she must wait to ask them. She mostly wanted to find out where he had been and if he had met up with Alex. If not, what would Alex do if he arrived and was unable to find them? Would he leave or would he search for them?

They had been so close to going home. Why, oh why, did this Abasi have to catch them now?

∞ ∞ ∞

Abasi's heart was beating so loudly in his ears he wanted to shout at it to quiet down, so he could think. Capturing a time traveler had been his goal for too many years. Twice he had been within seconds of capturing the old lady he believed to be the key only to have her slip from his grasp. It was most frustrating. Last fall he had been led on a merry chase across London by an entire family before losing them in the underground. Catching just one traveler would solve so many problems for him.

He was the largest antiquities dealer in all of London and enjoyed a well-earned reputation for dealing only the most sought-after goods. People did not understand how difficult it was to maintain a selection of verified antiquities for all those searching for them. He was constantly on the prowl for anyone who could assist in his quest for goods.

That is where time travelers came into his picture. If he could persuade them to help him, they could ferry a steady stream of goods from their original time period to modern day for profit. He would assist them in passing through London, and they would keep him supplied with antiquities. It would be a win/win, as they say.

He often wondered if his search was only a pipe dream and would never come to fruition. Thus, he was not entirely sure what to do next now that two such travelers were in hand.

Not everyone believed time travelers existed, but Abasi was convinced of it. His dealings last August with Zeek Duvall and the charming Professor Wilson had sealed the deal for him. Two signet rings had disappeared from the British Museum at the same time the good doctors were in the field looking for antiquities. Then Abasi's men had caught up with Duvall's niece and her family in Texas when their entire car disappeared into thin air. Yes, he was sure time travelers were real.

As they reached the edge of the park, Abasi noted that although it was still early morning, traffic was already filling the lanes next to Kensington Gardens. Waiting for him beside his parked vehicle was the festival worker who had spotted the suspicious-looking pair last night. The man was one of his informers. Had he not tipped off Abasi to the couple trying to pass tokens from the American Civil War, he would not have them under his control now.

Abasi dug in his overcoat for the cash pocketed there in case the man's tale panned out, and he had to pay him. He was so excited with the successful capture of a pair of time travelers, he would happily have paid the man double or triple. But no, he would stick to his original agreement, instead. No sense having another man outside his organization know exactly what he was up to. Better his informant thought the pair had not paid their bill with Abasi and that is why he wanted them.

He paid the man and sent him on his way, but the worker tipped his hat in an open taunt aimed at the pair of travelers as he left. Abasi did not approve. This was business, not some personal game. He would clarify that to the man if he dealt with him again.

Not wanting his men to be seen with guns in their hands by passersby, he motioned for them to lower their arms while they loaded the pair into the first of two black SUVs.

Abasi opened the front passenger side and got in. He turned around to eye his prizes in the back seat but faltered for a moment in deciding where to take them for interrogation purposes.

Part of him wanted to go to his office for privacy, but it would not be empty, and he wanted no one to overhear their conversation. The other part of him wanted to take them to his home which was only a few blocks away in Mayfair. Only his niece and her little boy would still be in the house since most of the extended family were already at work. Amal would never risk eavesdropping on him.

He had offered the young woman and her son a place in his house when she became a widow and had nowhere to live. An excellent cook, Amal earned her keep by cooking for the family. With no children of his own, her little son Fahrid was his pride and joy. Yes. His home would be the safest place to interview his travelers. If he needed to keep the couple for a period of time, better to secret them at his home than anywhere else.

That decision made he turned his attention to the pair in the back seat. They were not "happy campers" as Amal would say. "Will you tell me your names, kind s-s-sir and lovely lady?" His question hung in the air as the two simply stared at him.

"I s-s-see." Abasi felt his smile dim. They were not going to be easy. "I want to make a deal with you that would benefit us both. Pleas-s-e do not worry. I know I have not given you a choice to come with me, but if you hear me out, I think you will not be s-s-sorry I made you lis-ten." He smiled a toothy smile at them. "I am a fair man."

The man and woman must have agreed not to talk to him because their silence was as palpable as another body in the car. Abasi turned back to face front, unwilling to embarrass himself in front of his driver with their refusal to respond to his questions. He would not plead with them. There was more than one way to skin a cat. He would take them on a tour of Mayfair and judge their response to the area. That could tell him much they would not.

His informant had shown him the Civil War tokens the couple had tried to pass for entrance into the ice rink. Abasi recognized the coins as legitimately coming from the 1860s. After studying their manner of dress, he confirmed the era when he spied the initials CSA for Confederate States of America on the man's belt buckle. The couple's clothing was styled from another time, yet it did not have an aged look or feel to it that two-hundred-year-old clothes would have—unless the owner was a time-traveler.

They were unaware he had in his possession the hats, coats, and scarves they had worn before trading them at the festival. His informant had tracked those down last night and taken them from the two men who were proudly wearing them. What more did he need to prove they were travelers from mid-nineteenth century America? So, if that was where they were coming from, the real question was where were they going?

Were they English or American? The gentleman who commanded his men to let the lady go, had spoken with an accent that was hard to identify. It was not clearly British, but neither did he sound like the Americans Abasi knew. The woman's accent had placed her unequivocally in the British upper class.

There was an excellent chance at least one of them had seen Mayfair in the nineteenth century while traveling to or from America's war. So many things he wanted to know about these two people. Would he be able to get them to spill their secrets? Would they work with him?

"Victor, pleas-s-e to drive us to my home but take the long way around Mayfair. Our gues-s-ts would like to see the area, would you not?"

No response from either other than a few blinks. He pulled down his sunshade, so he could watch them in its rearview mirror. They were intent on ignoring him, so he was not sure they realized he could see them.

Victor was soon moving into traffic with the second SUV full of Abasi's men right behind them. As the vehicle picked up speed, the automatic locks clicked down making the pair in back look at one another in fear. Judging from the gasp the woman emitted, he was certain this was the first time she had ridden in a motorized vehicle. Her eyes were riveted on the landscape moving quickly behind them.

"Turn here onto Upper Brook Street, Victor, and take us around Grosvenor S-s-quare."

Abasi watched the pair in the back seat try hard not to appear interested in their surroundings, but he could tell they were stunned by what they saw. Or, perhaps more precisely, what they did not see. The gentleman's eyes widened, and the lady's hand went to her chest as if she needed it resting there to breathe.

The two SUVs paraded around the square, before Abasi directed Victor to turn on Davies Street and head toward Berkley Square. Eventually, they wound their way through the heart of Mayfair, ending at a three-story brick house on South Street. By the time they were parked in front of his home, Abasi had no doubts these two were time travelers. They looked shell-shocked.

He grinned.

Chapter 27

William admitted, if only to himself, that he and Caro were in a fine mess. He had awakened to noise outside their little clearing and thought maybe Alex had arrived. He had tucked Caro in and let her sleep while he went to find out. Not seeing anyone but some park gardeners, he returned only to find Caro being led off by two men. With no weapons on him and no time to search for any, he did the next best thing—used his authority to scare them off.

That had not worked out well.

He harangued himself for not realizing someone might be behind him. One would have thought time spent with an army might have encouraged better tactical thinking, but apparently not. Caro at risk had blown everything else from his mind.

Instead of freeing her, he was now caught in the same trap as she. His only excuse was that he had been terrified of her being separated from him. If she had been taken away before he returned, how would he ever have found her again? If their pocket watches were once more pulled apart, even Olde Gylda would not be able to find them. He had no idea if Alex or Gylda would arrive to save them, so they needed to save themselves.

As for Caro, the way she was clutching his hand told him she was thankful he was with her to share the struggle. There was some comfort in that. This was not the first scrape they had found themselves in, having an entire childhood of misbegotten deeds behind them, nor would it likely be the last.

He sat up a little taller. He needed to focus on keeping his wits about him. An opportunity to escape was sure to present itself. Abasi would not win. Then they would find Alex and Gylda and go home.

His resolve was severely shaken by the time the big black wagon they were riding in stopped before a townhouse on South Street. Having been in trouble countless times as children, Caro and William knew the best way to thwart the adults was to remain absolutely quiet and stoic. Without saying a word, they had fallen into that mode with Abasi, refusing to answer any of his questions. That tactic worked well. The man was angry with their silence.

William was not, however, prepared for the drive through Mayfair. As if riding in a conveyance with no horses pulling it were not sufficient to rattle him, the next few minutes touring Mayfair certainly were. Shocking did not begin to describe the feeling of seeing nothing where it should have been except for the parks themselves.

Caro's family home across from Grosvenor Square was no longer there. Where No. 12 should be, a large sign atop an unfamiliar building read *Gordon Ramsay Bar & Grill*. Her mouth dropped open for a moment until she caught herself. Then it formed a thin line below eyes that watered until he thought they might spill down her face.

She was not the only one to be treated with a jolt to the system. His family's townhouse fared no better. A lovely place just off Berkeley Square on Bruton Street, it no longer stood either. From the glimpse he got looking down the street, his family home was now a clothing store. The changes were so disorienting, his head ached. The street names were mostly the same, but that was where similarities ended.

Driving through what remained of the world he and Caro knew, they found houses where stables should be and stables for these horseless wagons where houses should be. All this was too confusing and most upsetting.

Their drive came to an end in front of a five story, red brick house five sash windows wide. A white stone doorway stood in the center and a set of four dormers topped off the structure. Situated on the corner of South Street, the number 28 sat above the door. In his day, the house would have been facing the King's Mews. Today, the street had a series of newer buildings lined up on either side of the street, but some appeared to be businesses, not homes.

William noted the building next door had a sign in front proclaiming it to be the Egyptian Embassy. That might come in handy for an escape. Perhaps if they asked for sanctuary there, they would be safe until Olde Gylda found them. Then he thought about that and realized he and Caro had no identity in the modern world. If they declared themselves time travelers from a couple of centuries ago, they would put themselves in worse trouble. If Bedlam were still around, they would likely be committed.

He was busy shaking his head trying to clear his brain when the door to No. 28 popped open and a small boy dashed out. Dressed in a sturdy coat with a knit cap on his head, he clutched a see-through bag in one hand that held two green apples. "Uncle, Uncle! We can go to the park now. I want to feed the green birds. It's not too cold. Momma said so!"

Already out on the pavement, Abasi's face lit up like the bright lights at the Winter Wonderland as he scooped the child into his arms and perched him on his shoulders. William and Caro looked at each other and back at Abasi, incredulous. What kind of villain played in the park with small boys? How did that fit with being abducted by gunpoint in the park?

"I must settle our fine friends into a . . . guest room, Fahrid." He pulled a set of keys from his pocket and used one to open the door that had gently closed behind the boy, ushering the little one back inside. "You must wait right here for me." He held the door open and pointed for the boy to sit on a carved mahogany bench situated in the entryway.

"Do not go outside until I come back and save some apple

for the wild parakeets, so they get their treats." This was said with a smile on his lips because the boy had sneaked an apple out and taken a bite of it. Looking guilty, Fahrid shoved the rest of the apple back in the bag and swallowed before nodding his agreement.

∞∞∞

From the doorway, Abasi watched his men remove the time travelers from the car without making the pair appear to be prisoners. He congratulated himself on having good employees who knew what he wanted without being told. Two of his black-suited men waited outside keeping an eye on the street as well as the two cars parked at the curb.

Once the couple had been surreptitiously pushed inside, Abasi directed the other two men to herd them to the lower level. With a glance back to make sure they followed, he led the entourage past a swimming pool and cabana area. The smell of chlorine and heat instantly warmed him. He noted the couple's wide eyes as they eyed this area of his home—more proof they were of another time.

The balcony guest room above the pool was an option, but he thought they might be desperate enough to jump off it to escape. He did not want them hurt. They were much too valuable. Unlocking a room behind the pool area, he waved them inside, shutting out his men who would be guarding the door.

He was pleased when the young woman gasped at the sight when he flipped the lights on. This was one of Abasi's favorite rooms in the house. It could open to the pool area for a reception or be a private guest room as partitioned now. Visually, the room was stunning. Part conservatory, part bedroom, it featured a private, terraced garden with bright flowers and tropical greenery displayed in splendor. The best part was that the area was guarded by a separate security system that could be armed to alert his men if they tried to escape.

"I believe you shall be comfortable here, my friends-s-s." Once again, they refused to answer him but simply looked at him with blank faces. It was unnerving and beginning to make him angry.

"I wanted to explain the bargain I have for you, but I s-s-see you are s-s-still uncooperative. Perhaps if you s-s-sit here and contemplate your s-s-situation, you will agree that your best choice is to do as I as-s-sk. I should think as far from home as you are, you might wish to do what is nec-c-essary to be free to go home. Perhaps I am wrong?"

Still no response from them.

"Uncle, Uncle! Are you finished? I waited right here where you told me to. Can we please go to the park now?"

Fahrid's shout was heard plainly through the door, making Abasi blink hard. He must satisfy his nephew, or he would know no peace. What was he to do? He searched the faces of his captives and found nothing but empty faces.

Fahrid would get his park time, and then he would come back to persuade them. There were ways to get what he wanted, and it was only a matter of time before they agreed to his plan. He held all the cards. They had no choice but to see things his way.

"Enjoy your s-s-stay, my fine friends, but do not think to leave here. You will not get far, I assure you, and my men can be most unpleasant should they need to impres-s-s upon you the reason you must s-stay. They are not patient people."

He opened the door and stepped out, calling to Fahrid, "I'm coming, nephew."

Leaning back into the room he added, "And one las-s-st thing, if you cannot find it in your hearts to deal fairly with me, then I will not deal fairly with you. Perhaps if you are s-s-separated and kept in different rooms? There you each can listen to the cries-s of the other being . . . chas-s-stened, and then you might decide it is neces-s-sary to cooperate with me." The woman moaned as he stepped outside with a dramatic flourish, slammed the door with a bang, and locked it with a sharp click of his key.

Let them think on that.

∞ ∞ ∞

Listening to Abasi's waning steps as he headed toward Fahrid, a shiver shook Caro's body. Her eyes found William's, and she could see the threat of separation was as loathsome to him as it was to her. How long would it be before that man lost his patience with them and beat them . . . or worse? Separated from each other would be intolerable, not to mention dangerous. What did he want from them? Perhaps they should have heard him out.

"Well, at least the room is quite lovely. I've never seen a bedroom surrounded by a conservatory before." William pointed a finger at the ceiling. "One can see the sky lying in bed. How charming." He waggled his eyebrows at her in a tease to lift her low spirits.

She ignored his attempt at levity. "I would enjoy it more if we were not prisoners, William." The room was quite warm, so Caro removed her outerwear and tossed it on a chair before she plopped on the bed with a bounce. "The bed is quite soft. If we were positive we would not be slaughtered in our sleep, I would suggest we take a nap. I am still very tired. Mr. Abasi, however, does not like our quiet game, so I do not think we should take the chance."

"You are right about that. He was working to hide his frustration with us, wasn't he? Just like old times with our parents and tutors."

"It is most effective." Caro giggled despite herself when William grinned at her. Memories flooded her mind of all the times they had been in trouble and pulled that tactic on those in charge of them. Still, no matter how unrepentant she and William had been, no one dared locked them in a room. Her smile faded at the thought of how serious this business was. They were no longer children, and they were literally worlds away from home.

"William, we cannot be separated. If Mr. Abasi were to move us too far apart, our pocket watches would not be able to find one another. We would never be able to call Olde Gylda and it would be like the years when we could not find you." Caro plucked her watch from under her clothes and thrust it at William. "Please take your grandfather's back so at least it isn't running interference again."

"No, no, I do not believe that is necessary, Caro." He folded the watch back into her hand and made her put it away. "We shall not be separated again, my love. Know that Alex and Gylda will not desert either of us no matter what happens. While we wait, we must use this time to see if there is a way out of here that will not alert Abasi's men."

He held out a hand to Caro who put hers in his before he pulled her to her feet. "Let's examine our fine prison, shall we?"

Chapter 28

Abasi's mind was not on Fahrid today. The boy chattered nonstop as they were driven to nearby Kensington Gardens in one of the black SUVs. Abasi found himself unable to utter anything but an occasional uh-huh to keep the boy believing he was listening.

Before he left the house, he sent his extra guards from the front around to the terraces in the back of the house to be less conspicuous. The captives would not try to leave by the front since they would remember the men left to guard there. If they tried to escape it would be out the back terraces and his men would easily nab them.

Despite Fahrid's shrieks and whoops of excitement, Abasi could not quit thinking about his time travelers and his mind wandered further once they arrived at the park. Fahrid skipped ahead and was passing the Peter Pan statue when Abasi's cell phone beeped. Motioning to Fahrid to hold up and wait for him, the little boy threw a hip to one side and gave his uncle an impatient glare. He flopped down beside the statue like the recalcitrant Peter Pan himself, pulled out his apple and took another big bite out of it.

The boy hated when his uncle got a call during their time together. Much of the time, Abasi let it go to message, but today he needed to learn about any further revelations his men might have regarding the captives.

The call turned out to be unrelated to his prisoners, but one he was happy to take. An antiquity he had been searching for was available if he had time today to go see it to assess it for himself. Why did all the things on his agenda converge at one time? He groaned thinking about it and hurried to set up a meeting with his contact in a little over an hour to secure the deal.

When he ended the call, he looked around to apologize to his nephew for interrupting their bird-feeding time and realized the child was nowhere in sight. Fear shot through him. Had he wandered off? Surely, Fahrid would holler if he were in trouble. If the child had been abducted, he would have noticed, right? The boy knew better than to go anywhere without telling his uncle.

Selling antiquities was always a dangerous business, but would any of his competitors go after a small boy? Guilt answered that question as he thought of the captives he held in his own home only blocks away.

Perhaps there were more time travelers than he realized? Were they watching him even now? Dread rolled over Abasi as he whirled about trying to find the boy, not knowing in which direction to go next.

Trying to calm himself, he reasoned that Fahrid was merely giving him the slip because he was mad at having to wait for his uncle's business call to end. That sounded more realistic, but not typical because Fahrid was just a little boy and a guileless one. What if he *had* been abducted?

Panic set in.

He called Fahrid's name as he jogged toward the usual wild parakeet location in the woods just beyond the statue. What was the boy wearing? He had not paid attention to the color of his shirt and did not know. Frantic now, he scanned the area. Meeting some older children laughing and teasing one another on the path, he searched their number for Fahrid. A brief sweep of the group told him none were small enough to be his nephew.

He turned off the path to the area where the parakeets

were usually found, but a shrill scream from behind him made him wheel and start back for the walkway.

Something crunched him squarely in the back, and he spun around intending to rip into the person attacking him. Instead, he came face to face with a laughing Fahrid who picked up a bruised, half-eaten apple from the ground that apparently had been the object hitting him.

The fight drained from him in an instant, leaving him limp. His nephew was in one piece and happy. Then he realized the child was accompanied by an older boy he had never seen in the park before.

"Uncle, Uncle, come meet my new friend." Fahrid grabbed the bigger boy's hand and dragged him over to meet Abasi. "You were busy yakking on the phone." Here the boy did an exaggerated impersonation of his uncle on a business call complete with his free hand waving in the air. Then he pointed at the older boy. "So, when I saw him pull out an apple to feed the wild birds, I followed him." The scamp shrugged his shoulders like none of it was his fault. "You were taking so long, Uncle, my apple was almost gone."

Before he could scold the boy for disappearing, the older one stuck out his hand for Abasi to shake and said, "Hi! I'm Josh. The little guy here looked bored, so I let him stick with me while he waited for you. I guess we wandered a little further feeding the parakeets than I intended. So sorry if we worried you."

Abasi was relieved and concerned at the same time. Who was this young man with an American accent Fahrid had taken a liking to? The older boy looked to be about sixteen years of age, with sandy-colored hair and an open, easy manner. Josh met his eyes and held them as if he were telling the truth of what happened, but could he by lying? He shook away the thought. It had been Abasi's own fault for not paying attention. He had no reason to blame this sincere young man.

"Thank you, Josh, for playing with my nephew. He does not like when my bus-s-iness connections call during our park time."

"Yeah, I remember how that works. Hey, I was happy to keep him company." Josh shook a finger at Fahrid, declaring, "This kid is a bird magnet. You'd think he was a tree branch the way those wild parakeets sat on his head and shoulders. He has quite a way with them."

Fahrid glowed at this praise and Abasi was a tiny bit jealous at the way his nephew was looking at his new friend.

"Thank you again, young man. Come along, Fahrid. It is time we headed home." The older boy took the hint, said good-bye, and started to saunter away. Abasi held out his hand for his nephew to come, but Fahrid wasn't going to make it easy.

"No-o-o, Uncle! Not yet." As Abasi reached out to grab him, Fahrid dodged his hand and ran to Josh, throwing his arms around the older boy's legs.

Embarrassed, Abasi stood rooted to the spot. Worse yet, Josh was looking at him now with a hint of concern showing on his face. Did he think the boy would be beaten or something for not behaving?

"Fa-ahri-i-id . . ." Even Abasi heard the pleading tone of his voice. He never pleaded with anyone. What to do? Fahrid never questioned his authority. Why now?

Josh saved the day by scooping up his little buddy and carrying him over to Abasi. Fahrid still put up a fuss, squawking and refusing to leave Josh's arms for his uncle's. After much fumbling and squealing, Josh promised he would play with Fahrid the next time they met in the park. That did the trick. Finally, Fahrid gave up and went into his uncle's arms. Abasi quickly boosted the boy over his head and settled him on his shoulders. Delighted, Fahrid screeched one last time and patted his uncle's hair, making everything right in Abasi's world again.

The two wasted no time in returning to the waiting SUV. This time Abasi found time on the drive home to make conversation with the boy, quizzing him about Josh. Fahrid knew nothing about the older boy except that he had been fun to play with and helped him feed the parakeets. Hopefully, that was all there was to it. Fahrid's shrill jabbering made Abasi's head hurt, so he was happy to see they were almost home.

He reached into his jacket pocket for his keys but came up empty-handed. He was still searching his pockets as they arrived at the front door a few minutes later.

Seeing that his uncle's keys were missing, the ever-impatient Fahrid pounded on the door and yelled for his mother. Aggravated, Abasi did one last search of his pockets and still found no keys. Had he put them down before he left the house? He did not think so. When he pulled out his phone at the park, had he pulled out the keys by accident and not realized he had dropped them?

He would wait until Amal answered the door to see if they were somewhere in the entryway before he made a trip back to the park. His office keys were on that chain as well as the house key. How inconvenient! He was to meet his contact at his wharfside office in less than an hour and now he had no key.

What if there were no second set of keys in the house to use to attend to his time travelers? Anger was making him want to spit. He closed his eyes tightly and forced himself to breathe deeply. Amal would know about the keys.

He could spare some of his men from watching the house to accompany him to the meeting, and they could talk in the private corner he kept reserved at the coffee shop next door. Lots of unknowns, yet one thing he knew for sure. He did not need this inconvenience today of all days, but he would make it all work.

He always did.

∞∞∞

Josh watched Fahrid and Abasi leave for home before strolling deeper into the trees to meet a tall, broad-shouldered man. Rick Duvall was busy feeding three bright green birds with a matching green apple that he held in one hand. When he saw his son approach, he held out his other hand, palm up, with a question in his eyes. Josh broke into an ear-to-ear grin as he dropped a set of keys into his father's outstretched hand.

"Nice work, my boy! I guess it pays to learn pick-pocketing from the best rogue in Regency London, huh?"

"I never thought I'd use that skill in my own time. I almost didn't get close enough to grab them." Josh's expression turned wistful. "I hope I can thank Jem someday. The dangerous way he lives his life in Seven Dials, he might not even be alive yet."

"I understand." Rick shooed the birds away with a shake of his hand and tossed what was left of the apple on the ground for them to finish. He wiped his hand on his jeans and turned to face his son. "It's hard to leave the friends we make in other times, especially when we realize they are long gone in our era."

"Geez, don't remind me!" Josh scowled at the unpleasant thought.

Several birds attacked the apple, and a squabble broke out over the treat. Rick clapped a hand over his son's shoulder and turned him back toward the main walk.

"Sorry, son. I forget that time travel takes some getting used to." Rick sighed and shook his head, his frustration showing. "This would all have been so much easier if we had gotten to William and Caro before Abasi."

"Ain't that the truth."

"When Alex visited and asked me to escort them through London because he and Gylda couldn't make it back here to meet them as planned, I thought it would take no time at all to send the pair on their way home. Why did I doubt Abasi would stick his nose in our business, like usual, and mess everything up? It's what he does."

"We were so close!" Josh kicked an aged apple core from the walkway that skittered across and plopped into the grass." If we had been just five minutes earlier, we wouldn't have had to watch Abasi and his men cart them off."

"Gotta admit, that was pretty hard."

"It was. We were coming from the wrong direction to stop William, too, so he walked right into it."

"I don't think he would have let Caro go alone with them

anyway, Josh. He would have gone with her regardless of what we did."

"Yeah, some guys are like that, huh Dad?" Josh said with a wry grin, thinking of all his dad had done to protect his family. "So, what do we do now that we have Abasi's keys?"

"We wait for the opportunity to use them."

Josh frowned. "How long will that take?"

"Well, while you were busy playing with the boy, I called Abasi and posed as someone wanting to sell an antiquity."

"How did you decide what to sell?"

"Your Uncle Zeek told me all about this guy. I feel like I know him much better than when he chased us all over London. Zeek explained what Abasi looks for in antiquities and what would excite him enough to leave his house immediately and seek a meeting with me." Rick elbowed his son in the ribs. "Hey, you do remember the merry chase we led Abasi on a while back, right?"

"I do. Will he remember us if he sees us together?" Josh cringed at the thought.

"At that point we were dressed for another time period. Your hair was longer, I was bearded, and your mother wore a long dress. I don't think he would put that together with the way we look today."

"I hope you're right." Josh paused and thought for a moment. "So, you called Abasi and told him you wanted to sell him some old stuff, and he agreed to meet you?"

Rick grinned. "Yeah, that's about it. I threw in a bit about a signet ring and my contact wearing clothing that looked like it was from medieval times, and I could hear Abasi salivating. His greed and interest in time travel will win out, and he'll make that meeting come hell or high water."

Rick and Josh shared a moment thinking about the infamous Abasi who was known for doing anything in his power to capture a time traveler. Their family, including Ashley and her husband Robert, had been chased in more than one hemisphere by Abasi and his men. All agreed the man was monomaniacal when it came to time travelers.

"By the time Abasi deals with all the roadblocks we've thrown in his way and arrives at his office, he will find himself waiting for no one. That will be the perfect time for us to rescue William and Caro."

"William is the doctor who worked with you during the Civil War, right?"

Rick nodded. "I left him in Missouri. He was sent to Tennessee, and I was sent to Kansas where I found all of you."

"Is he a good guy?"

"The best. You'll like him. I've never met his fiancé, but I heard about her so much from William I feel like I know her, too."

They reached the edge of the park and crossed the street toward Abasi's house.

"What's the plan to get Fahrid and his mom out, so we can get to our two?"

Rick's grin faded. "I don't have one yet beyond the keys to get inside a locked house."

Josh's jaw dropped. "No plan?"

"We'll have to wing it." He jabbed an elbow into Josh's ribs again. "Don't look so appalled. Winging it is half the fun."

Josh rolled his eyes at his dad and shook his head. "If you say so. I hope you know what you're doing."

Rick hoped so, too.

Chapter 29

"**M**r. Abasi is not shy about guarding us. His men are everywhere!" In exasperation, Caro threw herself into an overstuffed chair next to the bed. "Do you think we should perhaps start throwing things, screaming, or creating some other disturbance to call attention to ourselves? Perhaps someone is in the house who would let us out. Servants, perhaps?"

"If devoted to Abasi, they might bring even more trouble down on us," William cautioned. "We might try it as a last resort, though."

"I suppose." Caro rose and started for the three steps leading to the elevated side of the room. "Please excuse me for a moment, William."

His face a picture of puzzlement, William asked, "Where are you going, my dear?"

"If you must know, to the little room with the unusual white commode." Caro blushed and William grinned at her disquiet.

"I'm sorry, sweet Caro. I worry when you are out of my sight. Too much has happened."

She laughed. "I cannot argue with that."

Once up the stairs she disappeared to the left, going into the small, windowless room and closing the door. Earlier they discovered it featured a skylight that served the small space well and kept it from being dark during daylight hours. With no candles around anywhere, however, he wondered how anyone managed in there after dark.

William followed Caro up the stairs determined to find either candles or another light source for nighttime use. A moment later he discovered a door to the right of the stairs labeled *Utility.* They had not noticed it the first time. Caro had been so pleased to find a retiring room with a chair like the one at the festival, he had forgotten to continue his search of the area.

Caro emerged a few minutes later with a smile on her face. "It's getting dark in there, but I do so love the way the commode makes a swoosh, and all the refuse disappears. 'Tis quite magical."

"So 'tis," William grinned. "But look here, love. It's a door we didn't see before, and it's unlocked." He demonstrated by opening the door to reveal a very dark room. An ominous hum coming from the room created an unfamiliar energy. "Without candles we have no way to make it light enough to explore what is inside."

Caro pondered that for a moment, and then her green eyes lit up. "Do you remember when Mr. Abasi opened the door for us and then a moment later the room glowed brightly like lamps had been lit everywhere?"

"I do, but I do not know how he did that. Did you see?"

"I did not. However, there was a click like the one we heard when the worker at the festival flipped one of the switches in his metal box."

"Abasi stood beside the door." That was enough to make them rush back down the stairs to look at the wall next to the door where they had entered.

"Well, there is no box." Caro arrived first but was unsure if she wanted to touch the small plate beside the door. William had no such hesitation and pressed the button.

Nothing happened.

Then he flicked the little tab that stuck out and all the lights in the room went off. Caro gasped. He flicked it again in the opposite direction and all went back on—just like the festival worker had done with the black boxes.

Now Caro was excited. "What's this?" A small button beside the tab appeared to have a crack above and below it. Braver now, she wiggled the tab and realized it would slide up or down on the plate. As she moved the sliding tab up, the light in the room went brighter and when pushed down it became darker.

Amazing.

While Caro experimented with the controls, William dashed back to discover if the utility room had a similar feature. By the time Caro caught up with him, he was impatiently running his hand along the wall inside the room next to the door.

"Aha!" The lights flashed on, and both stood in wonder for a moment as their brains registered what they were seeing.

A large metal box hung on the wall like a small cupboard, but the most astounding thing was all the black cords that ran into the box. It might have been an octopus with all the legs running from it. This box had no lock, so William carefully opened the cover. Arranged in a similar fashion to the much smaller one they had seen at the festival, this box had two long rows of switches aligned with a larger switch at the top.

On the inside of the metal door was a paper that appeared to be a detail of the switches, labeling each with an area of the house. One was marked KITCHEN, one MASTER BEDROOM, etc., but the one that drew the eye was the largest switch on top. Its label read MAIN. As Caro pointed to the word, William nodded. They looked at each other for courage before William put his hand up and flipped the switch.

In a heartbeat, they found themselves in the dark. Caro's startled cry was enough to make William flip the switch back the other way.

When the light was on again, they grinned at each other despite their shock. This was power over their circumstances they had never hoped to have.

"If this turns off all the lights down here," Caro mused, "would it not do the same in other parts of the house?"

"One would think." William's gray eyes sparkled. "Shall we find out what happens before the light gets too dark for us to see our way out of the room?"

Caro's green eyes flashed a bit of mischief in anticipation of the plan. Seconds later, the room was pitch dark, and they were feeling their way out.

Something happened above in the house because voices were raised, followed by someone running across the floor, and feet banging down the stairs. Upon reaching their door someone tried to open it, but when they discovered it locked, they uttered a frustrated sound, swore softly, and left. Was that a woman's voice? Fahrid's mother or a servant, perhaps? No part of the person was visible through the tight-fitting door to be certain.

Hand in hand, Caro and William waited for what would happen next and were rewarded with the footsteps of several people pounding down the stairs before heading for the front door.

"Come along, Fahrid. We cannot stay in a house with no power. I cannot fix dinner, so we will have to buy something to eat before your uncle returns and everyone else gets home from work."

"No, ma-ma-a-a!"

Fahrid strenuously objected to the plan and whined his disapproval, but his mother was having none of it. "Pick up your feet, young man, or no sweets will come your way for a week."

Whether Fahrid liked sweets a great deal, or he believed his mother's threats, neither Caro nor William knew, but the boy and his mother sped out the door. Before it closed, they heard an unfamiliar man's voice that might have belonged to a guard.

Then quiet fell over the house as they continued to listen. No human movement from anywhere. It felt . . . empty.

"If we hope to escape, we'd better go now, Caro." William motioned to the fading light coming from the outdoor area. "If no one is here, we can smash one of those windows and escape out the back."

Caro examined the glass William pointed to. It was very

thick and did not look promising. "Wouldn't there be guards out there to stop us?"

"Probably, but we cannot sit here and lose our chance to escape, either." William was already about the room, testing whatever he could find for its ability to break glass. Apparently, he wasn't finding anything he judged solid enough to do the job because he was discarding every item he touched as fast as he picked it up.

"What about this?" Caro removed the shade from a lamp on a pole that stood taller than she did. The heavy base appeared to be made from marble.

"That might work!" William grabbed the pole with both hands and started off toward the windows at the back when he tripped on a cord that protruded from the base and stretched to the wall. Caro frowned and tugged on the cord. It popped out of the wall with ease, clearing the way.

As they reached the wall made of glass in the rear of the room, Caro discovered a handle that told her one section of glass was likely a door. William agreed that was the case because a garden path outside led to stairs connecting to an upper level. A flowering bush concealed where it went from there. Surely a way to escape would present itself if they made it outside.

Taking up a position in front of the glass door, William held the lamp like a scythe and took a big swing, crashing the marble base into the glass. With a horrible crunch, it did not shatter, but cracked like a piece of ice on a winter pond. William grimaced at Caro and prepared to swing again when a shout from outside made him freeze. One of Abasi's men tore down the stairs with fury blazing in his eyes.

He shouted at them to stop in multiple languages, before executing a demonic grin that stretched tightly across his face and showed all his teeth. He pulled a small gun out from under his suit coat and waved it to demonstrate he would be delighted if they continued their escape so he would have an excuse to shoot them.

Caro thought her heart might stop altogether it was

thumping so hard. William was furious and dropped the lamp at his feet with a thunk. Then he moved to the windows and closed the drapes on either side with a swish so the man was shut out.

Caro dropped to her knees from where she stood and started to cry. Tears of frustration, lost opportunity, fear, and a myriad of other emotions overwhelmed her.

William knelt next to her and took her in his arms. "I'm so sorry, Caro. You would not be in this situation if not for me. You'd be safe and sound at Woodworth celebrating Christmas."

That did it for Caro. She pulled back and gave him a glare hot enough to melt ice. "You ridiculous man! How often must I tell you I do not care about anything else but being with you?"

She dried her eyes with the back of her hand and used William as a crutch to rise to her feet. "I have had more than one man threaten me since this journey began, and that man outside would not dare shoot us, or he would be out of a job. You know that. I know that. And he knows that." She pulled a stunned William to his feet. "I just needed a moment."

William stifled a smile. His Caro was magnificent.

She marched back to the inside door through which they had entered, put her hands on her hips and challenged, "See if that lamp will knock this door down, hmm?"

∞∞∞

As Rick and Josh passed the house with the number 28 above the entrance, they spotted the Egyptian Embassy next door. Perhaps they could keep an eye on Abasi's house from there and not be too obvious. As they turned to walk up to the embassy, the door to number 28 banged open and three people emerged, all talking at the same time.

A woman's shrill tones sounded distinctly above the man's muffled voice. She dragged a squirming child in one hand they quickly identified as Fahrid. Josh hid himself behind his father, so he couldn't be seen, but he needn't have bothered since the child's attention was riveted on his mother.

"I'll be good, please don't take my sweets away. Please!"

"Stop it, Fahrid. I cannot argue with you now. Just get in the car." His mother's patience with Fahrid was clearly being tested, yet the man was the one who seemed to annoy her the most.

"Get in and drive, Omar. I do not care if my brother is angry with you or not. I will deal with him. He is more likely to be upset if he has no food on the table tonight. We eat in less than an hour and my cooking is now garbage with the power cut off."

The man's voice was low and sounded equally angry in its tones, but his words could not be understood. His arms waved in wide swaths around the woman, but she would not be dissuaded.

"I cannot decide what to purchase from their buffet until I see what they have, so we'll be back much faster if you simply quit arguing. Besides, the restaurant is only a few blocks away."

The man threw up his hands in a most dramatic fashion as a sign of acquiescence, unlocked the car with a beep, and opened the door for Fahrid and his mother. They were gone in a matter of seconds, the driver showing his disgruntlement with a shriek of his tires as they sped off.

Josh met his father's eyes with a wide-eyed gaze.

Rick smiled. "I believe that opportunity we needed just presented itself, son. We'll not have a better one, so let's make this quick."

Chapter 30

Desperation was prodding William when he picked up the long, skinny lamp again. The pole was unwieldy, but he didn't care any longer. The guard from the back had undoubtedly warned any others about their actions, so breaking out of their prison was a now or never thing.

Putting all his anger behind his swing, he gave the door a solid thwack with the marble end of the lamp. A chip of marble zinged off and a sizable dent showed in the middle of the door, but it held.

Caro uttered a few encouragements, and he readied a second swing, but a voice on the other side stopped him.

"William? Caro? Are you in there?" The voice was male, low, and just loud enough to be understood through the door.

Caro was quicker to respond than William who stood frozen mid-swing as if stunned.

"Yes, yes, we are! Who are you?" She put her ear to the door to hear them more easily.

Before they could reply, William uttered, "Rick? Rick Duvall? Is that you?" William's eyes were circles and his voice wobbled, making Caro grab his hand in support.

"Yup, my son Josh and I are here to get you out."

William and Caro were treated to the wondrous sound of keys being sorted and tried in the lock. "Just got to find the right key."

In less than a minute, the door opened, and William was face to face with his Civil War buddy.

"I don't believe this! I thought I'd never see you again, Duvall!" William grabbed Rick's hand in both of his and shook it like his life depended on it. Perhaps it did.

"Nah, Guardians make up a small world. You never know where we'll pop up next. Good to find you well, William." His attention shifted. "This must be the Caro you've told me so much about?"

"It is, indeed!" William put his arm around Caro's waist and proudly moved her closer to meet his friend.

"I look forward to chatting with you, Mr. Duvall, but right now could we please leave here before someone comes back?"

"You bet, ma'am." Rick's eyes twinkled at her insistence. He grinned and gave her a roguish wink. "In truth, I rather enjoy 'covert ops' as Josh calls them. He's over there at the front door acting as look-out. But you are absolutely right. We do need to hurry, cuz if the woman who lives here has her way, they'll be back in a flash in one of those big, black cars."

That made Caro shudder, and she practically ran to the front door, pulling William along beside her. He obliged without argument.

As the three reached the front door, Josh opened it and cold air whooshed in. "I forgot my coat and scarf!" The dismay in Caro's voice was palpable.

In spite of his hurry to leave, William was already turning back to retrieve that much loved scarf set when a not very distant squeal of tires echoed down the otherwise silent street.

"Leave it!" Caro cried, but William had not needed to be told.

The four dashed out the front door, no longer caring who might be out there to thwart them. As expected, one of Abasi's black cars screeched to a stop in front of the house.

Caro emitted a gut-wrenching cry, but before the driver had completely exited the car, a different vehicle skidded in from the other direction.

"'Bout time you got here, brother!" Rick jerked open the back door of Zeek Duvall's beat-up, silver Jeep Wrangler almost before it stopped. The other three dived headfirst into the back, piling up on each other. Rick slammed the door and jumped in the front. He grinned as they sorted themselves out in the back seat, thinking panic did indeed make people move faster.

Abasi's man threw himself back into his car when Zeek arrived but was thwarted once more in his pursuit when Fahrid and his mother took their time getting out. She pulled several large take-out bags labeled *Mayfair Grill* from the back seat and harangued the driver for not helping her. While her vitriol rained down upon his head, he fumed sullenly in his seat.

Fahrid had skipped to the front door to wait for his mother, but when the other car arrived with a screech, his bright eyes spied Josh. He jumped up and down and called to his friend, begging him to stay.

Meanwhile, the driver roared his motor as if that might speed up the exit of his passengers. It did not. He was doomed to watch Abasi's captives escape—the very ones he was supposed to guard. His job was surely on the line, and it showed on the man's face.

Rick enjoyed every minute of the tableau as it unfolded.

Not waiting for anyone to say the word, Zeek Duvall piloted his old beater past the shiny black SUV still stuck waiting for its last passenger to depart and lit out in the opposite direction from Hyde Park.

"We'll have to buy you a new car, Zeek, if you keep rescuing us from Abasi and his men. This old baby groans more every time." Shifting gears, the vehicle sounded more like it might take off for the skies before it finally accepted the higher gear.

"You wanna pay for a new one, hotshot, I'll be happy to drive it." Zeek replied, with a droll roll of his eyes at his brother.

"It's a deal!" Rick laughed and slapped him on the back.

"We headed for the park again?" Zeek was fast approaching the turn off to reach it the shortest way.

"Yep!" Rick held on as the car tipped slightly to make

the corner. Caro clutched William's arm, closed her eyes, and squealed in the same pitch as the wheels until the vehicle straightened out again.

"I should introduce you to my fellow Civil War doctor, William Lowther. And this is his fiancé, Caro. . . ?

"Wyckham," William and Caro said at the same time. "Hopefully not for long," William whispered in her ear. Caro squeezed his hand harder.

"Wyckham it is." Rick continued, "This is my brother, Zeek Duvall. He's an archeology professor who helps us out whenever we need him."

"We thank you, Mr. Duvall, for the timely rescue. So sorry to be a bother to you." William put his arm around Caro and pulled her in under his arm. "We only want to return home."

"Consider this my Christmas present to you and your lady, Lowther," Zeek caught William's eye for a fraction of a second in the review mirror.

"Thank you," Caro added in a breathy voice, looking even less sure about riding in this vehicle.

"What I wanna know, Uncle Zeek, is how you knew to pick us up like that. I was never so glad to see someone in my whole life."

"Your dad texted me to follow him on that friends' app ya'll use. Seems you guys needed backup once again." He stole a glance at Rick. "This is gettin' to be a regular thing with your family, huh?" Rick just grinned showing all his teeth.

"When did you text him, Dad?"

Caro wondered what on earth they were talking about now. How was it possible for anyone to know where someone else was in order to come to the rescue? None of this was making sense to her.

"Right after I called Abasi."

Wait. Was this about that thing people held to their faces and talked into? William pointed out those to her at the festival. Maybe that was it.

"And you said you didn't have a plan!" Josh reached up and

thumped his dad on the shoulder. "Thanks a lot for making me worry. I think I lost a couple years of my life back there when we left the house."

"Sorry, son. In this business you go with whatever opportunity presents itself, but backup never hurts."

Caro watched this exchange carefully. At first, she wondered if these people liked each other since they slapped and bumped and teased one another rather roughly. Then she realized there was actually a solid bond among them, and she started to relax. Well, as much as one can when one is running for one's life.

All talk subsided as if on cue when Zeek turned into a lane at the park called West Carriage Drive. Caro didn't see any carriages on the road, only other vehicles like this one. Just before they reached the edge of the Serpentine, Zeek pulled over to the side to let them out. He remained in the car, leaning over the seat to watch them exit.

"Safe travels, you two. Happy to have met you." His expression took a wry twist. "I have tons of questions I want to ask you, but maybe we'll meet again. Who knows? Bye for now."

Thanks and goodbyes were exchanged all around. Then Zeek sped off into the night as quickly as Josh and his dad, and Caro and William stepped out into a very dark Kensington Gardens. The only light came from the winter festival going strong on the other side of the park.

"We'd better hurry if we want to avoid Abasi catching up with us. I'm sure his men have let him know by now that you've escaped his clutches." Rick shooed them up the path toward the Peter Pan statue.

Was this really where they would meet up with Alex and Olde Gylda? Could they almost be home? Before that thought found purchase in her brain, a squealing tire coming from the drive made all four heads whip around to check it out.

Of course it was an Abasi vehicle headed their way. Dark had fallen, but not enough to block out the shape of one of his cars.

As if kicked with a riding boot, they all galloped off at a dead run, hoping against hope they had not been spotted. The car crossed the Serpentine, and they thought they were saved, but the SUV stopped, turned around, and circled back their way. Seconds later, car doors slammed, and voices were heard.

"I think they went up this path," shouted one.

"They must be returning to where we found them," called another.

A stitch formed in Caro's side as she ran, slowing her down. Her legs were shorter than those of everyone else, so she was having a hard time keeping up. She tripped on a stone on the path and nearly fell. William never missed a step as he swooped her up into his arms and kept running.

As they neared the statue, suddenly two other shadowed figures were running with them. Caro opened her mouth to shout to the others they had been found when one of them spoke in a familiar, cultured tone.

"So glad you and William are here, my dear. We thought we'd lost you."

It was Alex! And right beside him she recognized the shape of Olde Gylda.

"Hurry now, children. We've no time to spare before that dreadful man gets here." She grumbled, "I never get close enough to use my magic inconspicuously on him, but he has no difficulty getting too close to everyone else."

She held out a hand to stop them as they reached a clearing. "Put Caro down, young William, but be sure to keep a hold on her hand. Alex, you, too."

Was the old woman holding a Guardian Stone? *Yes!*

Caro's heart threatened to jump out of her chest from sheer excitement. She and William were going home!

In seconds, the four of them held hands as Olde Gylda began her incantation. *"Ar goll mewn amser. Ar goll mewn amser. Ar goll mewn amser."*

Once the winds started to swell, Caro looked over and saw Rick and Josh watching them from a short distance away. She hollered "Happy Christmas," but she was not sure they heard her until they both smiled and waved. That was the last thing she remembered before the world went dark.

∞ ∞ ∞

"Well, that was fun, wasn't it, Joshie?"

Josh always knew when his dad was in a great mood because he reverted to calling him Joshie like he had when Josh was still in single digits. He might have cared another time, but as it was, he was feeling pretty good himself.

They had managed to outwit Abasi again. This chase was even scarier than the one before when his family got away. The worst part, though, was the man and his goons had seen all three Duvalls and could probably identify each of them now. Even Uncle Zeek's old silver SUV would be on their radar. Maybe Zeek did need to trade the beater in—if anyone would pay anything for it. He snorted at the thought.

"You did well, son. I'm proud of you!" His dad's arm came around his shoulders and Josh had to admit the world was a better place with his dad beside him. Josh had missed him so much during the two years his old man had been stuck in the Civil War. It was infinitely better to have him back. Besides, he was learning lots of new things about time travel. That was way cool.

"Thanks, Dad. I liked your friend. I'm glad we could help." Josh's stomach grumbled. "Any chance we can grab some dinner?"

"I think you've earned a celebration. Where would you like to go?"

"I'm smelling food in the air. How about the Winter Wonderland festival? We're here, right?"

"Works for me. Let me call your mom and Zeek. It's Christmas Eve, remember. I'm sure they'd like to join us, so we can all be together."

"Wow, I forgot all about that until Miss Caro said it. Yeah,

Mom'll like all the lights." His grin widened as he thought of his mother and the way she celebrated the season with lights strung on every corner of their house back in Texas. "She always does!"

Talk stopped as Rick texted. They stayed quiet when they reached the road crossing the Serpentine, sauntering unseen in the dark past Abasi who was busy dressing down his men. With military precision they were lined up and standing on the road beside a second black SUV pulled up behind the first. What had they called it back in Texas? An Abasi Armada? Yeah, the name fit. He hoped he didn't see another armada for a while.

As they fell in with the crowd moving toward the festival, his heart felt lighter as the music and smells of the season wafted toward them. London would be a new place to spend Christmas, but a good one. He could feel it. His favorite festival food came to mind.

"Do you think they have funnel cakes here?"

At his father's nod, their pace picked up double-time.

Chapter 31

Excitement filled Caro before she even opened her eyes. She knew precisely where she was. The room smelled of fresh pine, the familiar sound of a ticking clock comforted her, and the rug under her body felt thick and luxuriant. Why then was she so cold?

Opening her eyes, she found the winds had dropped her inside the open doors by the same terrace from which she, Alex, and Gylda had disappeared at the start of her adventure. Cold air blew across her body, and snowflakes swirled in the breeze as they swept into the room with her.

Still, the sitting room was as she remembered it. The fragrance came from decorative holiday greenery, so she had not missed Christmas, or it would be gone by now. On the mantle sat the Ormolu clock announcing time passing with a steady beat. Individual snowflakes perched on top of the Persian rug pile like shining stars until the heat in the room popped them, and they transformed into beads of moisture. She sighed with pleasure. What a relief to be home!

Then an unpleasant thought intruded in her perfect homecoming. Where was William? For that matter, where were Alex and Gylda? Her adrenalin pumping, she bounded to her feet and did a full turn around the room, but she was, indeed, alone.

Closing her eyes, she tried to think back to their departure from Hyde Park. It was a frantic time, but she distinctly remembered William taking her left hand and Gylda her right. Alex was across from her with William and Gylda holding his hands. Where did everyone else go?

Then someone took both her hands in theirs and her eyes flew open in shock.

Disappointment followed because it wasn't William holding her hands, but Olde Gylda. The woman chortled in her rackety way. "I'm not the one you want here with you, am I?"

Unable to put two words together, Caro shook her head.

"Well, not to worry, child, your William will be along shortly."

What did that mean? Caro's eyes shot to the doorway, hoping William would be entering through it as they spoke. But no, only the wind and more snowflakes found their way inside.

"If you want to look your best for Christmas Eve, it's past time for you to go to your room to get dressed. The evening has already begun, and you will be needed in the ballroom before midnight." The old woman dropped Caro's hands, turned her around, and gave her a push toward the hallway. "Go now, dearie, and all will be well."

Caro looked over her shoulder into Gylda's eyes and suddenly her path was clear and simple. Grinning, she took the servant stairs two at a time and arrived breathless in her room, ready to become Lady Caroline Wyckham once more.

Pulling the cord for her maid, her mind raced to all that needed to be done to restore her appearance as fast as possible. She had a beautiful emerald-green gown chosen for the evening weeks ago just waiting for her in the closet. Most of the jewels she had brought with her had been decimated as they needed travel money, but her favorite pearl and emerald earrings and matching necklace were still in her drawer. Digging them out, she laid them on the dresser and dashed to the closet to pull out her gown. By then Betsey came at a run into the room and stopped in her tracks, a big smile on her face.

"You're back, milady!"

"I am, Betsey, but there's so little time to get ready for the ball! Do you think you can make me presentable in under an hour?"

The maid took in the bizarre clothing Caro wore and the tangled, dirty mess that was her hair and the smile dimmed a bit. Betsey gathered her wits and replied with a frown puckering between her brows, "You know I will do my very best, Lady Caro."

Caro's high spirits were undaunted by the girl's open assessment. "Then let's get started!"

∞ ∞ ∞

Checking her reflection in the full-length mirror, Caro had to admit Betsey was a miracle worker. Gone was the travel filth that had made her itch. Her fiery locks were washed, dried, and worked into a shining mass stacked high on her head with several tantalizing coils released to frame her face. The emeralds sparkled, making her eyes seem an even deeper green, and the pearls made her creamy skin glow. Even her long gloves hid the recent damage done to her tender hands and nails.

She had been only mildly excited when she ordered the emerald gown, fearing William would never be around to see it. Now, she could not wait to show him her transition from lad to lady. Giving herself one last twirl before the mirror, she picked up a white, gossamer shawl seeded with tiny pearls and glided to the door.

One thought niggled at the back of her mind. As Betsey worked on her hair, she had told Caro about a rumor among the servants regarding preparations for a surprise at midnight. No one knew what the surprise would be, so the mystery had kept the gossip flowing all day. What might it be?

Caro could not wait to find Violet who would know what was going on as only Violet could. Somehow nary a scrap of gossip was spoken without her friend hearing about it. The interesting part to Caro was that Violet was not a gossip herself. Always in the thick of things, gossip came to her like bees to honey. Still, whatever the latest gossip happened to be, it would not rival William's appearance at the ball after an absence of two years. What could top that?

Once in the hall, Caro closed her door and turned to find Elena and Violet coming toward her.

"There you are!" Violet ran the last few steps and threw her arms around Caro. "You have no idea how happy I am you're here."

Caro gave her friend an affectionate squeeze and stepped back, straightening her bodice and smoothing her skirts. "I missed you, too," she said dryly. "It's good to be back."

Alex's wife, Elena, was a bit droll in her response. "I will spare you the crushing hug, Caro, in hopes you might tell me where Alex is. I've been waiting for him in our room, but he has not come yet."

A frown puckered Caro's brow. "What has happened to Alex and William? They were with Olde Gylda and me when we left London."

Violet exploded. "What? William is back, too? Why don't I know what you two are talking about?"

Caro wanted to laugh at the irony of her friend not knowing the latest gossip, except the set of Violet's jaw told her that would be a mistake. Her dearest friend was not happy, and before another word was spoken, she unceremoniously dragged Elena and Caro into her room.

Slamming the door and with her hands firmly on her hips, Violet demanded to know what was going on. Sitting in a pair of armchairs like two naughty children whose bad deeds had caught up to them, Elena and Caro agreed with a nod they needed to fill her in. But Violet was not yet ready to listen.

"Where have you been, Caroline Wyckham? You go to your room to get a shawl after that horrid man kissed you beneath the mistletoe and you disappear for days." She inhaled a breath and attacked again. "Poor Charlotte has been beside herself trying to cover for you. She told everyone you were in the unused wing of this great monstrosity suffering from a fever contracted from the skating expedition. She and I made up doctors and nurses and fevers and tisanes and whatever else we could to hide the fact you were nowhere to be found. That you disappeared the same time as Alex was not missed by anyone either. Elena has been valiant in her defense of Alex, but it has been most awkward."

"Calm yourself, Violet, it is not so bad as all that." Elena smiled at Violet so patiently, Caro had to admire her equanimity. The sweet lady turned to Caro to continue. "The morning after you disappeared, I put it about that an emergency had required Alex to return to our estate. I told everyone he wished for me to remain here because of my delicate condition since he planned to return as soon as possible. That seemed to calm the waters." She patted Caro's hand. "It will discourage any gossip that you are here now and seen by all before he is."

"Well, that much is true," Violet agreed, still miffed. "But what is this about William? Where is he? Where have you and Alex been? What on earth is going on that I know nothing about all this?"

Caro sighed deeply and launched into an explanation of events that kept Elena and Violet enthralled for quite some time. Absorbed in the tale, Violet's face changed by degrees from angry hauteur to childlike discovery. She was absolutely gleeful over Caro's adventure and enthralled by the details of time travel until she was positively bouncing with excitement.

"I cannot believe the woman from your dream is the one who led you on travel to another time. And to find William!" Violet's eyes sparkled with joy. "Truly amazing! Be advised, however. I shall want all the details very soon."

"Speaking of William, should we not go below to the ball? Perhaps he and Alex are there waiting for us." Caro was itching to be reunited with William. Despite assurances from Gylda and Elena, she would not be happy until William was beside her again.

The doubtful expression on Elena's face was edged with worry. "My maid was told to alert me the moment Alex arrives, and she has not." She sighed heavily as she stood and adjusted her gown. "He and William will get here when they can. Until then, we must support Charlotte and be good guests at her ball."

"Now that we have our stories straight, we should be able to meet other guests with ease. I will try to look wan as though I need to rest frequently to support the fever explanation." Caro posed with the back of her hand over her forehead.

Violet laughed. "Maybe not quite like that, Caro. Elena and I will fuss over you so you can just be you."

"You're probably right." Caro grinned, impishly. "I never was much for dramatics. You and William were far more adept at play-acting."

When the three friends made their entrance at the ball, all three were disappointed, despite their words, that Alex and William were not there. Caro was especially unhappy to find her two former suitors both present. They flocked to her as if they were homing pigeons, and she, their rookery.

Even Caro's father descended upon her, a big smile holding court on his face. "I was positive you would recover in order to attend Charlotte's ball, my dear." He kissed her cheeks and held her hands, taking a close look at her face. "Although she said you were recovering, I was upset she would not let me or anyone else visit you. She was worried you would infect all her company, and we would all be sick." He released her hands and gave her cheek an affectionate pat. "Thus, it is a pleasure to find you well and looking so lovely."

"Thank you, Father. I am much improved." On tiptoe, she gave his cheek a kiss.

"I was counting on it, my dear." He leaned in and in his most imperious fashion, added, "Be sure to be here in the ballroom at midnight. I understand a big announcement will be made." Before she had a chance to inquire further, he chuckled and sauntered off to hail an old friend with a hearty slap on his back. What was she to make of that?

Charlotte was relieved and delighted when Caro appeared and cornered her to find out what was going on. Caro assured

Charlotte her curiosity would be satisfied in full as soon as they found some uninterrupted time for her to explain. It was a long story.

Caro had barely said that much when the attentions of Cornelius Tremont, who had been lurking in wait for her, became too overt to ignore. If the man cleared his throat one more time, she might march over and slap him. Gliding in beside her like he owned her, he placed a hand on her back and declared, "I believe this is our dance, my dear."

Oh, the impertinence of the man. She had not agreed to dance with him, and she certainly was not his dear. Unfortunately, she could not bring herself to give the odious man the cut direct for presuming a dance was his. She had no choice but to go with him to the dance floor; however, she was not above delivering an unrepentant scowl Charlotte's way to display her true feelings. Her friend kindly commiserated with her discomfort before moving on to join her other guests.

To Caro's horror, the dance was a waltz and the baron insisted upon holding her far closer than was allowed in polite society. To his credit he tried to make conversation with her, but Caro was not in the mood to indulge him. Thus, the dance that seemed to last an eternity finally ended as it had begun—in silence.

Undeterred, the baron returned her to Charlotte's side and promised to come back for the dinner dance. That was enough to make Caro groan audibly. Charlotte put an elbow in Caro's ribs to remind her not to lose control. Caro decided she would have to find some way to escape the man without undue histrionics so she would be unattached whenever William arrived.

Searching the room again for the missing men, her eyes were met by a sad-eyed Viscount Duncanby, who wore the hangdog expression of a stray dog kicked one time too many. What had happened while she was gone to garner such a mournful response? Violet needed to explain all that had transpired here since Caro had a feeling she was missing something important.

As Caro watched, Violet and her partner swept off the

floor with a flourish right beside Christopher, but he seemed not to notice the girl, much to Violet's chagrin. Well, nothing had apparently changed there. How could the viscount miss the way Violet sparkled in his company? Come to think of it, why was he looking over at Caro like she was the one who had kicked him? She did not remember treating him poorly. She had just avoided him.

After that, the evening passed way too fast for Caro. Midnight neared and still no William or Alex. Violet arrived at her side just as the orchestra stopped and her father stepped onto a raised platform centered against one wall of the ballroom. Violet and Caro exchanged questioning looks and sought Charlotte to see if she knew what this was about. Across the room, remorse showed on Charlotte's face as her friend gave her a helpless shrug.

The world wavered for a moment. Then heat poured over Caro's face and body as it registered with her that her bullheaded father must have something reprehensible in mind. His threats to see her married soon had been idle threats in her mind. Why had she not paid attention? He had told her quite clearly that if she did not choose a husband, he would choose one for her.

Now every bone in her body told her that is exactly what he was going to do. Unaware that William had returned, he was choosing for her. Glaring at him, she stepped forward, shaking her head for him to stop immediately. When the duke spotted her, he smiled. Thoughts of the possessiveness of Cornelius Tremont shuddered through her. No, her father could not do this to her. He would not do this to her, would he?

Rumors had circulated all evening about an announcement at midnight, so the room was thick with excitement that something important was about to happen. Seeing the Duke of Rowland on the dais, speculation in the crowd erupted like wildfire around the room. Furtive looks were sent her way as she was surely involved.

Blindly, she sought to make her way to the front to stop

her father. Violet protected one side and Elena the other, but people crowded in to see, making the way slow-going.

Determined to proceed, the duke charged into his speech with vigor. "Ladies and gentlemen, I have a most wonderful announcement to make this evening." The crowd was silent now, afraid to miss any of what the duke might say. "My thanks to Lord and Lady Woodington for giving me the opportunity on this special night to share the good news that my beautiful daughter, Lady CarolineWyckham, and my dear friend, Cornelius, Lord Tremont, are engaged to be married."

Chapter 32

An engagement announced in a ballroom was normally met with much cheering and clapping, but this news was met with shocked faces and an eerie silence. It was well-known that Lady Caroline Wyckham had turned down a long string of suitors in favor of waiting for the absent Lord William Lowther. A number of those former suitors were standing in this very ballroom.

William's parents and sister were here as well. Those in the crowd were seeking the families of Caro and William to determine how they should respond to the duke's surprise announcement.

Those faces turned Caro's way showed concern when they noted tears in her eyes. She looked colorless as if she might faint. Appearing beside her, Lord Tremont attempted to put an arm around her waist in support, but she threw him off as if his touch burned her. The room held its collective breath balanced on the head of a pin. No one knew what to do. Even the duke had lost his ear-to-ear smile and now stood uncertainly before all with a question in his eyes for Caro.

The big clock in the hall began to chime midnight, mercifully ending the unhappy tableau. Relief swept through the crowd as they no longer needed to deliver congratulations to the obviously unhappy couple. Instead, wishes of "Happy Christmas" circulated through the ballroom, shifting the uncomfortable focus from Caro.

Aware of the baron breathing down her neck mumbling words she chose not to discern, Caro felt her knees start to give way under her. Horrified by the announcement, Violet stepped rudely between Caro and the baron and slid under her friend's arm to support her. Charlotte glided from across the room into position on Caro's other side, leaving Elena to take up a rear guard, effectively blocking out the baron. Surrounded by her friends, Caro closed her eyes and breathed deeply in hopes she would not cause a bigger scene by fainting.

Without warning the double doors to the ballroom banged open, causing the entire room to turn in unison to see who was there. A stunned silence lasted about two seconds before the room burst into shrieks, oohs, and aahs.

William Lowther and Alex St. John might have been gods from Olympus the way the room responded to them. They were dashing in their black and white evening apparel. No one could have envisioned a more handsome duo, yet that was not the reason the temperature in the room was reaching fever pitch.

All eyes were busy darting between Lord William Lowther and Lord Tremont. Who would have predicted the moment the duke announced an engagement between the baron and Lady Caroline that her long-lost love would appear to claim her? Really, it was all too much. Judging from the shriek and rustle on the far side of the room, a woman must have fainted because there was a quiet call for a vinaigrette.

The ball-goers parted like the Biblical Red Sea as the two men strode to their respective partners. Caro was only partially aware of Elena sighing and falling into Alex's arms. She heard a groan from Cornelius Tremont as he retreated in the wake of the new arrivals. Her eyes were only for William and his for her. The room erupted when William took her into his arms and pressed her tightly to him. Even the high sticklers fluttered over the romance enacted before them.

William's parents nudged and elbowed their way through the crowd to join Violet in greeting him. In silent invitation, he stretched out an arm to include his family in their embrace, not ready to relinquish his hold on Caro for so much as a moment. All three fell in with a burst of love and thanks that their long-lost son and brother had returned to them.

The drama still not over, Alex stepped up to the dais beside the Duke of Rowland and whispered a few words to him. Looking deeply chagrined, the duke moved aside, and Alex clapped his hands to gain the attention of the room. Excitement flowed like a wave in this new direction as attention shifted again.

"Ladies and Gentlemen, may I have your attention. As you all witnessed here with your own eyes, Lord William Lowther has returned for a brief visit to us in good health from his work overseas. He is here to visit his family," Alex acknowledged them with a wave of his hand, "but specifically to marry the lovely Lady Caroline Wyckham." Sighs of delight were heard around the ballroom as William and Caro steadfastly held each other's gaze.

Alex paused to pull out an official-looking paper from under his jacket. "Earlier today, I had the pleasure of assisting Lord William in his quest for a special license so their wedding might happen this very evening before so many of their friends and family."

At this news, the audience swooned as one, Caro included. Smiles radiated from everyone. That is, from everyone but Christopher Duncanby and Cornelius Tremont. The baron had slunk to the back of the room, but the viscount's face showed a wistful acceptance.

The next few minutes were a blur for Caro. Her friends divided duties and dived into the spirit of the moment with a rush of happiness for the couple unparalleled in the history of the *haute ton.* Charlotte set off to order her kitchens to prepare a wedding breakfast, while Violet organized the guests before the dais as if they were in church. Chairs for the infirm were placed at the front, with those of firmer constitutions standing at the back. An aisle in the center was left for the bride and her father to walk. Many wondered if the duke was going to give his daughter away after his shameful treatment of her before those assembled. Violet masterfully rearranged the flowers in the room to provide an artful bower for the bride and groom to stand beneath as they took their vows.

Elena ushered Caro upstairs to take a moment to freshen her appearance and catch her breath. With Betsey's help, Caro's hair was tidied and rose water sprinkled on her face and wrists. One of the maids found sprigs of holly with white and red berries and sculpted them into the perfect bridal bouquet tied up with a luscious red velvet ribbon that trailed to the floor.

By the time Caro returned to the ballroom, all was ready for her. As her eyes roamed the room, she was stricken by how much all of this meant to her, and she had a moment of overwhelming emotion to choke back. Seeing the tears in her eyes, her father moved swiftly to her side and picked up her hand, delivering a heartfelt apology in her ear.

"I did not know William had returned, Caro, or I never would have moved to force you to marry. I'm getting on in years and all I wanted was security for you. Can you forgive me?"

He bent to kiss her hand and set off a coughing spell Caro quelled with a hand to his chest. Maybe she did have a bit of magic in her hands. When he recovered himself, he continued, "I am delighted William is here, and sorry I was the one who sent him away. I can see in the intervening time he has grown into a man worthy of you, yet I am sorry for all the misery I have caused the pair of you over the last two years."

His hand cupped Caro's cheek as he spoke into her eyes. "I love you, daughter, and I always will. I wish your mother were here to see how beautiful you are." He brushed away a tear that had begun to slip down his cheek at the mention of his late wife. "I would be honored to give you away even if by my actions tonight I do not deserve to do so."

How could she refuse that? She loved her father and no one else could take his place, gruff and obstreperous as he was. She simply stood on tiptoe and kissed his cheek. Then she took his arm and faced the dais.

William stood there, military straight, his face infused with love for her, patiently waiting for her to come to him. Alex was at his elbow acting as best man.

Seeing all was ready, Violet signaled the orchestra to begin playing *Jesu, Joy of Man's Desiring* before she started down the makeshift aisle as bridesmaid. Faces of the guests glowed in the candlelight as they looked past Violet and on to the bride.

With her father holding her hand in a secure grip, Caro took a deep breath and stepped toward a world with William beside her. As she reached the dais and took William's hand, she recognized the vicar from the Woodworth estate and wondered if he had been roused out of bed to officiate the ceremony. He fought a yawn before the words of the Common Book of Prayer had all been said.

Caro did not mind. Her attention was on the man beside her and his on her. Grey eyes met green ones and smiles followed when each answered, "I will."

When the weary vicar pronounced them man and wife, shouts of joy echoed around the ballroom, but none were happier than Caro and her William, joined forever as man and wife.

∞∞∞

"I knew the gel would marry the Lowther chap all along," Aunt Augusta proclaimed, holding court with her friends. "How could she refuse one as handsome and charming as Lord William?" That made perfect sense to the other dowagers who were already planning to tell everyone back in London about the amazing Christmas Eve at Woodworth. This would be a holiday to remember.

Somehow the magic of the event enabled the Woodworth kitchens to provide a champagne wedding breakfast complete with every delicacy one could imagine. Pulled into an embrace by nearly every guest who greeted the newly wedded couple,

Caro gave up any thought of keeping her lovely emerald gown from being crushed. Instead, she reveled in the perfection of the moment. Every detail was indelibly imprinted in her brain for eternity.

A sleepy Elena snuggled against Alex, still dapper in his evening clothes despite his travels. Her father carried on a lengthy conversation with the Lowthers as if two years had never divided these formerly best of friends and neighbors. Even Viscount Duncanby grinned at a giggling Violet with warm eyes.

Corney reappeared after the ceremony and sat glowering in a corner until an old lady with young blue eyes sat down beside him. She arranged her shapeless black gown around her legs before catching his gaze and holding it. Moments later, the man grinned and smiled at her as if she were his new lady love. Olde Gylda smiled back.

Caro had just given Charlotte a kiss on the cheek thanking her for all her help in creating the perfect wedding when her cousin Louisa and her husband Hugh approached. As she had suspected, Louisa glittered in the gorgeous diamond parure Caro had spotted in the jeweler's shop so long ago. The baron pulled out his heavy gold pocket watch to show her with a proud flourish that made Caro smile.

Her hand flew to William's watch tucked into the secret pocket of her gown. Pulling it out and flipping it open, it all but vibrated in her hand. Two heartbeats later, William was at her side with his watch, the present from Caro before leaving for India, open in his hand.

The two were in sync, now and forever.

They melted into each other's arms.

Time-crossed no more.

Dear Reader

I hope you enjoyed Caro's adventure and her search for William! Time travel offers so many avenues for new worlds to explore. I wanted Caro to have experiences she never could have had in her life as a duke's daughter in 1813 England. The Napoleonic Wars had been ongoing since 1803 and had two more years to go, ending with the horrific Battle of Waterloo. I wanted my hero William to have the ability to save some "lives and limbs" for the many soldiers who would be caught up in that strife yet to come. Thus, connecting him to Ashley's father Rick Duvall from Time-Crossed Wedding seemed a likely way for that to happen. Don't worry, Ashley and Robert's story, along with Alex and Elena's are coming in Book 4. These two novels cross over in time, so I put this one first because it begins ahead of the other stories in my timeline.

Research for Time-Crossed Christmas was time-consuming but very interesting. Lucky me, my husband has been a collector of books about the Civil War since he was in 3rd grade, so I had my expert and resources at hand. I admit over the years to listening patiently as he explained an event when we watched a movie or visited a battle site during our travels, but I had little enthusiasm for any of it. Perhaps that's because I remember a trip to Gettysburg as an Iowa high school student and dutifully taking pictures of statues and cannons but being more excited about lunch with my friends than any historical site. My attitude changed when we visited Gettysburg and Antietam a few years ago with another friend, a high school history teacher. Between their reverence for the sites and the compelling accounts given by guides, museums and even a horseback ride through the battlefield, I began to realize not only the magnitude of the political events, but the effects of the war on the people themselves, both soldiers and civilians. The Battle of Bean's Station in Tennessee took place after those of Gettysburg and Antietam on December 14, 1863, so it fit my timeline for the event at the center of William and Caro's Christmas story. Knowing what lies ahead of them in a war to come is the blessing and curse for time travel characters.

That said, most readers of historical fiction are bound to wonder at some point whether the account they read in a novel is based on actual events or is purely fictional. So, for the historian in all of us, let me attempt to answer a few of those questions regarding, "What's real and what's not in Time-Crossed Christmas?"

From The Regency Era:

—In 1813, Brown and Wilkinson were known for their pocket watches, and Love and Kelty Jewellers had a store on Bond Street in London.
—The East India Company, or some iteration of it, enabled an Englishman to earn a fortune in silks and spices, opium and tea, and many other Eastern trade route items for well over two centuries. About the time of this story their army was double the size of the standing army in England.
—Situated along the Great North Road, The Bell Inn in Stilton is a coaching inn that dates back to the 1500s. Dick Turpin was a legendary highwayman who hid at the inn for nine weeks while being hunted by the law. He was caught in a raid one night, jumped out the window, and escaped on his horse Black Bess. His ghost is said to haunt the inn which is still open for business today.
—I lost a day to researching Merlin's Mechanical Museum, not because I needed to, but because his inventions were ingenious for their time. John Joseph Merlin was an inventor and entrepreneur of the eighteenth century, but his influence and some of

the automatons he created are still with us today. The brilliant mechanical engineer Charles Babbage, often called the "father of the computer," would have been about the same age as Caro and wrote about going to see Merlin's Mechanical Museum as a child, so I thought Caro, too, could have seen an exhibit called the "Galloper," the forerunner of the merry-go-round.

From The Civil War Era:

—The Battle of Bean's Station as told in the story is as factual as I can make it with my fictional characters dropped into the mix.
—The Confederate General William E. Jones, known as Grumble Jones, was a real officer who earned his sobriquet, but his heart issue is entirely fictional to suit my story.
—Sutlers were the military peddlers of the time and were a necessary part of life for soldiers.
—Lots of progress was made for battlefield medicine during the Civil War, not the least of which was the establishment of triage, and the Union hospital wagons on battlefields designated by the yellow flag with a green H.
—The eggnog celebration is taken from a soldier's account of making eggnog for Christmas. It was quite an accomplishment for an enlisted man to gather all that was needed.
—Tokens were small coins minted and distributed in the US between 1861 and 1864 and are fascinating collectors' item. When people hoarded the legal tender of gold and silver coins during the war, tokens were needed to fill in the void to keep businesses and commerce from failing. By 1864 there were approximately 25,000,000 tokens in circulation, nearly all worth about one cent apiece and found in almost 8,000 varieties.

From The Modern Era:

—Winter Wonderland is a yearly event in Hyde Park that gets more spectacular every year.
—The house used for Abasi's home at 28 South St., Mayfair, Lon-

don, at one time belonged to the romance author Barbara Cartland, so it seems appropriate to use it in this novel.

—The wild green parakeets are ring-necked parakeets and found in several parks, including Hyde Park.

As a fiction writer, and particularly with time travel, I blend real people with fictional characters and place them in real settings at real events. Hopefully, the result is a better understanding of the era and the challenges real people faced in their lives during those historic times. Thus, any historical errors are mine alone.

If you enjoyed *Time-Crossed Christmas*, please look for more time travel romance to enjoy in the first two books in this series found on Amazon, *Time-Crossed Love* and *Time-Crossed Wedding*. Remember Book 4 with more of Ashley and Robert as well as Alex and Elena's story, will be coming soon.

Please consider writing a review wherever you purchased your book. Reviews help readers find books and help writers understand what you like to read.

I would love to hear directly from you, so please know you can always find me at Jane DeGray Author on FaceBook, Twitter, and Instagram, or email me at DeGray.Jane@gmail.com. Plus, don't forget to visit my web page and sign up for news and book releases at www.JaneDeGray.com.

Thank you for reading!

Jane DeGray

Acknowledgement

Special thanks to Jim May for sharing his Civil War expertise in helping me navigate wartime soldiering.

A huge thanks to editors Laurie Sauerbry and Meredith Wise for their keen ability to spot errors both developmentally and mechanically.

Your guidance is not only deeply appreciated but essential in the publishing process.

My love and thanks,

Jane DeGray

About The Author

Jane Degray

Jane DeGray, known to family and friends as Jane May, spent much of her childhood in Nebraska and Iowa with her nose tucked in a book. Her parents constantly caught her reading with a flashlight under the covers and had to pry books from her hands to get her to go to sleep at night. If you ask her husband today, he'll tell you not much has changed.

For many years Jane was fortunate to indulge her passion for creative works by teaching English literature, theatre, creative writing, and film/video to students in Nebraska and Texas. Later, while working as a casting director for independent film, (Lifetime's The Preacher's Daughter and The Preacher's Mistress), her attempt at writing a screenplay morphed into her first novel, Time-Crossed Love, and a series was born.

Today she spends her time writing novels, reading all she can, and traveling the world, always with the next story in mind.

Books in the Guardians of the Stones Series

Romance and adventure follow time-jumping Guardians of the Stones as they scramble to find and protect their time-crossed lovers and complete their humanitarian missions for the ancient witch called Olde Gylda of Hampshire.

Time-Crossed Love, Book 1

When modern miss meets medieval man, can time-crossed love survive?

Texas teen Ashley Duvall thrills to the romance of an archeology dig near Stonehenge when her Uncle Zeek offers her a spot in his university summer class. Her excitement fades as her big plans fail to pan out and it looks like it's going to be a long summer. That is until Ashley uncovers an ancient stone that sweeps her away to 1363 England where romance and the friendships of a lifetime await her.

Medieval man, Lord Robert Spycer, warrior son and heir to the Earl of Hertford, is haunted by dreams of a mysterious woman. She is blonde, blue-eyed, and beautiful but not his betrothed. Pining for a woman to love, he intends to marry his childhood match. That is, until Ashley lands in his life and upsets everyone's best-laid plans.

It's a midsummer night's designs gone astray that send mismatched couples scrambling for their true partners over the wishes of the powerful men who rule them. Will Ashley and Robert, with the help of a wizard, a witch, and their friends, win the right to be together or will they be forced into loveless marriages. Will love or power win the day? Will Ashley stay forever or go back home? Will time bring them together or thrust them apart?

Time-Crossed Wedding, Book 2

When time-crossed lovers Ashley Duvall and Lord Robert Spycer fall in love in 1363 England, Ashley realizes she needs to return to her modern world to explain to her mother and brother her choice to stay with Robert in his medieval world. Her family has already suffered the loss of her dad, missing for two years, and she cannot disappear and leave them wondering again. Little does she know that her medieval man will follow her or that Abasi, an unscrupulous London antiquities dealer, will be on their trail hoping to catch a time traveler as the pair flies to Ashley's home in Houston.

The lovers plan a small Texas wedding with only family but are chased by Abasi's men, sending their car careening through a Guardian stone into 1863 Lawrence, Kansas. Robert, Ashley, her mother and brother must fight their way back home through a Civil War border battle, but not without surprises from the past, a timely wedding, and a familiar witch.

Time-Crossed Christmas, Book 3

She waits in 1813 England. He's stuck in America's Civil War. Can time-crossed lovers reunite by Christmas?

Before Lord William Lowther leaves to seek his fortune in India, he and Lady Caroline Wyckham declare their love for one another and exchange miniature portraits of themselves, each encased in a pocket watch. Two years later, William has disappeared from his post, and Lady Caro's father insists she choose a husband from among her suitors by Christmas or he will choose for her. Lady Caro would rather be a spinster than marry anyone except William, but will he ever return?

Courtesy of the witch Olde Gylda of Hampshire, Lord William is now a Guardian of the Stones sent fifty years into the future to the American Civil War. Having been tasked with learning enough advanced medicine to save more lives and limbs in battles soon to come, William finds himself depressed and alone. His mentor has gone home, he's been captured by the other side, and he cannot contact Olde Gylda. Is it possible he can be reunited with Caro across time, or should he resign himself to build a life where he is?

At a Christmas house party, Guardian Alexander St. John recognizes the significance of a recent dream Lady Caro describes and alerts Old Gylda. Overhearing their plans to rescue William, Caro is accidentally swept away with Alex and joins him in his mission. Over a journey spanning two continents, several disguises, and multiple time periods, danger and adventure challenge at every turn.

Will time-crossed lovers William and Caro be reunited and home by Christmas?

www.ingramcontent.com/pod-product-compliance
Lightning Source LLC
Chambersburg PA
CBHW050712180626
46814CB00002B/399